I slid up to the checkpoint and rolled down my window. A punk wearing an orange latex one-piece stuck his frump in my face.

"Out of the vehicle," he snapped.

He yanked me by the arm, twisted it up behind my back, and shoved me face-forward against the bullet.

"Name!" he spat.

I swallowed what I wanted to say and committed the bastard's face to memory.

The punk grabbed my hair, forcing my face up to his. "What's the matter, honey?" he purred. "Cat got your tongue?"

He let go my hair, shrugging to his buddies.

"Guess he's the strong, silent type," he said. They all laughed.

Grabbing my shoulder, he half turned me around. The next thing I saw was a fistful of brass knucks coming at me like a pile driver...

**Mathew Swain:
The Odds Are Murder
by Mike McQuay**

# Mathew Swain:
# The Odds Are Murder

by
## Mike McQuay

**BANTAM BOOKS**
TORONTO · NEW YORK · LONDON · SYDNEY

MATHEW SWAIN: THE ODDS ARE MURDER
*A Bantam Book / January 1983*

ISBN 0-533-22856-0

*Published simultaneously in the United States and Canada*

---

*Bantam Books are published by Bantam Books, Inc. Its trade-*
*mark, consisting of the words ''Bantam Books'' and the por-*
*trayal of a rooster, is Registered in U.S. Patent and Trademark*
*Office and in other countries. Marca Registrada. Bantam*
*Books, Inc., 666 Fifth Avenue, New York, New York 10103.*

---

PRINTED IN THE UNITED STATES OF AMERICA

O     0 9 8 7 6 5 4 3 2 1

This entire series is dedicated
to the memory of Raymond Chandler,
who understood.


For Joy.
Treasure the pain.

# 1

They were all scared of the virus, every stinking one of them. What scared me more than the virus was the fact that I wasn't scared of it. Like the man once said, there's worse things than being dead.

The bar was old. Old the way I like old. It didn't grab you and jerk you in and throw you down. It let you come inside at your own pace and get acquainted gradually. The neon that filled the walls in pulse patterns was wasting away with age, flickering like electric fireflies, buzzing and spurting. The music oozing from the speaker walls was low and melancholy, like a drizzly fall night.

The bartender's name was Jerry. He was still young, but his thinning hair and noticeable paunch made me think that he was right on the edge of getting TKO'd by Father Time. He yelled at people to close out the wintertime whenever they came through the battered steel door, and he always looked like he had somewhere else to go. All that was okay with me, as long as he remembered to keep my glass filled without my having to ask.

Jerry, like everybody else, was scared of the plague. He wore a white muslin mask covering mouth and nose, so whenever he talked, it sounded like he was talking through a mouthful of food. The citizens around the bar were also wearing the masks, kind of like they were performing surgery on their alcohol. They sipped quietly through tiny red straws that fit into homemade cutouts in the fabric.

I wasn't wearing one. I was more scared of not being scared. A withered old man who sat around the bend of the bar wasn't wearing a mask either. He drank seltzer water. I'd seen his kind before. A doctor somewhere had told him that the booze would get him if he didn't stop; so he stopped, and all that was left for him was to sit in there and get what he could out of the smell of the place. The smell was everything—

1

all he had left. That's why he didn't wear the mask; it would have taken away the smell, his last hold on life. Every once in a while we would glance up and our eyes would meet, and we'd share a secret look—a look of understanding, of parallel fortunes.

A voice behind me. "Swain."

I ignored it and took another sip of my drink, hoping that the sound was just a hollow echo inside my head, a flashback of memory.

"Swain."

I let my eyes drift up to snatch a look in the segmented mirror that filled the wall behind the bar. A man stood behind me, reflected twenty times. A mob.

His hand came up to touch my shoulder, facial expression hidden behind white muslin. He was a bandit, a privacy thief. He was a road agent trying to drag me off into the bushes of my past and steal my golden forgetfulness.

"C'mon, Swain," the twenty voices said as one.

"Swain," I returned. "Isn't he the guy who died awhile back? The fool? Yeah. I heard about that one. Pitiful case."

"Damn it!" he barked. "Look at me."

I looked. Behind the mask he was dressed too good to be standing in there with the broken neon and the drizzly music. He was all sharkskin one-piece with a real purple velvet waistcoat. I could see the dirt on the walls just itching to jump on him. I still didn't recognize him. Didn't want to.

"I need to talk to you," he said.

"I'm not the guy you're looking for."

"This is important," he said, and it was then that I noticed the edge on his voice. It was a broken bottle pressed against an exposed neck.

"So is this," I returned, and held up my drink.

He grabbed the glass out of my hand and slammed it down on the bar, sloshing bourbon waves over the rim and onto the polished steel of the bartop.

Jerry was over in a second, glaring across the divider at us. "Problem here?" he asked.

I looked at my friend in the mask. "No problem," I said. "Just a case of mistaken identity."

His eyes were wild, jumping, tensed like a Latin verb. All at once they softened. They became a crayon on a lightbulb. "Have a drink with me?" he asked.

I looked at what was left of my spilled one and thought

2

about how I could probably catch pneumonia through my unlined pockets. "The magic words," I returned.

He nodded, a short, mechanical nod, then said to Jerry: "Two of whatever he's drinking." His eyes drifted around the room, stopping at a table off in the corner where we could both have our backs to the wall. "Over there."

"I don't deliver," Jerry told the man.

He waved it off. "Just get the drinks," he said in a voice that was used to giving orders. He was beginning to look familiar to me.

While Jerry fixed the drinks, my friend fished through his pockets until he came up with his shiny white credit disk.

I smiled and kissed my drink good-bye. "He won't take that," I said.

"What?"

"You're in the DMZ, old chum. Cash on the barrelhead."

"Cash?" He seemed incredulous, but went fishing again. Then he stopped dead, snapping his fingers. Reaching behind him, he did something in the back lining of his jacket. A neatly folded hundred came back in his fingertips.

He shook his masked head. "I knew this would come in handy someday," he said, and I figured from his organization that he was a professional man, either an accountant or a lawyer.

Jerry set the drinks on the bar. "Two Black Jack and water," he said, and blew a muffled whistle when he saw the money. "Hope I can change this."

"Just get as close as you can," the man answered. He picked up our drinks before I could capture mine and started walking toward that corner table. I sat for a minute and watched him, then finished off what was left of my other one. I stared at the empty glass.

Getting off my stool, I followed him.

"You really don't recognize me," he said when I sat down.

"Well, you have to admit," I said, "you're not making it easy on me." I picked up my drink and let my tongue wiggle around in it for a second before tasting it. I think I was anesthetizing myself for the coming conversation.

His fingers came up to play with the fabric of his mask. "Haven't you heard?" he asked. "There's a plague going on out there."

"You got a cig?" I returned.

3

He reached into an inside pocket of the waistcoat and pulled out a half-used pack. "Keep 'em," he said.

"Thanks."

I tapped out a smoker and had to borrow a light to get it going. I took a deep pull. It felt good. "So, do we play masquerade party all night?" I asked. "Or are you going to take that ridiculous thing off your face?"

He started to say something, stopped. Then his fingers tugged haltingly on the material. He was shaking badly. Finally he did it, pulling the fabric down to hang under his chin like a drool bib.

Even with the mask off, I almost didn't know him. It was a face that used to be cool and assured, a face that generated confidence and command. Now it was a face defeated. It was slack, the muscles having given up. It was a face that was gray like a jailhouse wall. It was Felix Bohlar, whiz-kid lawyer, now, apparently professional bundle of nerves. I had known Felix way back when we were both nickel and dimeing it. But that had been years ago, lifetimes.

I smiled over the rim of my glass. It was somehow reassuring to see someone in as bad a shape as I was. I belabored the obvious: "How's it going?"

"Someone is going to kill me," he said quietly.

"I don't want to hear about it."

His hand came across the battered aluminum table and grabbed my wrist. "You've got to help me."

I jerked my hand away. "I don't want to hear about it."

His eyes went wild again; they were totally unpredictable. The words fought his throat to get out of his mouth. When they finally made it, they were broken like a porcelain dish on a hard floor. "I've got nowhere else to turn."

I leaned up physically, glaring across the table at him. "Damn it, Felix. Don't you know where I've been the last four months?"

"I don't care," he said.

I was getting mad, and I didn't see a reason in the world to hold it in. He had shoved his foot through the dam and there wasn't any stopping it now. "Well, you damn well better care." My voice was up high, talking to the whole bar. "I've been in the funny farm, partner. I've been so far out of touch that being numb has gotten to be a way of life. I ain't human no more, Felix. They took it all away from me, just to get me

4

off the goddamn streets. And just so we can get it all out front, I don't give a hoot in hell about you or your problems."

He stared at me, waiting for me to calm down. And I could tell that I hadn't shaken him even a little bit. He was that desperate.

"I've torn the city up looking for you," he said.

I took a drag on the smoker, and *I* was shaking now.

Jerry came over to the table, dropping Felix's change next to his arm. "I don't want any trouble," he said sternly. "Business is bad enough, what with the plague and all."

"No trouble," I repeated.

"I mean it," he said, and walked off.

I looked at Felix, hating him for what he was doing to me. "This is a waste of time," I told him. "I'm beat down, out of the business, out of luck."

"You're not afraid," he returned.

"Of what?"

"The plague . . . anything."

I laughed at that. "No."

He balled his fists up, resting them on the table. He spoke to his reflection in the aluminum. "I am," he said. "God, Swain. I'm scared to death. I don't want to die."

"Go to the coppers," I returned. "You're a rich boy. You could afford them."

He looked around nervously. I had touched a tender spot. "I . . . I can't," he said in a near whisper.

"Why?"

"I just can't."

I sat staring at him. There was determination laid in heavy among the fear lines in his face. He was a drowning man who finally got hold of a piece of driftwood.

"Suppose I just got up and walked out of here right now?"

"I'd follow you," he said without hesitation. He licked his lips. "Do you think I'd come to this . . . part of town if I had anywhere else to go?"

I took a breath and looked around. Jerry was watching us very carefully from behind the bar. He knew where his priorities lay. I picked my cig up out of its ashtray and hit it again. There was no way that I was going to be able to get rid of Felix until I had listened to his story. And besides, it felt pretty good to be needed for a change.

"Okay," I said. "Let's have it. But let me warn you in advance that my license has been revoked, my out patient

5

status from crazyland is subject to review at any time, I lost my office and had to sell my bullet to keep a roof over my head." I showed him my teeth. "Still interested?"

His face lightened immediately. He was happily shifting his burden and knew it. Lawyers.

"I want to show you something," he said, and reached into a zipper pocket of his one-piece. He came out with a piece of paper, creased and folded very neatly. That paper had been folded and unfolded many times. Many times.

The door banged open at the front of the bar, partly pushed, mostly wind. Felix nearly came out of his chair. A woman stood framed in the doorway, a retinue of dirty gray snow swirling around her.

"In or out!" Jerry yelled at her. "But close that damned door."

She chose in, and the joint had its second dose of class in the same night. She was blonde and fair and carried herself like she was stuben glass. She was tall and wore a clinging movement dress that eased subtle patterns of rainbow colors across the peaks and valleys of a figure that didn't need mechanical doodads to call attention to itself. She was okay. More than okay. She didn't have a mask on either.

Everything stopped in the bar for a second as she made her entrance. Picking out a table a few meters from ours, she sat forlornly, facing away from the bar. Jerry apparently forgot about his no delivery rule, for he was over there playing Gentleman Jim in a matter of seconds. I turned back to Felix.

He unfolded the paper carefully, as if too much pressure would tear the creases, and slid it across the table to me. It was a piece of letterhead with the logo "SPRINGMAID CORPORATION" embossed across the top.

"Look at this," he said.

It was a list of names, written in the childish scrawl of someone who never has to write. Whatever this information was, Felix couldn't trust it to his computers.

There were twelve names, thirteen including Felix's. Eight of the names had been marked through in red. I glanced at it, then at him.

"The crossed-out names?"

"Dead," he answered. "All within the last six months."

"How?"

He sat back, fidgeting. "Accidents, natural causes, murder

6

with robbery, murder with passion . . . you name it. A mixed bag."

"A lot of coincidence," I said.

He answered me with a raised eyebrow.

"It could be," I said.

He leaned up then, index finger jabbing the paper. "If your name was on this list, would you be thinking coincidence?"

I shook my head. "No way."

He nodded in return. "There's only five of us left, Swain. And every day, I feel the noose getting tighter around my neck. You've got to help me."

"What's your connection with the Springmaid Corporation?" I asked, and took a sip of my drink. It tasted flat, metallic. I put it aside and finished the cig instead.

"I set up the incorporation for them and took my fee out in shares of stock. It's a common practice."

I picked up the paper and began reading the names, the living and the dead. "Any lost to the plague?" I asked.

"Not a one," he returned.

My eyes went to the paper again. There was something extremely odd going on here. Felix was screaming for my help, yet he wasn't volunteering any information. "What about motivation?"

"I don't know," he said, and I noticed that he was watching the woman who had come in with the dirty snow.

"Felix . . ."

His eyes went to mine. "I honestly don't," he replied. "That's why I want you to help me."

"Well, what exactly does this . . . Springmaid do?"

His lips tightened and he closed his eyes, shutting me off from them. "I'm not at liberty to discuss that," he said.

I started to say something, when a name jumped out at me from the paper. "Robert Hampton?"

"You didn't know?"

"Bob's dead?"

His breath came ragged. "They said it was an accident. He was frump-hunting wild dogs in the Detroit Preserve. Said he dropped his gun climbing over a brick wall." Felix put his hands over his face. "Took his whole head off. They had to identify him from fingerprints."

I tried to close that dam up from the flood of memories. "What about Lynn?"

He was moving around, twitching in his chair, like he was

7

afraid to sit in one place too long. "I haven't been in much contact with her," he said. "I . . . I think she's okay."

Words didn't seem to want to come to me, so I just sat there for a while, thinking about the loss of old friends and listening to the sad, runny music that was sliding in currents through the twilight haze of the room. It had gotten very cold outside, unbearably cold.

Jerry called out from the bar, "Is there a Felix Bohlar in here?"

"Y-Yeah," he spoke up and raised his hand like a schoolboy.

Jerry was pointing toward the back of the room. "Somebody wants you on the vis," he said. "You can take it back there."

He stood up shakily, unsteady. I grabbed his arm.

"Who knows you're here?"

His face was confusion as he shook his head slightly. "Nobody," he said, and started wandering toward the pay vis booth by the bathroom.

"Hey," Jerry called to him as he walked. "No more'n three minutes, huh?"

Felix made a noncommittal gesture and stepped up to the steel cocoon. Using his disk to get into it, he disappeared in the dark recesses of the chamber.

Through the soft darkness and blue white cig fog that drifted through the poor ventilation, I watched the big, heavy door close behind him, heard it click shut, even from across the room.

My eyes went to the paper again, to Bob's name. Somehow I kept hoping that it wouldn't be there this time. But it was. Bob and Lynn and I had been close, God, a million years ago. It all came back—young dreams, young promises, old pitfalls. Things never change; they're always the same. Always just exactly the same.

I forced myself to look away from it, looked at the classy woman just to gear my mind in a different direction. I was surprised to see that she was looking at me, a barely perceptible smile pushing up the corners of her blue-tinted lips. She had eyes, strange eyes. Eyes that dissected, that cut you into strata like a geologist with a rock. Her eyes were brown. Funny, I thought that blondes all had blue eyes.

"Christ!" Jerry was yelling, coming out from behind the bar.

I came back around. He was moving toward the pay vis. I

was up on my feet without knowing why. Then I saw it, a wisp of fine gray smoke was blowing out of the exhaust ventilator of the vis. It was much too thick to be cig smoke. I was running.

We got to the door at the same time.

"What the hell?" Jerry kept saying. "What the bloody hell?"

The door was locked up tight. I didn't have a credit disk to get in. Jerry just kept standing there yelling.

"You're going to have to get the door open," I told him.

"What? What?"

The smoke was getting thicker and blacker.

"A disk!" I screamed, and saw his eyes widen with understanding.

He ran for the bar while I stood there helplessly banging the unyielding metal. "Felix!" I called out. "Can you get it open?"

Hands were shoving me out of the way, and Jerry was jamming a disk into the slot. The whole bar was over there now, pushing to get up close, talking excitedly through the muffling fabric.

The door clicked, then sprang open. A cloud of dark black smoke bullied its way out of the chamber. It had that overdone-toast smell of burning circuitry.

When it cleared, we saw Felix. He was squatting on the floor, mouth open, eyes open, hands spread casually across his knees. Incredible amounts of blood had been pouring from his ears, running down his neck to blend with the purple velvet of his waistcoat. His mask had filled with blood like a tiny lake.

He was dead. There was no doubt about that. The vis screen itself had blown out, still trailing tracers of smoke. It was sound that did it though, high-range piercing sound that had blown out his ears and then his brain. For Felix, at least, the fear was gone.

I got down there in the booth with him and started going through his pockets, blood from the mask sloshing all over everything.

"What are you doing?" Jerry asked.

"Nothing," I said. "Just keep those people back."

I got out of my waistcoat and started dumping his personal effects onto it.

9

"You shouldn't be doing that," Jerry said. "I don't want no trouble here."

"Sure. Sure."

Felix had a pocketcom on his belt. I unhooked it and threw it with the other stuff. Jerry kept talking to me, telling me how he ran a respectable place. I kept nodding, not really listening. I think he was trying to get me out of there.

When I finally understood that, I grabbed my bundle and moved away from the booth, pushing my way through the crowd that was buzzing all around me. There was something still in my hand. I looked down at it—a small piece of paper, folded and unfolded many times, creased with indelible permanence.

My eyes drifted toward the classy woman's table.

She was gone.

# 2

I started for the door, not thinking, moving to the internal rhythm that had kept me going for so many years. Felix had clicked something on inside of me. I wasn't prepared to deal with it emotionally yet, but my body was already grooving. He was in trouble and he came to me for help. Now he was dead, murdered, and I held the death certificates of four others in my hand. I had to do something.

All of Felix's drink and the best part of his hundred was still laying on the table. I drained his Black Jack with one long swallow, and stuffed the green into the waistcoat bundle I had made. I needed operating capital. It wouldn't get me far, but it was a start. He probably had a bullet, too. That was the next thing to check.

I didn't have an overcoat, had sold it for booze money. Getting open the door, I was nearly knocked over by a blast of winter air. I went out into it.

The dirty snow was coming down heavy. It was a maniac snow, the kind that swirls angrily out of the sky and tries to whip you to death. It was gray and sometimes yellow, and if you got right down and looked at it carefully you could probably see tiny veins of red oxide running through the grossly distorted individual flakes. It was a mocking snow, a nonpurifying snow. It pinwheeled onto the decayed carcass of the dead city and piled more death upon it in thicker and thicker layers. And maybe if it snowed long enough it could wrap everything in a filthy burial shroud and consign it to the ashes. Fat chance.

The city loomed large and dark around me. It was quiet except for the howling, bitter wind. The night creatures were all off the streets, protecting themselves as best they could in their windowless mausoleums. If the weather didn't break soon, they'd be forced to prey upon each other to survive. Just to survive.

Felix's bullet was easy enough to find; it was the only one on the street. I hurried over to it, my feet tracking listlessly through the dingy carpet of snow that covered the remnants of ancient sidewalks in uneven drifts.

Getting up beside the thing, I fumbled through my bundle until I came up with the key. It was a new bullet, a shiny one, just like I figured. Felix had been doing okay.

Unlocking the door, I slid myself into the thing, gladly shutting out the predatory wind. My face stung with the cold; my eyes watered with it.

I guess it wasn't exactly kosher to be taking his bullet this way, but he sure didn't have any more use for it; and it could do me a lot of good. I'd look at it all as a retainer.

I slotted the starter and keyed the magnetic whine, feeling the bullet lift gently off the ground. I pulled on the lights. The snow controlled everything, a blowing nightmare dancing crazily in the spotlights of harsh white.

I eased away from the curb and into the crumbling streets just as a meat machine floated down out of the smog bank to deal with Felix's remains. It sagged gently onto the sidewalk in front of the bar, and the black-suited attendants hurried inside, their stainless-steel pallet balanced between them. Felix's clothes spelled money, so they'd fingerprint him instead of dumping him in the acid pit in the back of the machine. Then they'd call the coppers to see if someone could afford the cost of an investigation and burial. That meant that the money people would soon know about the loss of one of their own. It also meant that I'd have to be extremely careful about what I "borrowed" from Felix, since credit misuse was the only automatic death penalty on the books.

Home seemed like the place to start. There were things I needed to sort out in my head before I made another move. I didn't have far to go; Jerry's bar was within walking distance of my flat.

I had to take it easy. The oxides in the snow interfered with the bullet's magnets, buffeting me from side to side as I hummed along. I was so concerned about keeping an even keel that I almost didn't notice the people blocking the intersection of Tremaine and Vancouver.

There were about ten of them, lined up like toy soldiers in a neat military row. It was men and women, all stripped to the waist and smeared with blue paint. Plaguers. Advanced stage.

They called it the gray plague because it worked on the brain, a virus. It was something new, something genetic. It was apparently created by somebody with a little knowledge of DNA and a lot of disregard for his fellow man. The plague gave people full vent to their fears, their paranoia. As the disease came to term, those suffering from it lost all touch with any reality save the fire that raged nonstop in their minds. The most advanced cases traveled in packs. Like these.

I was on them, trying to brake quickly. The bullet spun, magnets going crazy in the snow. I slid into the intersection sideways and stopped dead center.

I sat there for a second, breathing hard, listening to the howling wind muffled by my windows. They moved up on me, silently lining out all around, their faces inhuman in the headlight glare.

They stared at me as the wind whipped their gnarled hair around the vortex of their heads, and they looked quite natural standing there in the midst of nature's madness.

They were calling to me without speaking. I could feel it.

I stared back at them, noticing the blue pallor of my own hands in the dim light of the dash. Their offer was almost attractive. I had learned in the nuthouse that madness can bring its own inner peace. No, the insanity didn't scare me. I had lived with it every day, knew it as the norm. The ultimate in situation ethics.

With total precision they took a step toward me, then another. Two more and they would be all over the bullet. It was a medieval festival, a passion play in blue and dirty snow.

They took another step.

I thought about Felix. I thought about Bob Hampton, about Lynn. I thought about the four soon-to-be-dead people whose names I had somehow managed to cop from the Grim Reaper. This wasn't the time.

"No," I said to them.

They started to take that last step.

Not yet!"

I leaned on the horn, the sound piercing, driving them back in a moaning frenzy. Keying the whine, I spun out of the intersection the same way I had spun into it. I could hear them bouncing off the side of the bullet, crumpling in heaps

13

to the soft ground. I hoped that if I killed any of them that it was at least quick.

I eased along Tremaine for another two blocks before reaching the building called ETERNITY. I pulled up right in front of the place—what the hell. If they wanted me, there'd be easier ways of getting me than trying to hang me with Felix's hummer. Besides, it would probably be stolen before the morning anyway.

Grabbing my waistcoat package from the passenger seat, I hatched the door and hurried out of the bullet, getting down the landing that led to my basement flat.

I slugged through the knee-deep drift that filled the stairwell, and handprinted through my door. I flipped on some lights, always surprised when I still had electricity. The place was one long room. It was narrow like a preacher's mind, with brick support pillars running in double rows down its length.

The kitchen was the front part of the apartment, my bedroom the back. I walked to the kitchen table and dropped my bundle in its center.

There was about half a fiver of Black Jack already taking it easy on the table. Uncapping his head, I poured myself a stiff one and sat down to go through the remains of Felix Bohlar.

It wasn't much: a ring of slot keys—probably home, office, and bullet—plus the usual array of cards that didn't fit much of anything anymore; a wallet, empty except for driver's ID and attorney-verification certificate; the all-purpose credit disk that I'd be a fool, a dead fool, to use; the paper he had given me; the pocketcom; and, of course, the green stuff.

Just for the hell of it, I punched up Springmaid Corporation on his com. As mysterious as Felix had been about it, I didn't really expect anything. And that's exactly what I got. The machine asked for the primary number code, and when I didn't give it, it short-circuited in my hand, sparking and fuming.

I threw it on the ground, as it spurted streamers of yellow fire. Cursing, I stamped out the fire, smashing the machine to bits in the process. Its wispy smoke had the same odor as the vis booth where Felix died. A Viking burial.

Whatever Felix was into, I was beginning to expect that it wasn't very legal, although I really believed him when he said he didn't know why the stockholders were being killed. He

14

was a lawyer and knew better than anyone the value of telling the truth to people who were trying to help.

Picking up my drink, I moved over to park myself on my worn sofa. Sitting down heavily, I drained half the glass. It didn't taste as good as usual. Black Jack and me had always been close friends, but lately he had been trying to dominate the relationship. Maybe it was time to teach him a lesson.

Setting the glass on the floor, I stretched out on the couch and listened to the quiet. I was into something here, the kind of something that I had promised myself I'd never get into again. And it wasn't all just duty or guilt either. There was a rush connected to it that was physical and mental all at the same time. It made me feel alive, like surviving a bullet wreck without injury. They say there's no such thing as an ex-alcoholic. I think my work is the same way.

I sat up long enough to unzip my calf boots and kick them onto the floor. For once all my wall heaters were working and it was halfway comfortable in the apartment. I lay back down with a groan and closed my eyes.

In the morning there would be things to do. I'd go see Lynn and offer what little comfort I could. Then I guess I'd have to track down the others. Warn them, something. I had to, at least, do that. It was the minimum I could get away with and still live with myself.

I could feel the sleep creeping up on me, crouching like some horrible lizard at the end of the couch, ready to move up my body and eat up my brain. I lied to Felix when I told him I wasn't afraid. I feared sleep, a lot worse than he feared the plague. Sleep brought dreams, dreams of madness.

They had tried me on public nuisance, but it was a ruse to open me up to psychiatric evaluation. I didn't have a chance. It was a railroad job by a powerful enemy with powerful money and powerful lawyers. They found me criminally insane and confined me to the public health facilities at Gainesville, right next to the federal pen.

The hospital was called Terra Firma. It was paid for by private contributions from people like the guy who put me away. It was maximum security and minimum care. It was an old cinderblock building with no windows. There were lots of rooms, but no doors or furniture. We got to eat sometimes and bathe when our sores got too bad. When the food didn't come we had to rely on the bugs, and there were plenty of those. We were all in there together, brain-fried electro-

15

junkies, psychotics, mass murderers who only spoke Fortran, and toward the end, toward the very end, a large number of paranoid schizophrenics. Looking back, I think it was the beginning of the plague and nobody recognized it.

They did something to me there, something horrible and insidious. They set me apart, like a moth on a pin. They believed that I belonged there, believed that there was no place for me in sane society. And in time, little by little, they made me believe it too. They took something away from me, some special feeling that a human being holds for himself, and in its place they planted a cancer of doubt. And when they were done, when I was no longer the man I had once been, they turned me loose. Once they had broken me, they were through.

They freed me to something less than life. They freed me to nightmares. I could almost shut it out in the daytime, shuffle it into the dusty parts of my brain that I never used. But at night, it always came creeping out to wreck havoc on me.

But tonight, I had the feeling that the sleep wouldn't be bad. Tonight I thought the sleep might be just fine, like a cig after a good meal. I welcomed the lizard tonight, stretched out my arms to embrace its scaly green skin.

And the sleep came, and it wasn't bad at all. I dreamed about blank walls. I dreamed about infinite blue skies. Then, somewhere in the middle of the night, I was jerked to wakefulness by sirens.

They weren't real close, a couple of blocks at best. I sat up and rubbed my hands across my face. Even the few hours I had gotten were refreshing, the first real rest I'd had in months.

There were frump concussions mixed with the horns, and I realized that the coppers had come upon my blue friends down the street, and were disposing of them in what had become the normal fashion: blow them to pieces with frumps, then napalm the remains. There had been a lot of that going around lately. A whole lot.

The kitchen light was still burning. Getting up sleepily, I moved to the door to shut off the switch. That's when I saw her.

There's a row of windows set up high by my ceiling that looks out at street level. I glanced up. There were a pair of legs in high heels standing there. They were nice legs, classy

16

legs, the kind of legs that should never have been standing out on the street in the middle of the night in my neighborhood. I couldn't see any higher than midcalf, so I couldn't get a look at who the legs were attached to.

On impulse, I grabbed the door handle and pulled the thing open, charging out into the snow in my socks. Taking the stairwell steps two at a time, I got up onto the sidewalk in a matter of seconds.

There was nobody there, nobody at all. I began to wonder if the nightmares hadn't come after all.

# 3

The morning came up gray and lifeless, and found me drinking coffee and smoking the cigs that Felix had given me back in the bar. The wind was still blowing like a fat saxophone player, but the snow had stopped coming down and was now seriously into drifting up the sides of the buildings.

I didn't much care for any of it—the cold or the ugly snow; but nobody ever asked me *my* opinion. Hell, I never even got to fill out a questionnaire.

I had been sitting up waiting for the morning, sitting in the dark. I was also waiting for those legs to come back. They didn't, but I wasn't ready to chalk it up to hallucination just yet. Something very strange was going on, and I wasn't ready to dismiss any of it yet.

When there wasn't any more doubt but that it was daytime, I punched up some vis coordinates that I hadn't used in a long time, and turned my kitchen chair around to face the fuzzy lit wall screen.

It buzzed for a long time before taking focus. The face that stared back at me looked like a putty mold that had been stretched out of shape. It was too long and much too narrow. Sleep-battered hair stuck out all over it in thick, coarse tufts, and the close-set eyes were trying unsuccessfully to get themselves open. His name was Marty Carver, but everybody called him Juke. Juke was a systems hustler; he lived by slipping through the cracks.

A hand came up to rub that rubber face, stopping to massage the eyes. "Whoever you are," he said, "I can't be held responsible for anything I might say before ten o'clock."

"This is the data bank," I replied. "And we've found you in our files."

Juke sat up with a jerk, instantly awake, face set in horror. Then he saw who it was and immediately crumpled to his former posture. "God, don't ever do that to me again," he moaned. "I'm no kid anymore, Swain. You could have given me a coronary."

"Bad night?" I asked.

"The worst," he returned. "Bad as it could be. Almost as bad as the night before."

"What happened the night before?"

His eyes kind of rolled out of those puttied-up sockets and he stared at me through the screen. "I stayed straight," he told me.

"Oh," I replied, and understood.

Juke took a deep breath and smoothed his wild hair. His face was waking up, solidifying a bit, like he had molded the clay back the way it was supposed to be.

"I heard you were out-processed," he said.

"You heard wrong," I returned. "I'm on the streets and looking for trouble."

"Looking for favors, you mean."

I didn't like the tone of his voice.

"Favor's a real iffy word, Juke," I returned, my voice as cold as my coffee was getting. "It kind of implies the possibility of rejection."

He pursed his old lips. "Let's be real honest with each other, shall we?" His face was drained, passionless, the face of somebody who needs nobody. "I've heard about you, Swain," he said. "And I don't like it. You're poison. I don't want to have anything to do with you."

I stopped long enough to light a cig and stick it between my lips. "That's not the way you talked when you needed somebody to hide you during the tax inquisitions."

He took a breath through his nose. "That was a long time ago."

I took a deep drag and talked through the smoke. "I'm a regular elephant," I said. "Also remember nursing you through hepatitis because you didn't have a safe name you could use to check into the hospital." I took a sip of my coffee, but it was too far gone.

"You owe me big, Juke," I said. "And I'm here to collect."

He thought about that, and he could have saved himself the trouble. There really isn't any such thing as a free lunch, and in a business like Juke's, if you don't pay your chits, you don't survive. It was as complicated and as simple as that.

"What do you need?" he asked after a minute.

"You still in the information business?"

His narrow eyes got narrower. "Let me get back to you," he said, and blanked without another word.

I sat back and enjoyed the cig, the vis cam on the table watching me impassively. Juke was going to scramble his call through an indirect route for security. He was a renegade, a nonperson. He had somehow managed to get himself expunged from all computer records and now, for all intents and purposes, simply didn't exist anymore. He was paper people, hundreds, maybe thousands of them. He created and discarded identities the way that I changed my socks, working the control systems against themselves. He was the fly in the ointment of control. He had himself salaried at nonexistent data-bank jobs; he collected money on nonexistent insurance claims; he got tax refunds on tax never paid. Juke was an outlaw, and if they ever caught him, they'd run him through their paper mills and make him into printout sheets.

The vis bleeped. I focused it. It was Juke. His picture was distorted, washed out.

"Pardon the reception," he said. His voice was distant, and about half a second behind the movements of his mouth. "I'm coming to you by way of Hong Kong."

"Should I speak Chinese?" I asked.

He smiled, but I don't think he thought I was very funny. "What's up?"

"I need some poop about a certain corporation."

"What about it?"

"It's called Springmaid, and I've got a feeling that it's not going to be easy to track down." I took a drag on my smoker and let it overhang the edge of the table.

"Why not?"

I thought about how much I should tell him, and opted for the easy way out. "I'm not exactly sure how legal the business is."

He used both hands to scratch his head. "Great," he said. "One crook to another, huh? You know, I'm not the only one in this world who can jack around the system. If these people have something nasty set up, they're probably damn good at hiding it."

"Don't think you can handle it?"

"I didn't say that, damn it." He stopped and looked hard at me, his thin, bloodless lips curling into a slight smile. "I want it understood right now that this job evens the score between us. After that, I'm out of your life."

"You're in for the whole ride, Juke. Start to finish."

"But that's it."

"Agreed."

He sighed in resignation. "They're probably amateurs compared to me anyway," he said. "What else can you tell me?"

I tapped some ash off the smoker with an index finger. "Just the name right now, but maybe more later."

"You don't want much, do you?"

"I have every confidence in you."

"Confidence," he repeated, and grimaced at the pun. "Okay. Just let your old Uncle Jukie do some checking around." He began wiggling his fingers in front of the screen. "A little dancing in the memory banks. We'll get you fixed up."

"Thanks," I said.

"I don't want thanks," he returned. "I want off your damned hook, and the sooner the better. I think I'm needing to get out of this city before it rolls over and dies."

"Just stay there in Hong Kong until it blows over."

"You know what I like about you, Swain?"

"What?"

"Not a goddamn thing."

He was waving to the screen even as the words were still coming out, and then he was gone. Picking my cig up off the table, I finished it slowly, drawing it out. What I wanted was a drink. What I got was more coffee.

Carrying my cup into the bathroom with me, I showered and put on my best one-piece. I was nervous about seeing Lynn again. It had been nearly ten years. She was the only woman I had ever proposed marriage to, which gave me a hundred per cent record of rejection in that department.

My one-piece was tan. I had a black imitation-wool waistcoat that was as warm as it got for me, so I slipped it on over the suit and headed outside.

The drift in my stairwell had gotten deeper and was piled high against the door. I waded through it and got up on the streets. The bullet was still there, whipped clean by the stinging wind, shining silver in the dull morning smoglight.

The wind made a hollow sound as it whistled up and down the bankrupt, broken streets—a desolate sound. Tremaine Avenue looked like the remnants of some ancient civilization out in the desert somewhere: all skeletal buildings half buried in forgetfulness. Ancient cultures built themselves on top of the decay of what went before. I wondered what would follow us.

Remembering the legs that I had seen the night before, I gave the bullet the once-over, just in case. It seemed to be okay. Slotting the card, I got into the thing, my cheeks and nose already numb with the cold.

Keying the whine, I rose above the drifting filth and hummed off, skirting the street drifts to stay as close to real ground as possible. Street crowds were sparse, practically nonexistent. They were all huddled in their buildings, wondering where their next meal would be coming from. It had been a cruel winter in the decay, Nature's way of getting rid of the weaker links in the survival chain. There was nothing I could do about that, so I chose not to think about it very much.

Even though I hadn't seen Bob or Lynn for years, I knew where they lived. I had kept tabs on them—why, I can't imagine. I think it was my one concession to romanticism.

She lived in a suburb called Dome-acile, a place where a good deal of the new money had gravitated during the last few years. It was a pretty good distance from my end of the city.

So I hummed through the serious decay and into the semidecay. I was just getting near the decent end of town, Fancy Dan territory, when I saw the roadblock.

Cordons of Fancy Dans wearing Confederate gray capes over their slick-shiny uniforms blocked Tremaine from sidewalk to sidewalk. They were stopping anybody who tried to get out of my neighborhood.

I came up on them slowly, lining behind the few other bullets that had the audacity to try to exercise freedom of movement in a free city. People on foot were being turned away. If they persisted, they were beaten.

They picket-fenced all around me, an army of rented punks who thought that intelligence was a measurement of the size of the frumps strapped to their hips. They all wore the masks, which was just as well, since I didn't want to look at their ugly punk faces anyway. The plague fear was on everybody; it was the same noose around the artery of the city that Felix had talked about around his neck. And it was tightening.

It was my turn in the gate. I slid up to the checkpoint and

rolled my window down a touch. A punk wearing an orange latex one-piece with large white frump holster and thigh boots strode officiously over to bend down to the window crack. He had a napalm rifle slung across his shoulder. His eyes stared dully, like polished rocks, as he looked me up and down, unable to connect me up with the new bullet I was humming.

"Nice day," I told him.

He straightened. "Out of the vehicle," he snapped.

"Why?"

He deliberately pulled his rifle off his shoulder. "You just do like you're told," he said, voice tensing. "And I don't mean tomorrow."

My hands tightened on the steering bars. I liked rented punks about the same as General Sherman liked Georgia. I hesitated for only a second. All at once there were enough shooters pointing at me to qualify me for the endangered species list—under M for moron. I shut down the hum and got out of the bullet.

They got all around me, got in close. "Turn around," the orange punk said. "Up against the hummer."

"Now wait a . . ."

Hands were grabbing me. My arm was twisted up behind my back, and they shoved me face forward against the bullet, my head bent over its roof. They frisked me.

"Got a live one here," the orange man said, breathing heavy, excited. He grabbed my hair, forcing my face up to his. Rancid puffs of frost were billowing out from behind his mask. "What's the matter, honey?" he purred. "Cat got your tongue?"

I swallowed what I wanted to say. This wasn't the time to be cute.

The punk pulled harder on my hair. "I asked you a question, honey."

I choked it down again, and committed the bastard's face to memory for future reference.

He let go of my hair, shrugging to his buddies. "Guess he's the strong silent type," he said. They all laughed.

Grabbing my shoulder, he half turned me around. "Look here," he said.

I turned to look and the next thing I saw was a fistful of brass knucks coming at me like a pile driver out of its mooring.

My head exploded white, but the shot to my kidneys was what sent me groaning to my knees. They still had my arms behind me. My face rested against the side of the bullet, its slick silver finish marred by the trail of warm blood that flowed from my nose and mouth to drip onto the stand of snow on the broken street.

The punk was down there with me, cackling. Someone else had pulled up my sleeves and was poking a needle in my arm. They were taking blood.

"I don't like your looks, smart guy. What's your name?"

"You know everything," I gritted through the pain that was grappling up my back. "You work it out."

He did a number on my kidneys again, and this time I went all the way down, my body arching involuntarily, the pain bolting through me, pushing the thoughts right out of my head.

The punk was down there again, shoving a small mike on a tension wire into my face. "Say something," he ordered.

"Go screw yourself."

He came down on me again, this time in the stomach, and I doubled over, vomiting my morning coffee to blend with the color of the snow.

They moved away from me, leaving me writhing there helplessly. The pain from the kidney shots was unbearable. I didn't think I could move my legs. I turned my head to face them. One of the Dans, all white uniform and brass buttons, was squirting the needleful of blood into a small jar full of clear liquid that he held in his hand. The solution immediately turned blue when the blood hit it.

"He's clean," the guy said.

The punk in orange grunted. He was busily studying the readout screen on the black box attached to his mike. His eyes got narrow with forced concentration for a minute, then they widened and I could hear him chuckling through his mask. He walked over to stare down at me.

"Voice print's back," he said, sounding like the winner of the Irish Sweepstakes. "You've had quite a life, Swain, fresh out of the loony bin and all."

I wanted to say something, but I could feel the water I was in getting hotter and, for once, saw no reason to turn up the burner. He looked at the bullet for a long time, running his still loaded fist lightly over its contours. "Pretty fancy bullet for someone in your financial straits, don't you think?"

"I saved up my lunch money," I returned weakly.

He bent over me again. "Then I suppose you got a registration for this vehicle," he said.

That was it; they had me cold. Grand theft: auto. Maybe even suspicion of murder. Enough to get me sent back to Terra Firma for a long, long time. The Dan walked to the back of the bullet and read the tag number into that little black box. Then he came back around to me.

"We'll have this all straightened out in a minute," he said sweetly. I was trussed up like a Christmas goose and they all knew it.

If I was going to do something, it would have to be right away. I could barely move. My legs were weak, unreliable. The punk crouched down beside me in the snow.

"Well, what's this?" he said, holding the box up in front of my face. "Your name's not Felix Bohlar." He clucked his tongue. "And you're certainly not deceased . . . not yet at least."

"Frank!" someone yelled.

He jerked his head around. They were all looking up, pointing.

"Oh, my God," Frank mumbled.

My eyes followed theirs, and I felt my own breath catch in my throat. Helis, a lot of them, were floating low, just below the smog bank. They covered the sky, covered everything. They were huge, an armada. Troop carriers, with "US Air Force" lettered neatly on the bottom. What the hell was going on?

I looked at the punks; they were all staring up, transfixed by the incredible spectacle that filled the gray, rolling sky. Frank still crouched beside me, his box held between him and me.

I struggled up on my elbows; he still wasn't watching me. I gathered what strength I had, then threw myself at him. Off balance, he fell back heavily, me on top of him. I only had a second. My hand went up and I jammed the box down hard on his face. It exploded in flaring, shorting wires.

Frank screamed and grabbed for his face. I quick stripped his rifle from his arm and turned it on the others, who were all coming at me.

I was on my knees, still not sure my legs would work. "I'll use this!" I screamed at them.

They stopped dead. Punks are very survival oriented. Using the stock as a cane, I struggled to my feet. Leaning

25

heavily against the side of the bullet, I leveled the rifle and stared them down cold.

"I want all of you down on the ground," I said, and the hot taste of bile and blood was rising up my throat. They hesitated. "Down!" I screamed. "On your bellies!"

They went down, about ten of them. Fumbling for the door handle, I got the thing open and slid painfully in. The key was still slotted; I juiced it to life.

Frank was still rolling around on the ground, holding his face. My jaw muscles tightened, and I fought down the urge to use the liquid fire to burn him to cinders. Instead, I laid down a large pool of it between me and them, all bright orange fire and black smoke that spit and crackled and drove the punks, rolling, for cover.

Opening up the magnets, I hummed out of there as quick as the snow would allow. In the rearview, I watched them scrambling back to their feet, trying to chase me down, but I had already distanced them.

Shoving the rifle out the window space, I rolled it back up and hoped that I hadn't been damaged permanently.

I wondered how I was going to get home later.

# 4

I went on to Lynn's; I didn't know what else to do. My mind wasn't working too clearly through the pain. The Air Force heli's still filled the low hanging sky, and I kept one eye on them as I moved through the streets. They had to be connected with the plague. I couldn't think of anything else. They were the outward manifestation of the trouble that had been rolling under the surface, the pus-filled boil that finally admitted to the infection under the skin.

My body hurt—bad. But the pain wasn't shooting streamers anymore; it was more of an overall gnawing. I could live with it, as long as I could get my legs moving properly again. My face was swollen pretty bad around the left side of my nose and mouth. I had used a handkerchief with spit to get off the dried blood. It revealed some pretty good purple and yellow bruises underneath. I'm a colorful guy.

The helis had thinned to stragglers by the time I got out of the city proper and on the private road that led to Lynn's neighborhood. The road was smooth paved and already cleared of snow, even though the wind kept trying to bury it in drifts again. The grounds surrounding the road had been cleared and leveled for miles in every direction. Tall cement guard-towers dotted the open grounds like lighthouses on rocky shores, making certain the complex was approached from only one direction. Their laser turrets followed me with undivided attention as I moved along.

Finally I came to a wall that was penitentiary high and sloping at a curling angle toward me. It was like a cement sculpture of a tidal wave. I saw no gate or guards—just the wall.

I gave a blast on the horn, but nothing happened. Getting the door open, I climbed painfully out. It was as good a time to check my legs as any. I couldn't move them much, and when I moved them too much, my whole spine felt like it had been used to pound nails into cedar.

Hobbling up to where the road dead-ended at the wall, I cupped my hands and yelled. "Room service! Anybody here!"

The wall in front of me juiced into a vis picture fifty meters high. A face filled that wall, a man's face, the smooth unlined countenance of a computer composite. It spoke in a mammoth, booming voice, that was a little too high-pitched to be authoritative.

"Hi," it said. "Welcome to Dome-acile. We don't seem to have your voice print on record, so we're going to have to ask for your name and business and the person you wish to contact on the other side of the barricade." The face smiled and raised its eyebrows. "I'm sure that you're a reasonable man and will comply, but just in case you're not, it's my job to inform you that a battery of laser turrets has you computer-locked on their scanners and will end your existence should I tell them so. I'm a nice guy, and don't want to do that, but I have to tell you that we're not overly fond of trespassers here, and if your answers aren't exactly . . . well, you get the idea. And while we're on the subject, I guess I should tell you that it would be a waste of both of our times to try to reason or bargain with me. I'm not real, so it would be kind of silly, all things being equal. So, to make a long story short, you have thirty seconds from the sound of the bell to either answer my questions or turn your vehicle around and beat it out of here if you can. Isn't this exciting?"

A loud, clanging bell went off immediately. The computer face pursed its lips and stared intently at me with its overgrown eyes.

I had a few seconds of incredible anxiety. I should have called Lynn first and let her know I was coming. What if she didn't give a damn about seeing me after all these years, or what if she hated me, or what if she didn't even remember me? Ten years molds a lot of bread.

"Fifteen seconds," the computer face said.

I leaned against the bullet to take some pressure off my legs. "Mathew Swain," I said. "Confidential investigations. I've come to pay a social visit to Lynn Hampton."

"There. That wasn't too hard, was it?" The face nodded. "Now comes the real tension." The eyes flashed. "We check you out." The face faded immediately.

I fidgeted. I lit a cig. The monster face was gone for a long

28

time. It was gone for an eternity. I kept waiting to hear the electric hum that would signal my death about a half second in advance. Time enough to repent.

Then the wall juiced again. Instead of the computer, Lynn's face was staring down at me from the height of fifteen stories.

"Matt?" she said, in a tiny voice that came out like thunder at a half mile.

"I always thought of you as being larger than life," I replied. "But this is ridiculous."

"I—I don't . . ."

"Let's just say that it's old home week," I told her. "What's the chances of a man coming in out of the cold?"

She smiled with a mouth that could have devoured me and the horse I rode in on. "Well, get your ass in here," she said, and I knew in that instant that there were some things that the years didn't change.

"How will I know which place is yours?" I asked.

Her weather balloon eyes twinkled. "You'll know."

She blanked, and the computer face replaced hers. It was smiling wide. "Welcome, Mister Swain," it said happily. "We sure are glad to make your acquaintance. You know, Mrs. Hampton has been kind of reclusive since her husband's unfortunate accident. I certainly hope that you can cheer her up a bit. Confidentially, I'm a bit worried about her, if you know what I mean."

"I'll do my best," I answered. "That is, if I don't freeze to death out here first."

A giant computer hand came up to slap a giant computer forehead. "Stupid me!" the voice boomed. "Please. Step back into your vehicle and sit securely. We'll have you inside in a jiffy."

Limping back to the bullet, I hoisted myself in and closed the door. I sat for about a minute, then heard a creaking sound above me. Leaning forward, I looked up through the windshield to see the arm of a large crane lowering something big on top of me.

I pulled out a cig, but before I could get the lighter out of my pocket to fire it, the thing flew out on its own to stick on the ceiling. Then the seatbelts jumped up as far as their tethers would allow and began dancing around like cobras to a snake charmer. Electro magnet, and powerful. I felt a pulling in my mouth, and for the first time found out that my fillings weren't real silver after all.

The magnet clamped on the top of the bullet and started taking us up immediately. There was pain in my knee where an old injury was held together by steel pins. I massaged the place and watched out the window. Looking down, the north Texas landscape spread out in a wider and wider area. I could see the government helis. They were on the ground, strung around the outskirts of town in a total bottleneck. The city was being blockaded. No one was being allowed to enter or leave. The noose was tightening.

Things were beginning to get nasty.

The crane took me over the top of the huge wall. Dome-acile lay below me, sparkling slightly in the dull morning light. It was a Christmas garden in shiny metal, a cabbage patch of stainless-steel geodesic domes set high atop stalklike protective tubes. There were about forty of them, and they were all just the same.

My bullet began descending. The wall couldn't be seen from the inside. The whole monstrous thing juiced a wrapa-round holo of gently rolling countryside and smogless sky. Security with the illusion of freedom. Interesting.

I settled with a bump on the snow-laden ground and the magnet unclamped, dropping my lighter back in my lap. I had changed my mind about the cig, so I stuck the lighter back in my pocket and hummed into the petrified silver forest.

It was strange to me. The domes were all laid out in neat, military rows, bisected by streets as straight as an alky who found religion. It seemed like the planners of the develop-ment could have done a little more eye-pleasing job for all the rich boys who laid out the big bucks to move there.

I looked up as I drove, the domes bulging out above me. They were extremely large, windowless, and their stalks seemed to be about twenty meters tall. Lynn said that I would know which one was hers, but I'd be damned if they all didn't look exactly the same.

Then I saw it. A block away, one of the domes began to glow in a soft, gentle blue, a pulsating blue. The silver was gone. It was a big, gooey lollipop calling me to it. Lynn's favorite color had always been blue. I drove to it.

I was shaking like a three time loser up in front of the hanging judge when I climbed out of the bullet. I was nervous. Just my luck after all those years to come upon

Lynn in the shape I was in. I limped up the flagstone walk and pushed the door buzzer.

The stalk was as big around as an oil pipeline. A section of it slid away with a hydraulic whoosh. It was thick steel, maybe five centimeters. I stepped inside and the door clanked shut so quick that I had to turn around and check my ass to make sure I hadn't left it out in the snow.

I was standing in a pleasantly warm up-tube. Setting my weight on the dial, it started up. The tube was settled in total darkness, except for the pale red glow of the instrument panel.

The tube rose slowly, silently. I leaned against the side wall when my legs hurt too bad. The machine stopped without a jerk, but it seemed to take an extra long time before the door hatched open to the house.

And she was there.

The years hadn't hurt her, not even a little bit. In fact, they added something. I think *elegance* is the word. She was tall, and in heels even taller. She was dressed in a floor-length tunic of soft red burgundy velvet over a body stocking of the palest blue that matched to perfection the color of her wide-set, vulnerable eyes. I was drawn to those eyes; they were not at all as I had remembered them. The innocence was gone, their childlike quality grown and aged. They were roadmap eyes that hid none of the pain that the years always bring. And I guess I realized just how childish my feelings and dreams about her really were. I felt a little something die inside me, and I hoped it didn't show on my face.

She had a large, wonderful mouth with soft pale lips. It was a mouth that smiled easily. It was smiling now.

"Come out of that machine and let me give you a hug," she said.

I hobbled out and could see my pain mirrored in those eyes. "It's good to see you," I said stupidly because it was all I could think of to say.

She moved to me and embraced me quickly, my face getting lost in long, black hair that smelled of vanilla. She pulled back to study my face. "What the hell happened to you?"

"Walked into a door," I told her.

She raised her eyebrows and sighed, hands cradling my face, cool hands softly cradling my face. "You haven't changed a bit," she said.

31

"I don't know whether I've been complimented or insulted," I replied.

Her eyes flashed me for a second, then she turned and took me by the arm and led me into the house. I realized at once why the grounds weren't laid out any better than they were. The place was large and round and held two stories' worth of housing. The first floor was mostly living area and kitchen. I assumed that everything else was on the second floor that connected by a wide sweeping spiral staircase that sprouted from the center of the room.

There seemed to be no walls per se. A holo filled all the walls, all around. It was as if we were standing in a whole houseful of furniture that was set outside. We were in Greece, mythical Greece. Fields of tall grass swaying to a soft, warm breeze glided gently around us. The Parthenon in all its newly built splendor stood proudly in the distance. About ten meters from us, several centaurs played a game of blind man's bluff with white togaed maidens, while a young man leaned against a juniper tree plucking a lyre. Their voices, mixed with the clear musical tones of the instrument, drifted to us on the soft cushion of the warm breeze.

The effect was total and quite pleasing. It almost made me forget that a real world out there was breaking off in large hunks right before my eyes. Almost.

Lynn was giggling softly as she led me to a low-slung sofa done in chocolate brown.

"What?" I asked.

She pointed me to the sofa and sat me down by pushing on my shoulders. Pain flared through my back, but I didn't let her see it.

"Now," I said. "What's so funny?"

She shook her head, her eyes twinkling. "You," she said. "After all these years when I sat around trying to picture meeting you again, I never pictured it like this." She put her arms in the air. "And God help me . . . this is you!"

"You've thought about me?" I asked.

Her face seemed to get sad all at once. "I'll get the first-aid kit," she said, and wandered off.

I sat back and looked around. Bob had done all right for himself, and for Lynn—better, for sure, than I could have done. There was a lot of real wood in the place, and oil-rich plastics.

"You want a drink?" she called from the kitchen.

I wanted a drink more than anything. "No, thanks," I returned. "But I'd sure take a smoker if you've got one."

"Regular or funny."

I wasn't much on dope, but I needed a little something to ease the pain rippling through my back. I didn't want her to know how much it was hurting. "Funny," I returned.

"Coming right up."

She wandered back into the room with a small medical kit that had a red cross on it and looked like it had never been used, and a pink-rolled reef.

Kneeling next to me on the couch, she leaned my head back over its edge. It felt great to be close to her, comfortable. It was like the last ten years had never happened.

She stuck the reef in my lips and lit it with a gold lighter. I drew the smoke gratefully into my lungs. It was sweet tasting, like cherries.

She leaned up close and studied my face. The pain came back to her eyes again. "What did they hit you with?" she asked.

"The kitchen sink," I answered.

"I believe it." She went into the kit and fished out a small yellow vial. "This won't hurt," she said, and I wished that I had a dollar for every time somebody told me that.

Breaking the vial in its center, she held it close to the cuts. A small puff of bright white smoke hissed out and enveloped my head for a second, and then it was gone. My face was immediately numb, and the rest of my body was getting that way from the smoker.

She took out a rag and began wiping the place. "Aren't you getting a little old for this?" she asked me.

I drew in another lungful of smoke, then handed the joint to Lynn. She took a small pull, then laid it on an ashtray on the table. I was beginning to feel pretty good.

"You haven't asked me why I've come," I said.

She had laid down the rag and was smoothing some sort of antiseptic cream on the bad places. I couldn't feel her fingertips. Her eyes never left her work. "You've come to offer me your condolences," she said.

"How did you . . . ?"

"You're really not that hard to figure out." She pulled away from me slightly and examined her handiwork. "The swelling's already going down," she said. "You've got a couple of pretty good bruises, but I think you'll survive."

I sat up straight, unable to meet her eyes. "I only just found out last night," I said. When I finally did look up, her eyes were distant, years distant. "I'm really sorry, Lynn. Really. Bob was a . . . good man."

She stood up abruptly and moved to a chair opposite the couch. "No he wasn't," she said quickly. "He was a son of a bitch."

# 5

The ashtray was a ceramic frog with a wide open mouth. Its long, sticky tongue would protrude, and when you laid the smoker on it, would suck the tongue back in and hold it for you. I picked the reef off the tongue and stuck it in my lips. I wasn't numb enough yet.

"You never understood Bob at all," Lynn said. "You were always so wide open with your friends that they couldn't do any wrong in your eyes. He hated you. Did you know that?"

I drew the smoke in and held it fiercely. I wasn't prepared for any of this. "Why?" I asked after streaming a long trailer of it out of my lungs.

She sat back in her chair. It was like a large, spongy hand that grasped warm fingers around her, wrapped her within itself. "He was born to wealth, Matt. He bought everything he had . . . including friends. That money link never meant anything to you. It was like you existed in a whole different sphere. He feared that in you. You were a threat to him, a denial of his way of life."

She pried the fingers from her body and reached across to take the reef from me. Taking a long pull, she handed it over, then eased herself back in the clutching hand. "He worked hard to become your friend, tried to buy you, to control you. That's so far removed from what you are that you never realized. When he couldn't control you, he went for the next best thing."

I stared at the reef and the gray, smoking ash that grew on its end. I put it back in the ashtray. I'd had enough. "You," I said.

Her wide mouth frowned, and it was as depressing as her smile was invigorating. Suddenly, I began to feel very old.

"He never wanted me," she said. "He only wanted you not to have me. It didn't take long to figure that out. He pulled the strings that got you drafted in the army. And when you

35

were gone, he had the time and the money to buy me away from you."

"*Buy* you?"

Leaning her head to the side, she stared at the centaurs. They were having races in the tall grass, shouting and laughing. "I didn't understand it at the time, but that's what it was. When he proposed, among other things, he offered me a quarter of a million in my own bank account to use however I wanted. It was independence, something that was very important to me back then, and he knew it."

"So did I," I said.

We shared a look, a second recognition for what was so important so long ago.

"Oh, Matt," she said. "I've wanted to call you so many times over the years."

"Why didn't you?"

She stood up, the grasping hand flying open. She walked up beside where I sat, but wouldn't look at me. "Shame," she said. "Embarrassment. Fear of rejection. You name it. He suckered me, Matt, brought me along like a prize pony. And all of it just to get at you. Do you know he told me you were dead?"

"What?"

"Showed me a paper and everything, killed in action." She folded her arms, watching the walls. "He proposed to me right after that. His timing was perfect, always has been. When you came back, I began to put it all together. I just couldn't face you after that."

I stared at the frog, watching the smoke drift indolently out of its mouth. "And I was too busy being noble," I said. "I kept tabs on you."

"Me too."

"What a world." I tried to stand up, forgetting about my back. I fell back again, my teeth clenching with the pain.

"What's wrong?" she asked, her hand coming up on my shoulder.

"Nothing," I replied. "I'll be okay."

Her lips tightened. "God damn you," she said. "You come strolling in here after all these years, and right off start giving me a runaround."

"It's not important."

"Wrong," she said. "Try again."

I put up my hands. "All right. All right."

36

I told her about the roadblock, and five minutes later she had me stripped to the waist, lying on my stomach on her living room floor, with a pad full of heat stingers gouging my back and spine. It helped. It helped a lot.

"You always were the most hardheaded person I've ever known," she said from above me.

"Why didn't you divorce him?" I asked the shag carpet.

She sat down Indian fashion next to me on the floor. "I had no reason," she replied. "Bob left me alone; I never saw him. You were out of my life. I'd never be able to find the kind of security that he offered. And I had lovers. Some long-term, others . . . well, you know."

"I know all right," I answered. "I know that you're the one who's giving *me* the runaround now. There's got to be more to it than that."

Running a hand along my back, she very deftly adjusted the pad and the subject matter. "You said you only heard about Bob last night. How did you hear?"

I stared at her from my sideways position on the floor. The years had built a lot more walls between us than I had realized. "Felix Bohlar told me," I said.

She chuckled without humor. "Felix is one of Bob's bought-and-paid-for friends," she said. "He'd kiss Bob's ass when the occasion arose, and in return, dear old hubby kept him on retainer and threw him a juicy morsel from time to time. Where did you see him?"

"He came and fished me out of a sleazy bar last night and told me."

Lynn leaned her head sideways so we could get eye to eye. "Why?"

I almost didn't answer, but she'd know I was holding back. "He thought that Bob was murdered."

She sat back up straight. "Murdered," she said, just like that. The word fell out of her mouth like a watermelon hitting the pavement from ten stories up.

I got on my hands and knees. The back pain had subsided to agony. I could live with that. "Could you get this thing off me?" I asked her.

She got to her feet and unwound the wrapping from my back, then helped me to my feet. I started getting my arms into my one-piece.

"Here, let me help you," she said, and held the sleeves up one at a time for my arms. "God, you're all scar tissue."

37

"Rough world," I answered, and pulled up my zipper to close the suit. I turned to her, took her by the shoulders. "Have you ever heard of the Springmaid Corporation?" I asked.

Her face got quizzical, and more than a little distant.

"What's wrong?" I asked.

"You're the second person to ask me about that this week."

"Who was the other one?"

"A woman," she answered. "I think it was a woman."

"You think?"

"She was in the shadows." Lynn pulled away from my grasp and put some distance between us. "What's going on?"

I looked at her. I hadn't intended to bring her into this if I could help it, but now it was different. Someone else was getting to her. Unzipping a side pocket, I reached in and pulled out the paper with the names on it. I walked up to arm's length and handed it to her.

"The names of the stockholders and board members of Springmaid," I said. "The crossed out ones have all died within the last six months."

She scanned the paper, her brow furrowing deeper the further she read.

"Felix died within minutes of showing me this," I said.

Her eyes came up. The stare was vacant. "What am I supposed to say?" she asked me.

I walked to the edge of the field to stare at the centaurs. They were staring back at me, their faces angry and suspicious. "All I know is that I've got a death list in my possession, and I feel like I have to at least find these people and warn them or something."

She walked up next to me and handed back the paper. "I know them all," she said. "They were all friends of my husband's from the Steering Committee."

"What's that?"

"It's kind of like a country club that Bob belonged to. Membership is limited to the richest and most powerful."

I turned to her, and the centaurs galloped away. "Never heard of it."

"I'm not surprised," she returned. "It's a totally secret society that guards its privacy and security relentlessly."

I refolded the paper and stuck it back in my pocket. "Sounds like a real fun bunch of folks."

"About as much fun as riding in the back of a garbage heli."

"What about the vis call?"

"What about it?"

"How much of it can you remember?"

She looked at me strangely, a look I couldn't read through. It was like she had walked in on her parents' making love and couldn't decide whether to be repulsed or fascinated. "It was . . . odd," she said finally.

"That's it?"

Her face fought a war with itself for a minute, then she just sort of sighed and ran both hands through her hair, pulling it back. "I can show it to you if you'd like."

I felt my mouth jump for the floor. "You've got a recording?"

"Old habit of Bob's that I picked up," she answered. "He was a financier, a go-between. The third man, you might say. He did so much business over the vis that the recordings avoided misunderstandings later on."

"Well, let's have a look at it."

"The tape is up in Bob's study," she said. "We can look at it up there."

Turning, she led me toward the stairs. The baluster was straight iron, the railing itself varnished ebony. The steps were heavily padded and carpeted. We didn't speak on the way up, things had already gotten too strange. She was holding back from me, holding a lot back. We had needed some time to readjust to each other. What we got was something akin to an introduction on the *Hindenberg*.

The second floor looked down onto the first like a mezzanine. There was no rail to separate it from a straight plunge down, though. Lynn saw me move in a little closer to the secure inside wall.

"Bob's idea," she said. "He called it his drunk catcher."

"Hell of a guy."

She led me to a locked door. It was steel. To get inside, she had to hand- and voice-print and give a special verbal code. The door creaked open, louder, I thought, than any door should ever creak.

I started to walk in, but she blocked the doorway with her body. "What do you want here, Matt?" she said, and her eyes were pleading. "What do you really want?"

"I'm just an old friend," I said, and tried to respond to the fear that formed the bottom end of her words, "just trying to do the right thing."

I tried to move past her again, but she grabbed my arms.

"Are you sure you want to get mixed up with all this? Are you really sure?"

"Lynn," I said, my voice harsh. "I'm here. Okay? I'm here."

"You might see more than you bargained for in here," she said. "And you'll certainly understand why I never divorced Bob."

There was pain in her eyes again, like he was even then reaching out of the grave to smother her. I squeezed her arm reassuringly and she stepped aside. I walked in, and will never walk into a room so easily again.

It wasn't an overly large place, which added to my immediate feelings of claustrophobia when I went in. It was painted black, flat black, and there were no lights in there to speak of. What lights there were were eyes—glowing eyes, glowing serpent eyes.

The room was a gnarled thing of twisted, outsized furniture and images of monsters. Everything except the monsters was painted that same flat black. All the furniture looked cold and sterile. It was either huge or tiny, but never human size. The chairs had twisted arms and tilted, off center backs, like something from a nightmare. Tables were round like beach balls or tilted on three legs at insane, useless angles. Bob's desk was a large tree stump, roots still reaching and intact.

And the monsters. The monsters were everywhere: dragons and serpents and hairy two-legged things. They were statues and holos and paintings, and they filled the room everywhere. The d.t.'s were never like this. Their eyes glowed, red or green, and smoke snorted in continual streamers from their nostrils. The place smelled of sulfur. Occasional tongues of fire shot from jagged-toothed mouths.

The walls were taken up with trophy heads of various breeds of dogs that Bob had killed. They were lined up ear to ear. Their tongues were out, mechanical drool dripping from them. Low growls emanated from them from time to time.

Bob was apparently fascinated with dismemberment. Wherever he had any space at all, he filled it with drawings that had his signature on them of people being tortured, cut up mostly, with everything from industrial lasers to hacksaws. The drawings were quite detailed.

There was no carpet on the floor. The floor was rubber, thick, hard, and slimy. Holos of dragons were jumping out at me from everywhere. It was like the fun house, but there wasn't anything funny about it.

Lynn came up beside me and took hold of my arm. "He would lock himself up in here for days at a time," she said, and I could feel her trembling against me. "Do you understand now?"

"You were afraid of him," I said.

She put her arms around me and I held her close and hoped that she couldn't detect the fears that gnawed at me like dragon's teeth.

She looked up at me and her eyes were wet. "Why didn't you fight for me, Matt?" she asked. "Why didn't you come and save me?"

I closed my eyes to try and shut out hers. I pictured the knight in shining armor coming to slay those dragons. I didn't have an answer for her.

She broke our embrace then, and moved away from me, composing herself. She walked solidly into the midst of the dark and twisted realities of Bob's rotted mind. Moving to a large painting of a Japanese-looking dragon chewing up a screaming man, she pulled at a corner and the whole picture swung out on hinges. It revealed several shelves of a tape library behind it.

"The call was so strange," she said over her shoulder, "that I filed it in the 'keeper shelves.'" She stood in front of the shelves, lightly running her unpainted nails across the rows of black cassettes that lined out before her.

"What are the other tapes?" I asked, following her over.

"Bob's private stash," she said. "I listened to a couple of them once. And they're all just vis conversations with Oriental people—Japanese, I think. I can't tell because I didn't understand the language."

"When did Bob learn to speak Japanese?"

She shook her head. "I didn't know he could. Anyway, I didn't listen to any more. Frankly, I didn't have the stomach for it."

I walked up closer to her. "I can understand that," I returned, and lay a hand on her shoulder. She shrugged it off.

"Here," she said, and pulled a tape off the shelf. "This is the one."

She turned around, not looking at me, and moved to the tree-stump desk. Its top was highly polished, and a computer console was inset squarely in its center. A realistic-looking cobra, coiled and ready to strike, was set off to one side. Its eyes were powerful arc lights that looked down at the desk top and lit it totally in a greenish-blue haze.

Lynn dropped the tape into the metal slot and punched up the console button. "I hope this makes more sense to you than it did to me," she said. She saw me looking around for the screen. "Watch the floor."

I walked around the end of the stump and stared down at the open expanse of rubber floor. All at once it became transparent, liquid. A body was floating in it, visible about waist up. It appeared to be a woman, but it was difficult to be sure. Shadows, moving shadows, kept drifting across the picture, giving me peek-a-boo looks at the caller, but never enough to make any real identification. In the background, behind the caller, there appeared to be crates of some kind, stacked up, filling every visible part of the screen. There was some manner of insignia stenciled on each of the crates. It was a simple picture, or lettering. I just couldn't be sure.

The caller spoke. "Am I talking to Mrs. Robert Hampton?" the voice asked. It was a husky voice, but mid-range. It could have been a woman, or maybe a man disguising his voice.

"Can I help you?" I heard Lynn's recorded voice say.

I looked at her. She stood, leaning against the stump and staring into space, at nothing.

Turning back to the vis, I stared at the caller. The shadows were maddening, plunging different parts of the face alternately in and out of the light. If I stared at it long enough, it began to play tricks with my eyes and I was looking at more of Bob's dragons.

"You are executor of your husband's estate," the voice stated flatly.

"Who are you?" Lynn asked.

The voice was cold, chilling. It was as inflectionless as a computer's and just as impenetrable.

"I am calling in regards to a specific section of your late husband's business interest."

"Listen," Lynn's voice replied, and it was slightly rattled. "I'm not that well versed on my husband's business affairs. Now, if you have a question, perhaps my lawyers..."

"I'm asking you," the voice said. "I want to know what your disposition of his stock in the Springmaid Corporation will be."

"I don't know who you are..."

"Answer the question," the voice demanded, and it was dripping with threatened menace, although its timbre never changed.

When Lynn's voice came back, it was controlled, but just barely. "I've never heard of the Springmaid Corporation," she said. "But even if I had, I wouldn't say anything to you about it."

Then the caller laughed, a low throaty cackle, like a chicken being strangled. Lynn moaned behind me. "Do you have any heirs?" the caller asked, and I thought I detected a flash of blue lipstick and blond hair.

"I don't have to listen to this," Lynn's voice said.

The figure on the vis tightened noticeably. "You'd better listen to this, if you've ever listened to anything in your life. Don't sell that stock. Sit on it. Leave it alone. Pretend it's a black widow spider that will bite you if you touch it."

The voice stopped for a second, measuring its effect. "And if you have heirs, don't will them any of that stock. It would be the kiss of death."

The screen blanked immediately and I was once again staring at the black floor. Lynn was sobbing softly behind me. I wanted to go to her, but I knew she wouldn't want it.

I wished I had a drink, just enough to steady my shaking hands.

# 6

Lynn's kitchen was made totally of surgical steel, the heavy-gauge stainless kind that they hone to an edge in scapels when they want to cut somebody up and mess around with their insides. It was all polished: fridge, cabinets, tables, utensils, everything; and it reflected the lights and our bodies in elongated reality mock-ups.

We sat across the table from one another, drinking coffee from clear glass mugs. The table was stainless steel also, cold to the touch, reflecting our faces in semicircles around its edges.

A small vis juiced just above the shiny sink. It was showing pictures of the Air Force cordoning off the city, choking it up, squeezing. The voice-over was saying how the President had declared a state of emergency and marshal law for the protection of the citizens. I was all for that, but I seemed to notice a number of large laser cannons tracking across the screen. It made you wonder just whose protection the troops were really there for.

I watched Lynn while she watched the screen. It was all there, all the stuff I remembered about her, but it was different. She was a stranger. I could sense that she felt the same about me. Hell, *I* felt the same about me.

"How bad is it out there?" she asked, not taking her eyes from the vis.

"Bad," I answered, and took a sip. It was too hot and too bitter, but it didn't matter. I drank it anyway. "The plague got started in the DMZ, in uncontrolled territory, and has spread slowly outward to where everybody's afraid of it. There are whole city blocks under plague control."

She looked at me. "So what happens now?"

"I guess we fight it," I answered. "The Air Force certainly isn't going to let us leave. I heard they've found an antidote, but it's scarce and expensive to manufacture. You may be able

44

to afford it," I said, and took another sip of coffee, "but I never could."

Her eyes flashed at me and her jaw tightened. "I refuse to feel guilty because I've got a few bucks," she said.

"I'm sorry," I said, and meant it. "Cheap shot. It comes from being poor too long."

"Forgiven," she said, and softened immediately. She was trying, she really was. Maybe too hard. We both knew that down under all the nonsense somewhere was a good solid relationship. And we were both trying our damndest to dig through to it.

"I think you're in danger," I said.

"You mean the vis call?"

I set the cup on the cold tabletop. As if that was her signal, Lynn picked up hers and began testing it, small, birdlike sips. She turned her nose up at the bitterness, but she drank it too.

"Try to understand," I said. "I'm in the midst of all this, and I haven't the slightest idea of what's going on with any of it. But if the woman on the vis was the same one I saw at the bar last night with Felix—I'd say you were in one hell of a lot of trouble."

She wrapped both hands around her cup, trying to warm up the natural chill of the room. "It's all so confusing," she said. "It's as if the whole world is..."

"Coming apart," I finished. "I know."

"So what do you suggest I do?"

I laid my hands flat on the table, felt the numbness seep gradually into them. Cold, all-encompassing. When I took my hands away, I left behind a faint steamy smudge from my body's warmth. Then it faded and disappeared.

"I don't know what any of this is worth," I said. "I thought I was dead already, on the skids. Then Felix came along and breathed some new life into me, some need. I've walked back into your life, and I'm not going to turn around and walk back out without a fight. I'm not real smart, and I tend to not know when to shut my mouth, but if you're willing, I'd like to hang around and look after you for a while, at least until I know what the lay of the land is."

She started. "You mean, like move in?"

The coldness of her tone surprised me. "Only in a professional sense," I returned.

She stood and walked to the sink, pouring out her coffee.

"I'll have to think about it," she said, like she was talking to the kid who mows her lawn.

"It *is* my profession," I said, unable to keep the edge out of my voice.

She flared around at me. "Was," she said angrily. "Was your profession. All you are right now is another shipwreck piled up on the reefs."

I stood. "Thanks for the coffee," I said, and started toward the down-tube.

"Wait."

I turned and stared at her.

"I didn't mean that," she said. "At least not like it sounded. It's just that I don't know whether you want to do this for me or for you, you know?" Her eyes traveled to the floor, then came slowly back up. "You wouldn't fight for me ten years ago. Why should I think that you will now?"

"Okay," I said, and moved back into the kitchen. "Maybe I deserved that, and maybe I didn't." I sat down. "I get four hundred a day, plus expenses. If you're not satisfied with the job I do, fire me and you only have to pay the expenses that I have receipts for, and no salary. If you don't want me, I can give you a list of qualified people you might want to use instead. But, it's my professional opinion that you need some protection right now, and I suggest that you do something about it."

She smiled, more at ease. "Okay," she said. "We'll give it a try. I don't mind telling you that the call has had me scared."

"Scared enough not to leave the house?"

"How did you know?"

I grinned. "Your wall told me."

She rolled her eyes. "Don't believe everything that Roger says," she replied. "He gossips about everybody."

She turned on the tap to fill her cup with water, and her attention was caught by the vis. "Come here," she said. "Quick."

I got up and moved to the sink. The vis was juicing a picture of a riot. Kevlar-suited cops and Fancy Dans were guarding the entrance to some sort of factory. A huge crowd was filling the streets, pressing angrily against the big iron gates that opened onto the grounds. The mob would boil up, seemingly out of control. And when it appeared that they were going to storm the gate, the cops would open fire with their frumps and lasers, scattering the crowd and leaving a

46

pile of bodies on the ground. Then the mob would form again.

"Jesus," I whispered. "The whole city's going up in flames."

"That's the Fullerchem plant," Lynn said.

"What?"

"Fuller Chemical," she said, somewhat irritated. "Harvin Fuller, owner and chairman of the board."

I looked at her. She nodded, eyes wide.

"Yeah," she said. "His name is on your list."

I turned and stared at the screen for a minute, watched the carnage that raged around the gates like yellowjackets swarming around a burning hive. The name Fullerchem meant something to me. I looked at Lynn, but my thoughts were somewhere else. Then it hit me. "They're the people making the vaccine," I said.

"What's that got to do with anything?" she asked.

I shrugged. "Hell, I don't know."

"What kind of detective are you?"

"The confused kind."

She took a drink of the water she had just drawn. She shivered slightly. "Yech," she said, and poured the rest out.

"What's wrong?"

She stuck her tongue out. "The water. It tastes awful."

I grabbed the cup from her and tapped a mouthful. I took a sip and rolled it around in my mouth. It was bitter, just like the coffee. Spitting it out, I put the glass up to my nose and sniffed. There was a slight odor, a musky smell. It wasn't natural. Something had been put in the water.

"What's the source of your water supply?" I asked.

"I don't know what you mean."

I put the cup down and took her by the shoulders. "Your water. Are you self contained here, or does it come from outside?"

"Outside," she said, and the fear was on her face. "Why?"

I looked at the sink, my own thoughts whirling. "I'm not sure, not really sure."

The fear turned rock solid. "Damn it, Matt," she spat. "Don't you start this shit again. What the hell's going through your mind?"

"I think that something's been put in the water from outside the walls."

"What?"

She was breathing heavy now, and I was right along with her. "I honestly don't know," I answered.

She pulled my hands off her shoulders. "You just won't stop playing the game, will you? This is business," she said. "I'm paying you for answers. Now, what do you think it is?"

"I think it's the plague," I said flatly.

The businesswoman was gone and the fear was back in control. "Why?" she asked, incredulous.

"To get you," I said. "And probably me."

She turned and walked about five paces from me, then abruptly turned back around. "That's insane," she shrilled, voice out of hand. "Infecting the water supply from outside would infect the entire development."

I thought about the woman on the vis. "I know," I answered.

She groped for the table, sitting down heavily. Her lips moved silently at first, like she was cranking up the vocal cords. When it came out, it was hoarse. "Oh, my God," she said. "What do we do?"

I turned to the sink. "Throw up," I replied, and stuck my finger down my throat.

# 7

The street crowds began to get thick several blocks from the Fullerchem plant. They mulled restlessly, angrily. They all wore the masks, snorting frost, the exposed parts of their faces and eyes stung red by the frigid wind, standing out in sharp contrast to the bright white of the masks. They bunched into tight groups, safety in numbers, waving their arms, yelling, anything to ease the problems that were overwhelming them through no fault of their own. The noose was choking now, in a very physical way, in a way that everyone finally understood and feared on a gut level. The razor's edge of panic was there now, poised, ready to slice into something vital.

And I had the plague.

"We'll never get through this," Lynn said from the seat beside me. She was trying to keep the panic out of her own voice, knowing full well that it was ultimately an exercise in futility.

"They said to come this way," I returned, not taking my eyes off the crowd that moved around the bullet, bumping us, their slack eyes staring listlessly through the windows. I moved slowly, nudging them aside as I went. The crowd was like a mud hole. If you stopped, you'd sink down into it and never get free.

They were everywhere, on the streets and sidewalks, thickening like beans left in the mike too long. They stamped through the snow drifts, scattered them, obliterated them. And the farther into the heart of the crowd we hummed, the angrier they became. What were ripples on the outer edges were rolling white-capped waves farther in. Mobs have their own personalities. They are a single brain, totally committed to a single thought. They were beyond reason, beyond discussion, beyond hope if they persisted.

We got through another block that way, and the plant was

49

in sight farther down the street. Fullerchem was right on the edge of the decay, and most of the street crowds were poor folks. But there were a surprisingly large number of goodtowners out there, too. And their faces were just as angry, their fists just as clenched. I'd gone as far as the bullet would take us. The mob was too thick. I shut us down.

"Why are we stopping?" Lynn asked, her voice climbing a ladder.

I shook my head, and wondered why I always had to be the strong one. "We're done for in the hummer," I told her. "Let's get out on foot."

"Out there?" she asked, pointing to the wall of bodies that flattened against us.

I looked out the back window. We were totally sealed in. I took a breath. "I'd be happy to entertain any other ideas," I said.

Her head began snapping around, watching the windows and the wall of flesh that was crushing in on us. "What if they won't let us in?"

"You've got an appointment."

"What if he doesn't want to give us the vaccine?"

I turned to stare at her. "Then you'll come back out here and take your chances with the rest of humanity. What the hell do you want me to tell you?"

Her face got hard, ugly. But it was what she needed. "Well shit," she said. "Let's do it."

"I heard that."

I notched the door handle and started pushing outward. The crush against us was too great.

"I can't get my door open," she said.

I started shoving against it. No luck. "Try the window," I told her, and rolled down mine.

It was a mistake. Hands were reaching inside, arms attached to misfiring brains. Lynn screamed. A hand in a sea of hands had reached in and grabbed her by the hair. It was pulling her head, twisting. And these were supposed to be the sane ones.

"Matt!"

"Damn!" I lunged across the seat, biting at the hand that had her. My teeth sank into, then through, the flesh, and it wasn't until I tasted someone else's blood in my mouth that it let go.

She jumped over by me, both of us twisted in a heap

between the front seats. Arms filled the windows, swaying, curling, like tentacles with attached hands. Lynn grabbed me and held on fiercely, her breath coming in short, ragged gasps.

Faces were pressed against the windshield, blank masked faces, inhuman faces. The anger welled up in my throat, and my legs came up to kick at the faces behind the glass.

"Get back!" I screamed at them. "God, go away!"

My heels were flailing, and the windshield shattered in short, awkward lines with blue tint. It shattered like a clear jigsaw puzzle, turning the people on the other side into the uneven, craggy aliens that they were.

I kept kicking, and the shatterproof glass began coming out in large sheets of interconnected parts.

"Come on!" I yelled to Lynn, and slapped her face when she wouldn't let go. "Let's get out of the fucking car."

I kicked out the rest of the glass and sat her up.

"Let's go," I said, and started pushing her up through the open place. People were reaching in through there. I kicked out some more to drive them back and shoved Lynn through the opening.

She moaned loudly, and blood was streaming from windshield fragment cuts in her hands.

"On the roof!" I yelled, and she was scrambling up on top of the bullet.

I came right behind her, trying to avoid the glass on the hood. I couldn't do it. I felt the cuts, ignored them, and scrambled onto my feet.

Their yelling rose in pulsating waves and they were grabbing for my legs, eyes fixed, nonhuman. I kicked out at those faces, angry at the emotional monsters that could steal away their humanity. I wanted to drive out the demons.

"Matt!"

I looked up at Lynn. A large, gray heli was floating up overhead. It was fixed with the Fullerchem emblem on the side: a test tube filled with flowers. It was coming for us.

Plant guards in shiny red exos stood on the deck, weapons ready. One of them had a blowhorn.

"DO YOU HAVE AN APPOINTMENT?" the voice blared out, laced with nerve-jangling static.

Someone grabbed my ankle, almost pulling me off the hood. I scrambled up on the roof with Lynn. She was frantic, nearly out of control.

"Yes," she was screaming. "Yes! Yes!"

"NAME, PLEASE."

She was shaking, lips trembling. We began rocking. They were shaking the bullet. I held her to steady her.

"This is Lynn Hampton, you son of a bitch," I called. "And you'd better get us up there right now."

"WHO ARE YOU?"

I lost my balance, nearly taking both of us to the ground. I choked back what I wanted to say, and instead, answered his questions.

"Mathew Swain," I called up. "I'm Mrs. Hampton's bodyguard."

"ARE YOU ON THE APPOINTMENT LIST TOO?"

The bullet was buffeting back and forth, the crowd caught up with the excitement. "Yes!" I screamed. "Get us up!"

"I DON'T SEEM TO FIND YOUR NAME . . ."

"Get us up! We'll talk about it then."

They densified their helipacks and floated low overhead, lowering a rope ladder down to us. It swung over by me and I reached out to take it. The crowd was climbing up on the hood, coming for us, wanting they didn't know what.

Lynn's face was altered, different, like a latex mask that still looks like the person but has none of that person in it. I took one of her hands and made it grasp the rope.

"You've got to hold on!" I yelled at her, hoping to crack through the ice that was hardening over her senses.

Hands scrabbling, reaching.

Her other hand came around on its own to take the rope. She was nodding.

"Let's go," she pleaded. "Hurry."

"Take it up!" I yelled, and a figure loomed beside me. I came around with a left and it took the impact, tumbling back on the people on the hood.

The heli was going up. It was being pelted now with chunks of sidewalk and trash and even snowballs. Lynn got her feet hooked on a rung. She was set.

I pushed another one off the roof and jumped for the rope, despite the cuts on my hands and the blood running freely down my arm.

Catching hold just above Lynn's hand, I came around to take hold of her, too. She was slowing her breath to long pulls, trying to get herself together.

They got some proper height, then began hoisting up the

ladder. A minute later we lay, panting with the excitement and the exertion, on the stainless steel deck.

The punk with the bullhorn moved over to us. His face was set hard and cold, like a plaster-of-paris mold. He had a moustache, but it didn't look like it went with the rest of his face. It was a moustache drawn on a photograph by a twelve year old child with a grease pencil.

"We need a voiceprint," he said. "Just to be sure."

I ignored him and turned to Lynn. The icy crust of fear was melting away from her. "You okay?" I asked.

She took one long breath, sat up on the deck. "I'm sorry," she said, smoothing her hair, trying to get human again. "I guess I didn't handle myself very well back there."

"You did fine," I returned, and she had. "How're your hands?"

She looked down, genuinely surprised at the blood and cuts. "I don't feel anything," she said.

"Shock," I answered. "You'll feel it pretty soon."

She shook her head, laughing quickly. "My hands used to be one of my best features," she said.

I laughed with her. "You've got plenty of other good features to go around," I answered.

She looked at me, the relief still in control of the fear; but I knew that it, too, like the numbness in her hand, would soon pass.

"If I didn't know you better, sir," she said coyly. "I would think that you're trying to sweet talk me."

"Maybe you don't know as much as you think?"

The plaster of paris punk bent down. "I want a voiceprint," he said.

I sat up next to Lynn. "Why don't you go play in traffic," I told him.

"I could toss you out of here right now," he said, low, through clenched plaster teeth. "And nobody would blame me."

I leaned out over the edge. Far below me, the mob swarmed mindlessly, expending itself in furious bursts of energy. Someone had gotten in the bullet, got it moving. The sea of anger began to part, to clear a space to the gates.

"Would you stop playing games," Lynn said, the mood quickly switching back. "Give the man what he wants."

I looked at her; the eyes were harder. I grunted and stood

up. My back was killing me again, legs stiff as advanced rigor mortis.

"Okay," I said, rapping my knuckles on the hard shell of his exo. "Let's do what we need to do."

Lynn stood up beside me. I tried to give her a hand, but she ignored it.

The punk led us to the cabin, then in. The outer shell was thick steel, heavily riveted. The heli began making a long, slow turn back toward the plant.

The inside of the cabin was plush, but a touch odd. Everything was nice, but it was all mismatched. Different styles and periods of furniture, contrasting colors, blue carpet and green-paneled walls. It was like drinking beer out of a champagne glass. Nut dishes filled with different colored pills were set everywhere.

"Over here," the plaster man said.

We followed him to a far wall. There was an apparatus attached to it that looked like a large ear. The man wiggled his thumb at the thing.

"Talk to Daddy," he said. "Name only."

Before I could think of anything wise to say, Lynn elbowed me out of the way and moved up to the ear. "Lynn Hampton," she said.

The machine whirred for a minute, waiting for the voice to shoot downtown to the data bank, then back. A green light flashed on beneath the ear. "Huggy-huggy," came its low mechanical voice through a speaker grill.

When Lynn was through, I stepped up for my turn at bat. I said my name and got the green light, but it didn't talk to me. Good thing, too.

"That's it," the punk said, and turned to the cabin door. "Make yourselves at home. We'll take care of those cuts at the plant."

I followed him to the door, stopping him just as he was going out.

"Everything's okay now?" I asked. "We're cleared to go in?"

He nodded mechanically. "You're cleared."

"And we're the visitors, and you're just the hired help?"

His stiff eyes narrowed. I could swear I heard them creak. He nodded again.

"Good," I said. "Then this is for you."

I came around with a good right, a frustrated right, and

54

caught him just under the chin to where I could hear those plaster teeth snapping together.

He went down on his can on the deck, automatically reaching for the burner on his hip.

"No no no," I told him, wiggling my finger back and forth. "How would your boss like it if you went around blowing up some of his distinguished visitors? It wouldn't look good at Christmas bonus time."

His shooting hand went instead up to rub his sore chin. "I'll remember this," he said, struggling to his feet.

"Great," I replied. "And while you're remembering things, remember to stick your blowhorn where the sun don't shine."

I turned and went back into the cabin, slamming the door behind me. Lynn was sitting on a low-slung couch, the simple green tunic she had changed into torn and dirty. She was staring at her hands.

I walked to the window to watch twenty meters down at the crowd. That's where I should have been, down there with them, instead of floating above it all in a private heli.

"You were right," Lynn said from behind me.

"About what?"

"My hands. They *are* beginning to hurt."

"We'll get you fixed up in a minute." My hands hurt, too, but I found out a long time ago that pain is a very relative commodity. I slowly rotated my back, trying to work out that particular pain. Below me, the crowd had cleared a runway to the gate. Felix's bullet sat at the other end of the gauntlet, about a block from the gates. They were going to try and break through. Cops and punks were clustered on the walls and in front of the gates, ready to do battle.

"Are we contagious right now?" Lynn asked me.

I turned to her for a second, then back to the window. "Naw," I replied. "The virus incubates for a couple of days. You're not contagious until it makes you sick."

"You sure?"

A laugh found its way out of my throat. "One of the advantages of spending all your time in barrooms is that you get to hear all the gossip, and believe me, the plague has been the major gossip for a long time."

"How long before... before..."

"It depends on the person," I replied. "The virus itself isn't fatal; it's the paranoia that gets people, the madness."

"How?"

The mob below was chanting in unison: "Ram it! Ram it!" They were rising to a fever pitch.

"Suicide," I told her. "Accidents, murder . . . they prey on each other through fear. I've even heard of people starving to death because they feared poison in the food."

"That's horrible," she said.

"It's all that and more," I replied. The chanting was getting louder, rising to us like the ammonia smell from a cesspool. "Are you going to handle this business with Fuller all right?"

"I suppose so," she answered, and in the reflection of the cabin glass, I watched her dig a comb out of the small purse that dangled from the cinch around her waist. She started combing her hair. "I'm under control, if that's what you mean."

I nodded at her reflection. "Don't mention anything to him about what happened at your place. I want to feel him out first."

"Why?"

"Trust me. Let me do most of the talking, and go along with what I say."

"But . . ."

I waved it off. "You hired me to do a job, remember? Let me do it in my own way."

She didn't answer. Instead, she took a compact from the purse and began a minor repair job on her face. Below, the mob had peaked. They wound the hum all the way up on Felix's bullet, then turned it loose. It sped through the open ground, building speed. The crowd filled in the spaces behind it like a human zipper. They were screaming frantically, out of control.

It was really moving by the time it got within range of the gates. It didn't matter. The death rattle exploded all at once, from fifty hands, loud, deafening. It brought Lynn up out of her seat. Everything poured into the bullet and surrounding crowd: frumps, lasers, napalm; and where it had been was now growing a monstrous orange and black flower of destruction that blossomed into the dirty gray sky. The price of admission.

I suppose I should have been happy. That was the end of the evidence against me. The end of Felix.

# 8

The hallway was a dark, ill-defined place. The outer walls and ceiling were lost in some soft, all-consuming haze, like $CO_2$ smoke, but not physically substantial.

Lynn and I walked into it, toward the glowing red circle at its end. We had gotten cleaned up some, and our hands had been doctored and bandaged.

Lynn looked over at me, a halfhearted smile curling her lips. "I meant to tell you," she said, softly, like we were in a church—or a funeral home. "Harv is a trifle . . . strange."

"You sure know how to pick friends," I returned.

The hallway was dripping with a sickly sweet smell, like a room full of dying violets. Holos of pills floated everywhere. Large pills, mammoth. They floated languidly through the hallway, swaying to soft music that came from nowhere. They tumbled gracefully, capsules in soft pastels, reflecting bands of white light in slick, sensuous patterns. The overall feeling was highly erotic. If the pills were women, they would be belly dancers.

"Nothing like enjoying your work," I said.

She shrugged. "It's the key to success."

With no definition to the room, there was no way to judge how far we were moving. I keyed on the red circle, watched it grow larger. When we got closer, I saw that it wasn't a circle at all. It was a large throbbing heart.

We came up on it, as tall and wide as double doors—red pumping with the heartbeat sound. I reached out and touched the thing. It was wet and mushy.

"So now what?" I asked.

She put her hands on her hips. "I guess we go in."

"How?"

She tilted her head and looked at me sideways. "Put one foot in front of the other?"

"Wonderful," I replied. "Everybody's a comedian."

57

I walked right up to where my body was touching it. Then there was a vacuum sound, and the thing sucked me into it. A second of darkness and fear of suffocation, then it spit me out into a room.

The place was extremely long and narrow. It was shaped like a cylinder, like I was standing on the inside of a large pipe. The walls glowed a shifting pattern of primary colors, easing through the spectrum then back again.

Lynn came through the opening, bumping into me because I had never moved.

The room was bare up where we were standing, but the farther it went, the more cluttered it became. It was like a junkyard, with electronic gear and old broken furniture piled everywhere. I don't think the place had ever been cleaned.

We started walking.

There was a desk at the end of the room. It was overflowing with trash: food wrappers and half-eaten things, cups and papers, pieces of junk.

A man sat behind the desk, nearly lost behind his mountain of garbage. A hand came up to wave at us as we walked.

"Come on in," he called. "Welcome."

The going got tougher. We were having to step over things, crates of test tubes, boxes of pills, all covered with thick layers of dust. There were clothes strewn around, like someone had worn them until they had gotten dirty, then simply took them off and discarded them to their fate.

And pills. There were pills everywhere, in bowls and boxes and old nut dishes. It looked like someone had ransacked a legal drug parlor.

We got up to the desk, and the man was up and around it, kicking packing crates out of the way to get to us. He was short, shorter than Lynn anyway, and was wearing some purple overalls without shirt or shoes. He had a chubby, cherub face, rosy-cheeked and angelic. His hair was wild, unkempt, hanging nearly to his shoulders. His beard was long and straggly like a robin's nest. He looked just like an overgrown kid—except around the eyes. The eyes were impassible and moved with a snakelike precision that bothered me. But then, I'm naturally suspicious.

"Lynn!" he yelled. "God-DAMN, it's good to see ya." His drawl was hard, native west Texas all the way. He sounded like he had just fallen out of a mesquite tree.

He moved right over and embraced her like they were long lost relatives. Pulling back, they kissed on the lips.

"How are you, Harv?" she asked, smiling.

"Totally wasted," he said. "Absolutely bonkers."

He looked over at me like he had just seen me for the first time. Those eyes clicked up to appraise me. There were several seconds of contact, then his hand shot out to take mine.

"Harv Fuller," he said, like a salesman trying to hype Florida marshland. "How's it goin'?"

"Rapidly," I returned, answering the pressure of his grip despite the cuts. "Name's Swain."

"Right proud to know ya, Swain," he said. "Any friend of Lynn's . . ."

"Well, I'm more the hired help," I replied.

"Do tell," he said, and nodded at that, nodded like he knew everything there was to know about everything. "Heard you had a little trouble gettin' through the gate."

"Yeah. I think you've got some serious public relations problems out there."

He shrugged with his chubby cheeks. "The axle greases that way sometimes," he said, and picked up a bowl full of blue and yellow capsules.

"Pill?" he asked, and shoved the dish in my face. "These little babies'll turn ya inside out, kinda move things in slow motion, and make ya wonder if ya locked the door on the way out. Developed 'em myself."

"No thanks," I told him.

He turned to Lynn. "Pill, darlin'?"

She flashed an automatic smile and shook her head.

He shrugged again, grabbed a fistful of the things and began throwing them into his mouth like peanuts. His eyes got distant for a minute, like a fighter who just took a roundhouse right on the jaw; then he jerked, wagging his head.

"Whoa," he said, and took a deep breath. "Sneaks on up on ya sometimes, y'know? Hell, ah got so many chemicals runnin' through my body, that when ah die, they're gonna hafta bury me at a toxic dump."

He looked at each of us in turn, then jerked his head again. "Christ on a stick, ah'm forgettin' my hospitality," he said. "Here." He slipped up a couple of yellow plastic packing crates, dusted them off with a red-and-black-checked bandanna that he pulled out of his overalls, then made a sweeping gesture with his arm. "Have a seat."

We sat.

Going back behind his desk, he shoved enough stuff aside so that we could see him between the twin mountains of foil and half-chewed burgers and white sacks.

"Hell of a way to make a livin'," he said.

"I missed you at Bob's funeral," Lynn said quietly.

All at once, his face got all red and bloated, and his hands went to his throat, tongue protruding. It was like he was choking. He came up out of the chair and fell across the desk, knocking his little mountains all over us and the floor. He lay on his back, flopping.

I was up, moving to him.

"Do something!" Lynn yelled.

"No, no," he choked, taking a hand away from his throat and waving it crazily. "I'll be . . . all right."

I just stood there, staring down at him. After a minute his spasms began to subside and his breathing became easier. Within another minute, he was breathing normally and sitting back in his chair like nothing had happened.

"Pardon," he said, while I watched the color drain out of his face—deep crimson back to its normal jaundiced off-white. "Happens from time to time." He twirled his finger. "All that shit that runs through me sometimes doesn't get along." He picked up a bowl full of red capsules. "Pill?" he asked.

We shook our heads and watched him take some more. "Started this business when ah was still a kid," he said, smiling dully, eyes glazed. "Ah just *loved* playin' with the chemicals, findin' new ways to turn the folks around. Y'know, ah've invented four hundred and thirty-seven different drugs, and all but eighty of 'em have gotten the legal stamp."

"What about the others?" I asked.

He flashed me a quick smile, and his dull eyes twinkled. He ignored the question. "When ah started, people thought ah was a maniac, or an imbecile . . . or worse." He gave a sharp laugh. "Funny how things turn out."

"Yeah," I said. "Funny. Do you know that Felix Bohlar is dead?"

"No," he said. "Felix? He was a young man. What happened?"

"He was murdered."

Fuller raised his eyebrows and sighed. "Jeez, they're droppin' like flies."

I watched him for a minute. It was strange. He hadn't asked us why we'd come. It was as if he were waiting for us to make the first move. I decided to see what he was willing to talk about.

"Can I ask you what may seem like a dumb question?" I asked.

He tossed another red pill into his mouth. "Ask away."

"How come you're the only company that makes the antidote for the virus?"

He cocked his head like he was surprised at the question. His smile faded somewhat. "Well, that's kind of a strange set of circumstances," he replied. "The vaccine is no secret. It's a matter of public record. But there's a certain . . . ingredient in it that no one but me seems to have much access to."

"Which is?"

"It wouldn't mean anything to you," he said.

"Try me."

His eyes got distant again, foggy, and when he came back around, he looked at Lynn. "Ah'm beginnin' to get real interested in why you came here," he said.

"How come it's so expensive?" I asked.

He turned to me. The smile hadn't faded. "It's expensive to make," he answered. Then, "Oh, ah see what you're gettin' at—old Harv-boy makin' a killin' off other folk's misery. Well, ah'll tell ya the truth. Ah ain't makin' doodly off this stuff. Costs a bunch to produce it, and ah'm takin' just barely enough profit to make the operation worthwhile. Ah'm jest doin' it because ah'm a nice guy. Ah care."

I shifted around on the crate, wishing I had some support for my back. "You've killed more people outside today than you've probably saved with the vaccine."

I heard Lynn groan beside me.

"Y'all are wrong there," he said. "Ah haven't killed nobody. We're all free to choose, ain't we. Those folks out there have killed themselves. Silliest damn thing ah ever saw. Hasn't got a thing in the world to do with me. Ah'm jest a businessman tryin' to get along like everybody else."

"Surely there must be something . . ."

"Okay," he said. "You tell me. Ah guess ah could make the stuff and give it away for free. Ah'd go outta business in about a week that way, and we still couldn't vaccinate more than

61

ten . . . fifteen thousand people tops. The state government hasn't got the money to pay for it, and the feds . . . they're camped around the city right now waitin' to level the whole blamed place if it looks like things are gettin' outta hand."

Lynn stiffened. "What!"

"You got it," he returned. "It's a hard world, but if you've got a suggestion on how to handle this, ah'm willin' to listen."

I didn't have any suggestions.

"Fact is," he said. "We may all be history. Done for." He picked up the bowl again. "Pill?"

I shook my head. Lynn took one. Fuller picked up one to match hers.

"Jest to be sociable," he said, and tossed it into his mouth. His face creased for a moment, in thought. "Ah been thinkin' these last couple of days." He paused, but his eyes didn't leave us this time. "Them madmen are all over the damned streets," he said. "More all the time. What happens when there's more of them than there is of us?" His eyes suddenly went wide and he snapped his fingers. "Have y'all been vaccinated?" he asked.

"Well, no," Lynn said, a tad too quickly. "We haven't."

He sat back and grinned wide. His bare feet came up to rest on the desk top. The bottoms of his feet were black with dirt. "One of the advantages of bein' in my position," he said, "is that ah'm able to help out mah friends from time to time." He grinned over at me. "We are friends, aren't we?"

"Till the end," I replied.

"Good." He pulled his feet off the desk and stood up. There was a long, narrow shelf attached to the wall behind him. It was cluttered with medicine and pill bottles. "Now let's have a look-see," he said, finger moving from bottle to bottle.

I shot Lynn a glance. She returned it with a look of expectation. I could physically watch her face sag with relief.

"Here we go," Fuller said, and pulled a big, brown bottle off the shelf. Grabbing it, he spun around and slammed it down on the desk top. "Bingo," he said.

He let himself fall heavily into his chair and creaked back with it. He relaxed like he was asleep for a few seconds, then snapped straight up. "So, where were we?" he asked.

"The bottle," Lynn helped.

"Bottle?"

She pointed.

He looked at the brown bottle like he had never seen it before, then his eyes widened with recognition. "Right," he said. "The bottle."

Twisting off the cap, he handed it over to Lynn. "Here ya go, darlin'. Take a big ole swig."

She held the bottle out there, her face unsure.

"Go ahead on," he told her. "Jest tip that baby up and take a good swalla."

She looked at me. I nodded. Taking the bottle to her lips, she drank down a gulp, then passed it over to me. It was my turn to look at Fuller.

"You too, buddy," he said, and emphasized the word *buddy* a little too strongly for my tastes.

I took a drink. It was thick and tasteless. I'd like to say that I felt guilty about it, that I wanted to be outside those gates with the people like me; but it would be a lie. I grabbed it up and drank it down, and never once thought about anything but saving my miserable hide.

He smiled, satisfied after I handed him back the bottle. I could tell by looking at him that he thought he had it all worked out—Lynn and her new boyfriend had come to him to get set free. Well, maybe that wasn't so far from wrong.

"I want to talk to you about the Springmaid Corporation," I said.

For the first time his smile faded completely. He leaned up on the desktop. "Just who the hell are you?" he asked, and the accent had faded with his smile.

I took the paper out of my zipper pocket and handed it to him. The well-creased folds got some more exercise. He scanned it. "You from the..." He started a sentence, then started again. "What's this to you?" His eyes wandered with suspicion toward Lynn.

It was my turn to be vague. "From the looks of this list," I told him. "It seems to me that you're in a great deal of trouble."

He threw a handful of green capsules into his mouth, gulping audibly. "Ah don't know what you mean."

"What I mean is that the life expectancies of the stockholders of the Springmaid Corporation look to be a bit . . . shall we say, on the narrow side."

He made a face and shook his head. "Coincidence," he said.

Listening to my own initial words echoing back to me, I

knew that he didn't believe them any more than I did. "What are you people trying to hide, anyway?" I asked him.

The smile was back. "Swain," he said. "This is no way for friends to be talkin' to one another."

I stood up and leaned against the desk, staring at him. Not smiling. "Let me lay it out here to where you can understand it," I said. "Felix gave me this paper"—I leaned across the desk and snatched it away from him—"and died five minutes later. Today, someone tried to kill Lynn." I straightened, glaring. "Now, I don't know about your friends, but I'm kind of funny about mine. I like having them around and in one piece. Now, somebody's out to get you people, and with or without your help, I'm going to do my damnedest to stop them."

His face went somber, but it wasn't mean. He nodded. "Maybe you got a point," he said. "Now, that's just a maybe, but ah's allowin' that you might be right."

He stood and turned to put the medicine bottle back on the shelf. The muscles on his bare back rippled as he moved. He was in far better shape than his attitude would indicate.

He turned around, lips pursed. "What can ah do to help?" he asked.

"Tell me about Springmaid," I returned immediately.

"Can't," he said. "It ain't jest me; there's others involved." He sat back down in his chair. "Tell you what ah will do. There's a kind of a . . . club . . ."

"I already told him about the Committee," Lynn said.

He gave her a Mount Rushmore look, blank but meaningful. "Okay," he said. "Suppose we all meet out there tonight, all the names . . . left on the list. If everyone agrees, we'll talk about Springmaid."

I nodded; it was all I was going to get. "Sounds like a deal," I answered.

Lynn stood up, happy. "Thanks, Harv," she said, and leaning across the desk, gave him a hug. "You've made me feel a lot better."

"Well, darlin'," he said. "You know ah'd do anything for you. Anything for a friend."

"We'd better get going," I said. "I know you're a busy man."

He chuckled at that one. "Loaded down," he replied. "It was nice makin' your acquaintance."

I nodded, and turned to go.

"Swain," he said, and I turned back around.

"A thought jest occurred to me."

"Uh huh."

"If what you say is true, about the list and all, then one of us—one of the names on the list, is probably the one doin' the killin'."

"That's probably about it," I responded.

He picked up a bowl of green ones. "Pill?" he asked, and responded positively to his own question.

# 9

Since Felix' bullet was wasted, Fuller gave us a ride back to Lynn's place in one of his company's helis. Floating up to Roger, the wall, we cleared air space and went in. They took us right up to the stem door of her dome.

A minute later we were taking it easy on her couch, while the holo walls floated us at bird level gently through an Arabian Nights landscape—old Baghdad, crammed with towering minarets and veiled maidens astride flying carpets. They'd wave to us as they'd pass.

"Is it true?" she asked me. "What Harv said about the killer?"

"You mean about the killer being one of your friends? Probably." I sat up straight. "You got anything to eat around here?"

She frowned in surprise. "You can still eat after all we've been through?"

"Every day," I replied. "It's an old habit of mine."

She stood, brushing a long strand of black hair from her ripped tunic. "I'll see what we've got." She walked toward the kitchen. "I know that Harv's weird," she called over her shoulder, "but his heart sure is in the right place."

"Sure," I replied. "Big as all outdoors."

She disappeared into the kitchen, her voice drifting back. "Do I detect a note of sarcasm in your voice?"

"Natural suspicion," I called back, and didn't mention the clutching hand of doubt that pulled on my insides. Harv Fuller talked a lot, but he never gave anything. Not anything. "Don't worry about it."

"Well, he did vaccinate us."

"That he did." I wondered about that, too. Nothing's free in this world. Not a thing. I wondered what the going price on life saving was to Harv Fuller. I was afraid that we'd know soon enough.

Lynn reappeared in the doorway with two foil-wrapped packages in her hands. "You have two choices," she said. "Steak or soy burgers."

"Real steak?" I asked.

She shook her head. "Mag-sub."

I'm sure that maggots are very high in protein, and they tell me that mag steaks taste better than the genuine article; but I was never able to get myself up for it. I guess we all have our little prejudices. "Soy burgers sound great," I said. "What do you have to drink?"

All at once, her eyes got large and she ran up to me, dropping the food bundles onto the coffee table. "What about the others?" she said. "The others who drank the water?"

"Take it easy," I returned. "While you were upstairs changing to go to Fullerchem, I got hold of your wall and told it the situation."

"And?"

"He drained the water lines and contacted the other houses."

"What did he tell them?"

I took her arm, and pulled her down to sit on the couch. "He told them the truth, that any of them who drank the bad water has probably contracted the disease."

Her face bunched up. "That's it?"

"What else is there?"

Her hands were moving, waving as she talked, nervous. "Isn't there something else we can do for them?"

"Not unless they're good buddies with Harv Fuller."

She stopped fidgeting. The absolute finality of every action we were taking began to finally sink in. "They're as good as dead," she said.

I reached up and took her face in my hands, made sure we were eye to eye. "It's never over until it's over," I said softly. "Anything can happen."

"Shouldn't they be quarantined at least?"

"We're giving them the chance to do that themselves," I replied. "The only other alternative is to call the coppers, and the prevailing sentiment for them right now is to burn first and chitchat about it afterward."

"Suppose they don't quarantine themselves?"

I took a breath. "Let's worry about one thing at a time. Now, about that food," I said, and stood up, deliberately turning away from her. A large open market stretched out below me in Baghdad. It teemed with bustling, yelling life. Its sweet stench hung like a spring mist in the room with us.

"You in a hurry?" she asked, picking her food back up and going once more to the kitchen.

"Couple of errands to run," I said. "If I can borrow your bullet."

She went into the kitchen to mike the soy. I turned and stared at the open doorway. She didn't answer me. When she reappeared, she was strung out again, her face tight and fearful. She walked right up to me. "I'm scared, Matt," she said. "Please don't leave me alone."

"Got to," I replied. "You'll be okay."

Her eyes got hard again. "Damn it. You work for me, and you'll damn well do what I say!"

I shook my head. "One of the tricks of my business is that you only take advice if it's good." I jerked my thumb toward the holo wall, but we both knew that I was pointing at something else, something a lot less idyllic. "I've got business out there, and anybody else I have to look out for besides myself is going to cut down my efficiency by that much. It's an edge I can't afford to lose."

She started to say something, but a buzzer went off in the kitchen before she could get it out.

"Food's done," I said.

She turned and left the room without a word.

The interchange where the freeway emptied into John Wayne Boulevard was practically impassable. An endless conga line of bullets shimmied out of the city, trying to get away. Life is never that easy.

Federal troops, done up like ghosts in stark-white rad suits and black-goggled gas masks, turned the traffic back upon itself, tried to keep the flow of blood in the wound. There were heated arguments and occasional skirmishes, but no one got through. The lines were drawn; the battle would be fought to conclusion right there.

So the streets jammed, then flowed back, back into the teeth of the voracious north wind. There was very little snow left on the streets. The wind was so bad that it had blown most of it away to pile against the first vertical surface it came to.

I worked myself into the traffic jam and moved with it. The going was tough. Everybody on the streets was driving like the world had already ended. They zigzagged all over the roads and plowed into one another, small wrecks that usually ended in fist fights among the occupants of the bullets. The burned-out remnants of private helis were strewn here and there along the roadside, some still smoking and flickering tiny fires. They had tried to cross into restricted airspace and were shot down by the troops. The whole scene reminded me of some of the Central American villages we had "liberated" during the war.

The farther I got from the barricades, the easier the going became. By the time I got back into the city proper, the flow wasn't too bad. The streets were strangely deserted though, like nobody lived there anymore; but a close look at the buildings showed faces pressed against the glass. Hollow faces—portraits of spirits. I kept thinking about something that Harv Fuller had said. What happens when there are more of them than there are of us?

I needed to get back to my flat, but I sure as hell wouldn't be able to run the punk barricades on Tremaine again. There was a way to do it, but it turned my stomach just to think of it. I kept running alternate plans through my mind until I was in sight of the barricade, but couldn't come up with anything better.

Not wanting to tackle the boys on Tremaine again, I turned right on Military and found a place to set it down near the corner of St. Charles, the next thoroughfare into the decay.

There was a department store facing Military that had a holo-window display of the spring line of flak suits and self-defense equipment. A Fancy Dan done up in fluorescent green stood guard over the revolving door that led into the place. An alley full of trash frozen in mid rot and rats starved from frozen food ran between the store and Fusion Electric's payment building next door. I hatched out of the bullet and sighed. I just hoped that none of my friends saw me.

I sauntered up to the punk and looked him over. He wasn't as tall as me, but the uniform looked stretchable. He was wearing an Australian bush hat, the brim turned up on one side, with a large ostrich feather stuck in it. The word WOMBAT was stitched on his right breast. The things I do for the business.

"How you doing, cowboy?" I asked him.

He stared straight ahead, like maybe his head forgot how to

swivel. "Move along," he mumbled through his mask. "No loitering."

"Sure like that hat," I said. "Mind if I try it on?"

His eyes moved to take me in, and his hand crept toward the equalizer on his hip. "You lookin' for a tough time?"

I shook my head. "Very original. Tell you what. I'll give you a couple of bucks for the hat. What do you say?"

His hand was caressing the butt of his frump. "I say, blow. Right now, or you're gonna be steaming up the pavement."

I put my hands up. "Hey! Take it easy. I'm walking." I turned and took a step, then turned back around. "See, I'm walking."

His hand eased off the frump and I made my move. Diving back at him, I snatched the hat off his head and shoved him against the holo window, the merchandise pictures inside bobbing up and down with the impact. I ran.

He was up behind me, obscenities running out of his mouth like diarrhea. I rounded the corner into the alley shadows. Then I turned, my balled fist stiff-armed out in front of me.

A second later, he charged around the same corner at full speed and introduced his nose to my knuckles. He went down like a submarine and I was all over him. It was so easy that it was embarrassing, like beating up a kid or something.

He tried to go for his frump, but I got it away from him and stuck the barrel in his mouth. A mangy rat the size of a small dog scurried across his arm and disappeared into the piles of trash that glutted the narrow passage.

"Should have given me the hat," I said.

"Farg zimick reck," he replied around the obstacle in his throat.

I stood up, pulling him to his feet by the front of his one piece. His eyes were like glazed doughnuts, his mouth a permanent frown.

"Okay, hero," I said, and backed away from him. "Take off the clothes."

"Go to hell," he spat.

I matched his frown. "Listen," I said. "I'm not any happier about this arrangement than you are, but it's up to you. I could just as easily knock the bejesus out of you and take the clothes anyway."

His resolve weakened a bit, and he started shifting his weight from foot to foot.

70

I shook my head. "I'll tell you the truth, cowboy. It doesn't much matter to me one way or the other."

Even though the front of his day-glo uniform was filled with shiny gold buttons, it was held together by a zipper. He rasped it down. "What are you going to do?" he asked.

"I'm the dry cleaner," I said. "I'm just here to pick up the laundry."

"I'm cold."

"You're fixing to be a lot colder."

He took off his black gleaming knee boots, then unbuckled his frump holster. I picked up the Aussie hat from where it had fallen and put it on after wiping a handkerchief around the inside of the sweatband. It was awful. It was like sticking my head deliberately in a barrel full of horse manure.

He undressed down to his mask and stood, naked and shivering, with his arms wrapped around him. I gathered up the clothes in a bundle and stuck them under my arm.

"What am I supposed to do now?" he asked.

"That's your problem."

His eyes were wide, fearful. "If I go out on the streets like this, they'll think I've got the plague and burn my ass."

"I'm sure you'll work it out," I replied, and turned to walk out of the alley. "I have faith in you."

I went back to the car and hummed out of there. Stopping another block up the road, I changed in the bullet, tried to transform myself into a Fancy Dan.

The uniform made my flesh creep just to know that it had lain so long next to punk skin. I hoped I wouldn't catch anything from it.

I climbed out of the bullet feeling like the granddaddy of all popinjays. I wanted to believe that even in the clothes I would still look too smart, so I pulled the brim of the hat down a little to better cover my eyes and walked on toward the barricades on St. Charles.

I moved down the block with my eyes fixed, straight ahead. If anybody was looking at me, I didn't want to know about it. What street crowds there were were small and directed. They all had a reason for being out.

The checkpoint was only a block away. About fifteen punks were milling around—all reds and bright yellows and patent leather. They also wore the gray capes, and everyone of them but me had on a mask. We all fit in together, like a yard full of peacocks, except that the collective intelligence of the group was probably an insult to the bird population of the world.

I walked up to them, my face stinging and red from the wind. Most of the street was blocked by bullets, with only a narrow passage in the middle to get through. No one was trying, though. The people in the good side of town didn't want to go into the decay and the people in the decay were afraid to come into the good side.

One of the Dans had a pocket holo that he had set on the hood of a barricade hummer. It juiced a woman half-a-meter tall, who was doing a slow, methodical strip tease. The punks were enthralled, like cows watching a bumble bee. The projection had red hair. They were betting on whether or not she was a natural redhead.

The projection slipped out of a sequined dress and was wearing some sort of leatherlike harness that looked like it should have been on a horse in the Kentucky Derby.

The Dans began to get excited. They were yelling and handing cash around to the bagman. A fat one in a black kevlar uniform with bright white trim all around seemed to be in charge. His face looked like a raw piece of beefsteak behind the mask.

"Keep 'em comin' gents," he blubbered from behind the fabric. "The little lady is gettin' down to it."

The projection sat on the hood and began to slowly slip out of a pair of black nylons.

"Mind if I go through?" I asked the beefsteak.

He glanced quickly at me, his eyes fleshy slits. "Who the hell are you?" he asked, then turned back to the show. "Whoo-ee! Will you lookee there."

"Ten on double red," one of the punks yelled, and handed a bill across to the guy I was talking to.

"Come to papa," the punk said, and snatched up the cash.

"Work over at Neiman's," I told him. "I'm on break and had some business down there."

"That's crazy land, buddy. What kinda business you got in crazy land?"

"Personal business."

The lines around his eyes creased deeply. He just stared at me until the yelling turned him around. The stripper was standing up, dropping the top of her outfit.

The fat man threw up his hands. "Will ya look at them milk

factories!" he yelled, and did a little dance right there on the street.

Then they all got quiet and leaned up close, waiting for the payoff. The woman danced around and shimmied for a minute, then hooked her thumbs into the release rings of her harness.

"She's gonna drop 'em," someone whispered reverently.

"So's it okay if I go through?" I asked the punk.

He didn't even look at me. He wiggled his hand around. "Yeah," he said quickly. "Sure, sure."

I slipped past him and started off down the street. After about ten steps, I heard a cheer go up from the punks. "All right!" the fat man screamed. "Both ends!"

# 10

The complexion of the streets had changed. It wasn't anything you could put your finger on, but more of a sensation, like the flush that pinches your face just before you come down with something. The city was dying and everybody knew it. All that was left was to unplug the life supports and let nature take its course.

As soon as I got back to my place, I got out of the punk clothes and took a shower to get the cooties off me. I'd have to put the uniform back on soon enough, but I wasn't about to wear it any longer than I had to.

Getting out of the shower, I dried off and slipped into a one-piece, and started gathering some other clothes together to take over to Lynn's. I had lost my suitcase on Freefall City, but I had a big yellow shopping bag from the market and used it to carry my gear in.

I understood very little of what was going on around me. It was too much of a sensory overload. I knew that I didn't trust Harv Fuller the way Lynn did. I knew that I was going to have to find out as much about Springmaid on my own as I possibly could. I knew that the plague was bad and getting worse. I knew that I was going to have to take out the woman who was after Lynn. And, God help me, I knew that down under the surface all of it was tied up together somehow.

Where to start?

I moved back toward the front of the place, and punched up Juke's coordinates on the console on the kitchen table. My old friend Black Jack was still sitting there from the night before. All at once, my mouth got very dry.

I was just reaching for the bottle when Juke's form took hold. When he saw me, his eyes got wide.

"Don't say anything," he hurried out.

"I . . ."

"Not anything. Just listen." He was nervous, more agitated

than I'd ever seen him before. Moving fingers came up to remold the putty of his face. "I don't know what this deal of yours is," he said. "But I don't think you're telling me everything."

"Juke . . ."

"Listen," he barked. "I'm not going to talk about any of this across the fibers. You meet me somewhere. We'll exchange information."

"Where?"

"You name it."

"I have an appointment this evening," I said. "Let me buzz you after and set it up."

He nodded quickly. "You're going to owe *me* some after this is over," he said, and then he was gone.

I disconnected and looked at the bottle again. The moment had passed. Sitting down heavily at the table, I let my fingers dance idly across the vis keyboard. There was a step I had to make here, and I was hesitating, afraid to get in over my head. Afraid I couldn't handle it. Afraid.

Then I heard the sounds. Outside.

Frump blasts. Distant at first, but coming closer. Shouting began mixing with the concussions. All of it coming closer.

Jumping up, I ran for the door. Getting into the snowfilled stairwell outside, I moved slowly up the steps, checking. They were a block away, but moving up fast. There were about thirty of them—plaguers. Plaguers with frumps.

I climbed the stairs, fascinated. They were running, charging. They were all dressed like clowns in white grease paint and shiny red noses. They were running and jumping and doing somersaults—and blasting the hell out of everything in sight.

They had everything but a calliope. Plaguer children climbed on the big ones shoulders, pinwheeling off to crash painfully on the hard ground. One of them had a large hoop, and others would take turns running and diving through its center. And as they went, they etched a path of destruction behind them. Instant urban renewal. They blasted as fast as they could fire with the frumps, and the streets and buildings and snow-covered trash cans went to pieces all around them, disappearing in flashes of orange fire and ink-black smoke. It was a circus parade in hell, and Death was the ringmaster.

I kept waiting for the coppers to show up. Then I realized

75

that they wouldn't, that they had already written all of us off. Jesus.

They were on me before I knew it; I had been magnetized by the spectacle. I stumbled back down the stairs, but not before I got a look at the faces beneath the makeup. They were faces turned inside out, faces surgically opened to expose the raw, twisted pathways, the back alleys and slimy sewers that all of us hide and ignore in the dusty caverns of our brains. To look at those faces was to look in a mirror that showed only the fears and gut-wrenching hatreds of which we're all capable. Those faces were at once the most horrible and compelling sight I'd ever witnessed.

I sank into the stairwell, snow to my knees, fighting visions of Terra Firma, fighting back all the visions that threatened to turn me into a raging beast of the streets. I backed into the shadows, tried to become one with the blessed darkness. I hugged the cement wall with my back, tried to imitate its rough, pebbly texture. And then the explosions ripped around me, sky flaring orange above. A devil's rain of cement and brick chips pelted me, jagged building shrapnel attacking. I put my arm up to cover my face, and the stairwell was roiling with thick, choking smoke, and I sank to my knees, gagging, up past my waist in sooty black snow.

And then it was gone.

The circus parade had moved on down the street, moved toward the punk barricades several blocks up.

I stood slowly, rubbing my eyes to get the smoke sting out of them. And I didn't mind the sting. It reminded me that I was still alive. And kicking.

My door had locked tight behind me. I handprinted back in to the buzzing of my vis. I moved to it, coughing the carbon out of my lungs.

I punched up the juice and watched Maria Hidalgo focus in. Her dark eyes bled concern above her high, aristocratic cheekbones. She was dressed in a slick green exo, her war armor. All was not well with the underground warlord of the DMZ.

"What's the matter with your eyes?" she asked as soon as she caught sight of me.

I coughed again, waved it off. "Smoke," I replied. "I'm okay."

"I've been trying to get you all day."

I took a deep breath, coughed once more, and felt my lungs clear. "You got me now. What's up?"

She flinched visibly. "You mean besides the end of the world?"

I sat down, looked around for a cig. Couldn't find one. "That bad?" I said.

Her face drained of whatever color was left in it. I had never seen her like that before. She was always in such control. "It's all fallen to pieces," she said, and then there was a noise off cam.

Her head jerked to it. There were explosions, smoke drifting on screen. Maria disappeared from view. I listened to the skirmish, to people screaming, yelling. It was maddening, like looking in a window when everything is going on in another room.

Bodies, moving fast, passed in front of the screen. Jumping up, I found some cigs on an end table and lit one with a shaking hand. The noise died down on screen, and the smoke cleared. Maria returned. There was a small trail of blood running down her cheek. Her eyes were wide, almost in shock.

"We've got to get out of here, Matt," she said. "There's nothing more I can do. My people have all got it; this whole end of town's got it. And soon, every place else is gonna have it, too. And then the feds are gonna make it look like we were never here at all."

"What are you going to do?"

Her hand came up to wipe at the blood. She held her hand out to look at the stain. "Get to the underground bunkers," she replied without inflection.

"Then what?"

She sighed. "Watch each other. Very carefully."

I took a drag; let it out. "Good luck," I told her.

"Good luck? Haven't you been listening to me? It's all over. Done. Finished. The streets are going to become hell like you never imagined it."

"Yeah, I know."

"Come with me," she said. "There's nothing you can do up there. You'll at least have a chance for life down underground."

I tapped some ash off onto my floor, watched it drift lazily down. "What?" I said. "Sitting around watching one another go insane? I don't know if I could handle that, Hermana.

77

Besides, I have a hard time with closed-in places. I like to have somewhere to run."

Her face got solid. "We're talking survival here, Swain," she said.

"We're talking choices," I answered.

"I'll miss you, novio," she returned softly.

"Yeah," I said. "Remember me on April Fool's day. Let me ask you a question?"

"Hurry."

"I'm trying to get a line on a woman," I said. "Blonde, long-legged, and classy."

"I'm not an escort service."

"This is serious," I returned and dragged my cig. "She's a mechanic, a pro. Slick and clean. Makes her hits look like accidents. Is she one of yours?"

Maria shook her head. "We deal in retribution, not hits," she said. "And if we did, we wouldn't use anybody that stuck out like the lady you just described."

"Well, how much of that could go on here without your knowing about it?"

"What, professional stuff?"

"Yeah."

She shook her head. "None," she said. "This is my town. All criminal activity is controlled through me."

There was another explosion, and the picture rocked on the screen. "I have to go," she yelled through the smoke. Waving quickly at the screen, she blanked, leaving me alone again. It was all unraveling, quicker than I could have believed possible. The city was going to pieces, shattering like a piggy bank dropped on the floor. And I was searching through the broken chips, looking for a lucky penny.

I juiced information on the vis and got the coordinates for the department of health. Punching them up, I had to let it buzz about thirty times before I got focus.

A woman's face filled the screen. It was pulled tight, strained with anger, slash lips stretched tight across bared teeth. Her hair knotted in tangles around her head.

"What?!" she screamed when she saw me.

"Is this the department of public health?" I asked her.

"What the fuck do you *want*?" she said, and her head was constantly turning this way and that, eyes just occasionally meeting mine.

"Information," I said.

78

She put up her hands. "Oh Christ!" she yelled. "In the middle of all this shit, *you* want information."

"About the plague."

"Ohhh," she trilled. "What else?"

"Listen. I won't take up much of your time."

"Time," she spat, like the word was made out of rat poison. "Now *you* listen. We're in business because of private donations. We got a staff of five, three of whom didn't even show up today. We got a computer that's so old we bring it in on a wheelchair. We got a thousand people trying to break down the door right now because they think we can do something for them. And when they get through that door, and they *will* get through it, they're going to tear me up because I'll be about as much use to them as burning candles in the church. Now, let's talk about time."

"Why is the antidote so scarce!"

She just stopped and stared at me. "Okay," she said. "I'll play. Why not?" She took a breath, pulled her hair back out of her face a little. "We're a public health organization, right?" She sat up straight and put on a mock businesslike face. "Yes, sir. I will be happy to serve you."

A voice off screen. "Jeri, they're breaking through."

The woman cleared her throat. When she spoke, it was in a crisp voice. "The antidote, taloxin, contains a derivative of whale oil."

"Whale oil?"

She shrugged. "Whales, as you know, are an extinct species; so you can imagine that the oil derived from their blubber is also rather scarce."

The off-screen voice again. "They're in . . . they're coming!"

Jeri calmly turned her head in that direction. "Lock the office door," she said quietly. "Brace it."

Then, back to me. She smiled slightly. "Sorry for the interruption, sir. Where were we?"

"How come Fullerchem has the antidote?" I asked, trying to keep from thinking about what was going on there.

She shrugged again, her eyes strangely distant, resigned. "Guess they found a whale," she replied. "Is there anything else?"

"Just get yourself out of there," I said.

"Oh, but sir," she said, looking at a wristwatched arm. "Quitting time isn't for another hour. Thank you for buzzing." She blanked me with a warm smile, and I hoped that whatever place it was that she went to in her mind was the best place for her to be.

I stood up, crushing my cig on the kitchen floor with the heel of my shoe. I needed to get out of there. Grabbing my yellow shopping bag, I threw the Fancy Dan outfit inside, not wanting to put it on any sooner than I had to.

Going out the door, I moved into the cold and the wind. I had left Lynn's bullet a block on the other side of the St. Charles barricades. I started hoofing.

The wind was bitter, slashing. It bit my face, numbed it to where it felt like it wasn't there anymore. I pulled my waistcoat tight around my neck, clutched the bag to my chest, and kept walking.

Smoke swirled wildly in the streets ahead. The barricades. I walked up on them, tossing the punk uniform out of the bag as I did. I wouldn't be needing it anymore.

The barricades were gone, blown away. Bodies and parts of bodies, Dans and clowns alike, were strewn everywhere. The street itself was torn and pitted by frump blasts that etched the cement like lunar craters. Many of them were still smoking.

So, the stopper was out of the bottle; the thumb was out of the dike and the craziness was spilling into the sanity. I made my way around the charred and broken wreckage of the checkpoint, lighting a cig on a smoldering piece of melting plastic.

Moving on, I made my way to Lynn's bullet. It was done in, blasted. A small fire still burned on the inside, trickling smoke out of the busted out window places. I warmed my hands on the fire for a minute and began looking around for a city helibus.

Above me, a government heli floated down low. I could make out people on the decks. They were watching the street through binocs, talking quickly into small boxes. In another time, they would have been on a horse, a large pale horse with fire for eyes and pestilence for hooves.

I forgot about the bus and took a taxi instead.

# 11

The smog night was dark and cold. There was a full moon behind the pollution layer, but we had to take Nature's word for that one; we never got to see much of the moon. The full moon has a bad effect on peoples' psyches. That was all we needed. A dose of lunar rays to paranoia is kind of like prescribing heroin to cure someone of morphine addiction.

Lynn wasn't real happy about the death of her bullet, but in spite of everything, she was a rich girl and could get another one. So it wasn't the end of the world to her. We borrowed a small one from one of her neighbors, and headed back toward town, and the Steering Committee.

I was expecting this hideaway to be on the city's outskirts, but she kept humming us farther into town. I guess that's what I get for thinking.

The streets seemed quiet enough, like the quiet of the grave. There was some military on the streets, but they were few and nonthreatening. And we were quiet, too. We slid silently through the decaying city, the air thick and heavy between us. Something was bothering Lynn, something that had nothing to do with what was going on around us. It stood right there between us, looming and impassable, like the Great Wall of China. I wished that I could scale that wall, but I didn't know how.

Lynn drove. I kept looking around. "Right down in the middle of it, huh?" I said.

She just smiled a half-smile that was about as real as the maggot steak she had tried to feed me earlier.

"Are all the others going to be there?"

She turned to me, staring through the layers of darkness, her face appearing as flashes in headlight and street pole glare. "All but one," she replied.

"Which one?"

She tapped nervously on the control pistols. She really was

81

fidgeting. "Sig Harris," she said finally. "He's hiding out somewhere, trying to wait it out."

"What's his story?"

"No story," she answered quickly. "He's an old man, and he's scared. Made his fortune in electronics. He's got the money to hide himself and try to weather the storm, and that's what he's doing."

"You sound defensive," I said.

She shook her head. "Not really. I like Sig. He makes his friends call him Siggy, and he's a sweet old man." She shrugged. "Guess I just feel a little protective of him."

"Birds of a feather," I said, and regretted it immediately.

"Am I supposed to be offended?"

It was my turn to shake my head. "No," I replied. "Rich people are entitled, just like everybody else. Maybe I've been hating too long for my own good."

"Maybe," she returned, but her *maybe* had a ring of *definitely* to it.

I began watching the neighborhood. Lynn was getting close to my end of town. She hung a right onto Euclid, and I held my nose as we drove past the police station. There was a pretty good crowd around the front of the station, a crowd of citizens wanting in. The doors were shut tight to them.

I got a surprise when she turned into the station's security park. "What the hell are we doing here?"

"You'll see."

We hummed up to the big sliding gate and Lynn voice-printed before punching up the special number code on the typer box. The door refused to open until I also had voice printed, and then it was only with reluctance. My fame had preceded me.

The garage was wide and long, the ceiling low, nearly touching the top of the bullet. It was about half-full of other hummers. It glowed with yellow vapor haze that filled the inside of the place like a kerosene flame fills a lantern. It was thick, unornamented cement with big square support beams that cast long shadows of various darkness and intensity, depending on the positions of the light sources.

I got out and closed the door, its tin-can sound echoing through the cavern, almost sounding solid and substantial. The ceiling was so low that it brushed the top of my head if I stood completely upright.

"I never come here on a full stomach," I told her, and my

words played back to me from the length of the room. "You're lucky we haven't had dinner yet."

"Is your stomach all you ever think about?" she asked, and closed her door.

"It is when I'm in a police station," I returned, and knew she'd never understand.

She led me through several aisles full of bullets and into a long hallway that said LOBBY in flowing neon script; an arrow pointed down the hall, as if there were anywhere else to go. We followed the arrow.

"What do you know about the others?" I asked, wanting as much as I could get on them before a meeting.

"Not much. They were all Bob's friends. I never went to many places with Bob, so I never really got to know his friends."

"Give me what you do have."

She was wearing a simple black one piece with matching long coat of quilted down. Her fingers diddled constantly with her zipper tabs. "Harv you know already," she said, her eyes set straight down the hall, not watching me. "Amanda Pitcher's going to show. She's an art dealer by trade, owns several galleries in several cities."

"What's she like?"

Lynn's eyes touched me for just a second, but ran away again. Whatever was bothering her was just eating away. "Mid-forties," she said. "Good dresser. She can talk to you all night and make you think you're her dearest friend in the whole world, and two hours later you're analyzing what she really meant by everything she said. Know what I mean?"

"I think so."

"She can be vicious, too. You know, the old story of talking about whoever's not sitting at the table."

"Did she get along all right with all the men in the group?"

"If you mean that literally, I would say yes. If you mean emotionally, I'd say that the ones you'd need to talk to would be the members' wives."

I smiled at her; she had answered my question. "What about the other guy, what's his name?"

"Marion Jasper," she said. "But he won't answer to anything but Jasper. He's middle-aged, but can afford to take care of himself, so it's hard to tell his real age. He's a vice president over at Continental Insurance, and is apparently able to parlay gold futures like they were horse races."

I started to laugh.

"What?" she asked.

I waved it off. "Nothing," I returned. "I used to do a little work for Continental from time to time."

"Oh. Well, anyway, Jasper's real prissy, selfish. Considers himself a great sportsman. Used to go hunting dog with Bob all the time."

"Was he with him in Detroit?"

She frowned. "No. That kind of surprised me. Bob didn't even ask him, and they used to love going to Detroit together. Does that mean something?"

"Probably not."

A one-way door was set at the end of the hallway. It was unsecured, which made sense to me. Nobody would go in there unless he had to. A small buzzer controlled the lock. Lynn pushed it and the thing clicked open.

We walked into a dark, quiet station. All the real lights were out, and the only illumination came from the neon rate-boards on the walls that juiced protection and detection prices in soft reds and greens. The prices changed from time to time, upgraded. And every time they did, a bell would ding, like an egg timer.

The cops in their black kevlar uniforms congregated in small groups around the large wide-open lobby. They looked beat, their clothes torn and dirty. It had been a tough day on the streets. Some wore the masks, others didn't. I think the ones who didn't felt like they had to be comfortable somewhere. They eyed us suspiciously, fearfully when we came in, hands within grabbing distance of their lasers. Odd. I was beginning to feel that the lines separating the plaguers from the sane ones were growing very indistinct.

The coppers talked in whispers, as if somehow the darkness of the room had made the proceedings sacrosanct. The barred tellers' cages were closed, as was the cashier's tower in the middle of the room.

Outside, the shadows of the people trying to get through the doors could be seen flitting around the frosted glass, but their sounds were completely muffled. I knew how those doors were made. They were built during the terrorist years in the twenties and thirties, and attempting to break through them would be worse than useless.

I kept my eyes on their gun hands. "The natives are restless," I told Lynn.

She looked at me the way she would look at a five-year-old caught with his hand in the cookie jar, and moved on. I trailed behind, smiling at all the nice policemen in as docile a manner as my rocky face could manage.

She stopped in front of a door marked MUTANT DETEN-TION, and began entry procedures so complicated that they entailed placing an electron ring on her head to take an EEG.

Bill Dooks, the head cashier, was leaning against a nearby wall smoking a huge reef. His eyes stared myopically at the dark swallowed ceiling. His green counting visor dangled by its elastic band from the change machine on his belt. While Lynn got us through the door, I walked up to Dooks.

"Is it Christmas, or what?" I asked him.

His eyes never left the clouds. When he answered, his smoker bounced up and down between his lips. "How are you, Swain?"

"Surviving," I replied.

Pulling the reef out of his mouth, he dealt with the ash. "Lot to be said for that." He looked at me then, his eyes distant like the woman's at the health department. He held the doper out to me.

I shook my head. "What's going on here?"

He leaned his head back against the wall. I wondered what was so damned interesting up on that ceiling. "The feds are in charge now," he said. "They're running whatever show there is to run."

"Why?"

He laughed, a short choppy laugh, almost a cough. "When you invite the bear in for dinner," he replied, "he eats whatever he wants." He shook his head. "It doesn't matter. We couldn't get our boys out on calls anyway. Things are too out of hand."

"So, what are you all doing here?"

"Same as you," he returned. "Surviving."

Lynn called to me, and I turned to see her holding the ring out. I went over and let them humiliate me for a few minutes, then the door slid open with a clang.

It wasn't an Old Town mutant cell at all, of course. We were in a dressing room of some kind. It was partitioned off into a number of small cubicles with slide curtains for doors that never completely covered you while you took off your clothes. There was always something particularly obscene to me about watching someone undress from the knees down.

"Now what?" I asked.

She gave me the first genuine smile I'd seen from her in hours. "Now you get naked," she said.

I gave her my best self-righteous look. "Are you trying to compromise my virtue?" I asked.

"I never compromise," she answered, and walked into one of the booths.

I took a breath and dutifully marched into the closest cubicle. A holo of an Africk in a starched white waistcoat was standing in there with me.

"How do you do?" he asked.

I looked at the projection. "How do I do what?"

"If you will kindly disrobe now, and drop your clothing, one article at a time, down the chute, we will have you quickly on your way."

"I will if you will."

He apparently didn't hear me. He just kept standing there—waiting.

"Would you stop messing around," Lynn's voice called from her booth.

If I had to, I had to. It was, of course, cold in there. And by the time I got down to the bare facts, I had raised enough goose bumps to qualify as a major mountain range. When I was done, I started dropping clothes down a stainless-steel chute set into the wall that made a sucking sound every time something went in it.

When I was done, a red light went on in the booth, and the projection walked around me in a full circle. He made a great show of nodding when he was finished.

"Thank you," the holo said. "Your clothing will be returned to you when you are ready to leave. You may wear this in the meantime."

The chute coughed up a package wrapped in plastic. It hit the floor right by my feet. Opening it, I found a cinched toga, pale red, and slipped it on. It came to just below my knobby knees, just like the curtain. I moved out of the booth to find Lynn already standing there.

"Finally," she said.

I narrowed my eyes and stared at her. "You weren't peeking, were you?"

Her eyes started to laugh, backed away. I could almost get

there, almost get through those secured passages into her brain; but there was something that always held her back.

"Let's go," she said.

There was a secured down-tube set off to the side of the room. We voice printed in and set our weight on the dial. The thing started moving; it was a long way down.

By the time we hit bottom, I was keyed up to see what the place looked like. I wanted to know what kind of fantasies the very rich would indulge themselves in if they had the chance. What I got was nothing like what I expected.

The tube hatched us into the DMZ, or at least what looked like the DMZ on the surface. The whole place was a faithful recreation of several blocks of decayed city. There were streets, cracked and broken, that stuttered past buildings in ruin—crumbled brick and cement piling onto the streets. Buildings without windows, going up three stories and disappearing into the smog-billowing ceiling, like a tree growing up through a house. There was garbage strewn on the streets, but it wasn't real garbage. Rats scurried through that garbage, but they were just holos. Fires burned in the distance, giving off black smoke that bore no taste or smell or feel. There was no smell at all—just the sterility of a museum.

Street people wandered through the debris of the dead city, their ragged clothes clean and pressed to tight creases. The rich folks were dressed in togas just like mine and they strolled through the Theater of Ruin, stopping now and again to watch fights and fake muggings that were staged just for their benefit. I began to feel angry, violated in some horrible way. Life, my kind of life, was all some monstrous game to these people—the rich kids trying to get hold of the one thing their money could never buy: poverty.

"You don't approve," Lynn said, catching the expression of disgust that had settled on my face.

"No," I answered. "I don't approve."

"Neither do I," she responded. "I rarely came here."

"But you did come."

"You never give it a rest, do you?"

"Never."

She started walking into the antiseptic, acceptable substitute for life. "Come on," she said. "They're supposed to meet us in a building on the corner of Fourth and Hudson."

I followed, catching up to her. I knew Fourth and Hudson,

knew someone who lived there. I let my eyes wander around some more. This *was* the city, was just like it. I got angrier.

Lynn was talking, her words just barely sliding into my range. "They got the idea from Marie Antoinette," she said.

"Who was that?"

"A French queen. She kept a farmhouse near her summer palace and stocked it with peasants, so that from time to time she could experience the simple pleasures of the poor."

"What happened to her?"

She stopped and looked at me. "She was beheaded."

I smiled. "Good."

We got into the streets and it chilled my blood. It was so real, like walking through a dream and knowing that it's a dream, but getting caught up in it anyway. We passed a trash can full of plastic imitations of decomposing food. Mechanical flies buzzed around the can, moving politely out of our way as we passed by.

I recognized the street. The imitation was perfect, which made it that much worse for me. There were bars along the way, bars that I frequented. They were filled with rich boys who talked about the money market instead of the monthly drug rations. There were whores on the streets, both genders, and they all wore the gaudy street flash. But down underneath it all, they were scrubbed clean and smelled like jasmine and would never, ever know what it was really like to have to fuck to stay alive. I hated them, hated every one of them.

The corner of Fourth and Hudson had a broken light pole that always shone red. This one was the same, but its stuck color was green. By the pole was an overturned letterbox. In my neighborhood, an old man with no arms or legs lived in there. This one was filled with pillows for people who wanted to sleep on some of the beds in the buildings.

The address was 410 Hudson, the same building where my friend Sanchi lived. We climbed the cracked steps and entered the dingy foyer. It was dingy all right, but the dirt had been painted on. Sanchi's apartment was on the ground floor. I ran to it and threw open the door. It wasn't decorated anything like he had done it; it was much too nice. Sanchi wasn't there either. But, then, he couldn't be. He had frozen to death the winter before.

"Up here," Lynn called, leaning over the creaky banister of the staircase. "They're on the third floor."

I backed out of Sanchi's place, closing the door softly, the way he liked me to do it. Turning, I went to the steps and joined Lynn on the second landing.

"You look strange," she said.

"I'm okay!" I snapped. "Let's just get moving, all right?"

She frowned and started up the next flight. There was very little light and a lot of shadows and the stairs made noise when we walked on them. But there was no dust in the air, no smells from the must or the community toilet down the hall.

We got up to the third floor. The stairs continued up, ending abruptly in the third story ceiling. Lynn walked a few paces down the worn, flowered carpet and stopped in front of the door marked 311.

"This is it," she said.

I joined her just as she was getting the door open.

They were all in there, sitting around a rickety wooden table.

They were eating a dog.

# 12

They all looked up when we walked in, and they were wearing their board room faces, no giveaways. Harv Fuller, hair and beard flowing down to slide across the fabric of his yellow toga, stood up no sooner than he caught sight of us. His eyes were a milky haze.

"Welcome," he said, voice full of blowing dust and cotton balls. "Come on in and have a sit."

The room was small, the walls graffitied full of brown water stains. Mechanical roaches roamed the place at will, crawling up everything but the people. The window was wide and overlooked the street, the never-changing color pole.

We moved to the table to sit down. Lynn was nodding greetings to everyone, but their eyes never left me. I was the one they were interested in, afraid of.

Harv reached over and took my arm in his grip, squeezing. He had powerful hands. "Let me introduce you 'round the table," he said.

"Fine."

He gestured to the woman who sat directly across from my place. "Amanda Pitcher," he said. "This here's Mathew Swain. Mr. Swain's a . . . detective."

The way he had said that last word, I knew that he had thoroughly checked me out already. Well, what the hell? I'd have probably done the same thing.

"Glad to know you," I said.

"The hell you are," she responded in a gravelly voice. She was a small woman, her hair pixie short. Her eyes were gray and protruded slightly, like a lizard's. Her lips were thin, but not unpleasant if she wanted it that way. Right now she didn't. She looked at me the way she would look at a pimple on her forearm.

"And over here . . ."

The man jumped out of his chair, arm thrust out to me.

"Name's Jasper," he said, and his voice boomed in and out like waves, like he was trying to dominate the entire room with his presence. He was large, about my size, good-looking in a stern kind of way. He could have been cast from bronze, but it was probably electroplated tin. He was the kind of man you never turned your back on or left alone with your wife. We shook hands, and he surprised me by not trying to break mine. I was glad of that. Lynn and I had discarded our Fullerchem bandages, but my hands were still a bit tender.

I nodded to him, kept my mouth shut after the woman.

He tightened his lips across the bars of his teeth and nodded up and down. "Bet you'd be a hard man to take down," he said.

"I get by," I returned, and broke our grip.

Fuller let go of my arm and slapped his hands together. "Well, now that we're all acquainted, let's sit down, eat a bite, and get ready for the show."

"Show?" Lynn said.

He pointed a finger out the window. "Right out there," he said. "A show."

"Best seats in the house," Jasper added.

We sat.

The others had already started eating. The dog wasn't really a dog. It turned out to be duck molded in dog shape, and it was really pretty good. I've got a fine taste for things I can't afford.

Fuller had his pill bowl sitting right next to him on the table, and snapped one into his mouth from time to time. To drink, we had champagne poured from bottles of Leaping Deer, a bathtub whiskey that was a medical miracle because it could cause instant cataracts.

Nobody wanted to start the conversation; they didn't want to give without getting. I finally couldn't stand it anymore.

"I guess you know why I'm here," I said.

"Suppose you tell us," Amanda Pitcher returned, and her lizard eyes continually moved over my face. Her eyes never held still.

I put down my fork. "Okay," I said. "I'll play." Pushing the plate away from me, I took a quick drink out of a blue plastic cup. It was tasting too good to me. I shoved it away also.

They were into their serious routines. Fine. I tilted my chair back on two legs and talked directly to the Pitcher woman.

"You people are all marked for death," I said, and waited

91

for the reaction. There wasn't one. "First off, I felt that I needed to at least warn you of that."

"Why?" Jasper asked through a mouthful of food.

I turned to stare at him. "Guess I'm just funny that way," I told him.

Pitcher laughed sharply. "Nobody does anything for nothing," she said.

I ignored her and went on. "I personally don't care what happens to any of you, but Lynn has been dumped in the hopper, too, and her I *do* care about."

"Isn't that sweet," Pitcher said.

Fuller reached over with his fork and speared what looked like the dog's head, bringing it to his plate. "Now come on, Mandy. Leave the gentleman alone. He's bein' real sincere."

"Sincere's ass," she said.

I slammed a fist down on the table, knocking over one of the glasses. "That's it," I said, pointing across at her. "I don't know what gutter you learned your manners in, but if you want it fast and loose, that's okay by me. This isn't any game, lady. You're going to be dead, probably within a matter of days. Dead, like in all gone. And I'd probably be the first one to dance on your grave, but right now, keeping Lynn alive probably means keeping you alive, too."

"That's right," Jasper laughed. "Get mad."

"Your corporation is tied up in all this—the reason for it all. To help you, I've got to know what Springmaid is all about. I'm going to find out one way or the other. It's going to cut through a lot of bullshit if you tell me."

They all stared at me.

"The question," Harv Fuller said after a minute, "is whether or not you're the one best suited to help us. We all know all about you all."

"I'm in, whether you want me in or not."

There was a noise out on the streets. Everyone's head turned. Down below us, a well-dressed man was cornered by the letterbox with the pillows. He was surrounded by five limb strippers, large white refrigerator units strapped to their backs, gleaming long-bladed knives in their hands. He seemed petrified. I started out of my chair.

"Relax," Jasper said, smiling wide. "All part of the show."

"Well, we *don't* want you," Pitcher said. "Who in the hell do you think you are, coming in here and interfering in business that doesn't concern you?"

I glared at her. "You can stow the intimidation, lady. I'm immune."

Jasper's smiling face suddenly took on the nasty edge that was hiding back in there all the time. "Remember where you are, *Mister* Swain. This is our world . . . and we run it."

"What are you people hiding that's so damned important that you'll die for it?"

The man on the street was screaming as the limbers drew their circle in tighter and tighter, taunting him, playing. A large crowd had gathered across the street. They were laughing and pointing, occasionally applauding a certain line or action.

"Nobody's asked me," Lynn said, and when I turned to her, her face was set hard. "I'm in this with the rest of you. *I* want to know what's going on."

They all just sat there, like they didn't hear her.

"What about the heirs of all the others?" I asked. "Maybe they should be here, too."

"The others all willed their stock back to the corporation for even distribution among the other stockholders," Fuller said, and Jasper glared him down.

He shrugged at them. "Lynn does have a right to know," he said. "It's only fittin'."

Lynn stood, getting a commanding view of them all. "You mean, I'm the only one who inherited Springmaid stock?"

"The only one," Pitcher said.

I looked at each in turn. "That means that the more people who die, the more stock you people get."

"It was just a means of protecting the security of the company," Jasper said.

"Why? Why does the company need protecting?"

There was a shriek outside. The limbers had finally charged their victim, the knives silencing his screams in a second.

"All right," Jasper rasped in a hoarse voice.

They laid the guy out and gutted him. Taking the heart first, then the eyes and hands, then the kidneys, liver, pancreas, and lungs. Lynn, still standing, kept her back turned.

"You told me it was a show," I said to Jasper.

"Shhh," he said. "Android. Don't worry."

I strained my eyes. It certainly didn't look like an andy.

The limbers didn't fight over the organs. They apparently had a rotation system that allowed everyone a shot at the better values. Very industrious bunch. Next stop would be the closest hospital that would pay top price, no questions asked. The crowd across the street was oohing and aahing.

Lynn turned back to them. "You can't keep this from me," she said.

"So sue us." Jasper smiled, his eyes never leaving the window.

She turned to Fuller. "Harv?"

He took a couple of pills. "Ah agree with *you*, darlin', but we're all equal say here. Ah go with the vote."

"Lynn gets a vote," I said.

"That she does," Pitcher said quietly.

A familiar sound was drifting down the street. Police clankers. Moving fast. The limbers heard it, too, and were back on their feet, getting their booty into the chill on their backs. Those extra seconds did them in. Greed among the lower classes. An object lesson.

The coppers were on them, their armor-plated machines sounding like an army slapping loudly against the broken streets. The limbers scattered, scurrying in all directions, but it was too late. The machines bore quickly down on them, frying them in their tracks with short bursts of pink-hot laser light at close range. They went down quickly, insides cauterized. I guess it's a quick enough death. I had no trouble with the limbers. They did look like andies to me, their humanlike deaths choreographed and programmed.

The crowd across the street applauded loudly, Jasper joining in. Then they drifted away, on to the next amusement, as stretcher bearers in street clothes came to remove the remains and hose down the street.

I looked at Jasper. "Are you sure that . . ."

"Don't be tedious, Swain," he said, frowning.

Lynn's face hadn't lost its hard edge. She was still indignant about being left out of the decisions. "So, what's the story?" she asked. "What are we going to do?"

"I know what we're *not* going to do," Pitcher said, her lizard face void of expression. "We're not going to tell your boyfriend all about our business affairs."

"Now, Mandy," Fuller trilled. "We ain't officially decided on that yet."

She blinked those lizard eyes. "Why don't you shove it, Harv," she said. "There's no way I'm going to let this feckless idiot get anything on me. Where the hell's your common sense?"

I felt my fists ball up. I was vibrating. "I may be an idiot, lady, but I usually get what I want. And right now, I'm hoping that you're the one doing all this. Because if you are, it'll give me the greatest pleasure to take you down."

"Are you threatening me?" she said loudly.

I leaned across the table to glare at her. "I'm just telling you the way things are."

She started to say something, but looked into my eyes and stopped.

"So, let's vote on it," Jasper said.

Pitcher set her jaw and smiled an iron smile. "I vote that we send Mister Blood Money here back to the mud hole he crawled out of."

"If we've got a problem," Jasper said, "I think we can solve it very well on our own. I have no reason to believe that this man can do anything for us. I vote with Mandy."

Pitcher nodded in his direction.

I looked at Lynn; she smiled at me, an old-times smile. "Swain works for me," she said directly to Pitcher. "*Works*. I've known him for years and he has my complete trust. I want him in."

Everyone turned to Fuller. He sat motionless, either deep in thought or brain-nova'ed. He jerked slightly, then stood. Throwing a fistful of pills into his mouth he paced a tight circle in the small room. "We're all tied up here together," he said. "Business . . . associates. It'll jest get in the way. Mr. Swain here is a professional, an expert, and despite his piss-poor record of late, he's done some fine work in the past." He was silent for a few seconds, then his eyes brightened. "Besides, Lynn's payin' him, not us. What have we got to lose. Ah vote he's in."

Amanda Pitcher made a very unpleasant noise down deep in her throat and turned to stare out the window, at the show that wasn't there anymore.

"That leaves it tied," Jasper said. "Stalemate."

"Not quite," I returned. "Not everybody's voted yet."

"Siggy," Lynn said. "We haven't got Siggy's vote."

Fuller returned to sit at the table. "When I vissed him this morning, he said that he was abstaining from any vote."

"No," I said, and stood up. "That doesn't wash anymore." I looked at Lynn. "You coming?"

"Where?"

"To have a little chat with Siggy Harris."

She stood up. "What if he doesn't want to talk?" she asked.

I smiled broadly at Amanda Pitcher. "He'll talk," I said.

# 13

We got out of there and headed back to Lynn's place. It was late, already past eleven, and I still had to get back with Juke about setting up a meeting.

The line of bullets still trying to get out of the city was backed up for miles on the freeway, their headlights stretched out bright like some sort of incredible Chinese holiday. We finally had to get off the road and go overland just to make any progress at all.

"I can't believe they wouldn't tell me anything," Lynn said, and it wasn't the first time she had mentioned that.

"Don't worry," I told her, as I tried to keep control of the hummer on the rocky terrain. "We'll straighten it out."

"Do you really believe that?"

I glanced at her in the dark, a shadow in a world of shadows, black against black. "I have to," I said.

We slid around the wreckage of some helis, weaving in and out of the twisted steel landscape. Somehow, it seemed appropriate. I saw the jutting dark towers of Dome-acile's defenses and began looking for the access road.

"Listen," Lynn said, her hand poised in the dark air.

"What?"

"Listen."

I shut down the hum and opened my window a crack. There was a voice booming down from the sky, from the bulbous shape of a government heli:

"ATTENTION PLEASE . . . ATTENTION. THE CITY HAS BEEN PLACED UNDER MARTIAL LAW. REPEAT: THE CITY HAS BEEN PLACED UNDER MARTIAL LAW AND A TWELVE O'CLOCK MIDNIGHT CURFEW HAS BEEN IMPOSED. GO BACK TO YOUR HOMES. GET OFF THE STREETS. ANYONE IN VIOLATION OF THE CURFEW IS SUBJECT TO THE SEVEREST PENALTIES. NO ONE MAY LEAVE THE CITY. RETURN TO YOUR HOMES . . ."

The message was repeated over and over. None of the freeway bullets seemed to think it was directed toward them. They kept forging ahead, as if everyone of them thought they were a special case.

I keyed the hum and moved toward the flat roadway. Bumping up a drainage ditch, we hummed toward Roger and home. It looked like there would be no traveling tonight.

"Why do you think that Bob didn't will his stock back to the corporation like the rest of them did?" I asked.

"I don't know," she said too quickly, and I began to get that feeling again that she was keeping something from me. I let it drop.

Roger greeted us immediately. His composite face seemed creased in worry.

"Problems?" I asked him.

His fifty-meter head shook slowly back and forth. "Things seem so bad right now," he said, as the crane creaked down to get us. "My people aren't happy. It bothers me."

He seemed genuinely concerned. "You're doing everything you can do," I told him, as the magnet clamped onto the bullet and began to lift. "Your people are in good hands."

"Then why do I feel so strange?" he asked, and we were over the wall, moving down the other side, and Roger had turned into a landscape that didn't exist.

"Do we need to return the bullet?" I asked once we were back on solid ground.

"Joanie said I could keep it until I got another," Lynn answered, and she was really distraught again.

"Do you think you can get us in to see Sig Harris?" I asked, just to get her talking about something else.

"He likes me," she answered. "And I like him, but I can't be sure about anything anymore. Everything's gotten so strange."

"You can be sure about me," I said. "I'm on your side for the duration."

"I wish I could believe that."

"So do I. Maybe it would make you start trusting me."

I heard her rustling around in her seat. "What does that mean?"

"You tell me."

We slipped up on her dome, and I left the bullet parked out front instead of safing it in the parking garage. As we walked up the flagstone path to the tube, she tentatively linked her arm through mine. "I want to trust you," she whispered.

"I know."

She got us in and we took the ride up in silence. I could sense her fighting some sort of internal battle, could feel her trembling slightly against me. I put an arm around her shoulder, and she responded by moving closer. We both wanted the walls down so badly, wanted to reach out through the craziness for something solid and real.

The living room was dark, the walls juicing a nighttime scene looking out from the ramparts of a stone castle onto a sleepy village. The air smelled of impending springtime, sweet and damp. I moved for the light switch.

"Leave it off," she said, and led me to sit on the big couch. I needed to get Juke, but it wasn't anything that couldn't wait.

I sat, sinking deeply into the cushions. Lynn sat close, just touching me. The old memories began to stir for real, and I remembered part of the reason I had kept up with her for so many years. The small glow from the walls lit her face, wrapped it in a soft haze, a simple radiance. And I knew that whatever I was feeling, she was feeling it too.

"Matt," she said, and it was like I had never heard my own name before. I reached out and touched her face.

"It's been so long," I said. "God, I still feel the same."

"You won't desert me?"

"The duration, remember?"

"I'm so afraid."

I took her face in my hands and kissed her softly on the lips. "The walls have to come down," I said. "All of them."

Her hands came out to take hold of the lapels of my waistcoat. I wasn't sure if she was pulling me closer or pushing me away. I don't think she knew either.

Finally she came to me, embraced me. She began crying, her head on my chest. I stroked her hair, got lost in the smell of it.

"Say it," I told her. "Get it all out."

She looked up at me, the tears in her eyes glistening like sun on the ocean in the dull light of the room. "I don't think Bob is dead," she said.

I wiped her eyes with my fingertips, then held her close again. I knew it would be something weird. I just knew it.

She was still crying; muffled sound, like a distant motor noise, drifted from my chest.

"You want to talk?" I asked her.

She raised her head slowly, composing herself. Moving away from me, she sat stiff-backed on the edge of the couch, her hands twisted together on her lap.

"Bob used to have this little fantasy," she began. "You might remember it."

I grimaced. I did remember. "He always talked about faking his death, so that he could start over with an identity that was his alone. One that he picked."

She nodded, eyes on the floor. "He became really obsessed with that toward the end. I think he may have seen the pattern of the murders, and simply decided that it was as good a time as any to play it out."

I stood up and took off my jacket. Folding it over the back of the couch, I sat again. "Not much to go on," I said.

Her hands came up to wipe at her face, put it back together. "That was what I thought, too," she replied. She looked at her hands in the semi-light, at the mascara smeared on them. "I must look a mess."

"You look great," I replied, and meant it.

"The feeling was always there, you know? Even when I kept telling myself that it wasn't really possible. For instance, he had put all of his business in order, fixed it so that it could run without him."

"But even that . . ."

"I know," she interrupted. "But then last week I heard from my accountants." She paused for a minute, her tongue flicking out to lick dry lips. "They asked me if I had been making any cash deposits lately into my bank account."

"Someone's been putting money into your account?"

"Lots of it. Thousands."

I stood and walked to the edge of the holo castle, looking out. There were riders in the distance, riders on horseback. They were using the cover of darkness for some sinister purpose.

"You think it could just be part of some deal that Bob had going with someone else?" I asked over my shoulder.

She answered my back. "Possibly. But the deposits didn't start until a few weeks after his death."

"Did you identify the body?"

"No. They said it was too horrible. I was grateful at the time, but ever since I've kicked myself for not doing it."

I turned around and walked to her, looked down at her. "And tonight you found out that you were the only one who was left Springmaid stock in a will."

She stood up and we were very close, almost touching all over. "Almost as if he intends to come back for it sometime and doesn't want it in the wrong hands."

I put my hand lightly on her arm, making the connection. "Why did you wait so long to tell me?"

"Oh God, Matt," she said, lower lip trembling. "I was afraid you'd run out on me again."

I pulled her to me, fiercely, held her tight to stop the shaking. "Damn you," I whispered. "You couldn't get rid of me with a stick of dynamite. Don't you understand that?"

Her arms came around me and we moved together, swayed to music that only we could hear. "I was afraid to hope," she said. "My life has been one long interval of pain. I'd learned to live with it. Then you came back and stirred up all the ashes again after all these years. I felt life coming back into me, and it scared me to death. Because when you feel, really feel, the pain can be that much worse." She was crying again. "Please," she sobbed, "don't love me if you don't really mean it."

I took her face in my hands, locked our eyes together. "I mean it," I said.

She raised her lips to me and I took them and there was softness and tenderness and fire and urgency and all the good dreams in the whole world all at the same time. And she melted against me, opened herself fully, all the floodgates to all the dams that keep all the secret things inside where we never let anyone get to them. Not even ourselves. Especially not ourselves.

And when the kiss ended, we were on the floor, sunk deep in the big, fluffy carpet, and the riders on the wall were coming closer, their dark horses snorting into the sweet night air.

I found her breasts and caressed them with my hands, felt her nipples rise through the fabric of her tunic, even as I rose to meet her. Her hand was grasping the zipper of my one-piece, reaching inside to stoke the fire that was building within me. And our clothes were in a heap beside us, and in the pale light she opened herself to me, more beautiful than even my dreams of her had been. She was reaching for me, guiding me into her, moaning softly like a lonely child. And then I was inside of her, and our breath came as gasps; our sounds were secret sounds that came down through the floodgates to share only with those who have the keys to those locks. And there was another sound mixing with our sounds, an outside sound. A sound so loud that we could hear it even through the metal of the dome; even as we were screaming out the final agonies of our happiness, the dark riders were charging the castle.

We lay panting, still wrapped like vines on the floor. "What . . . *is* that?" Lynn asked, voice still hoarse.

I wanted to shove it away, wanted to lie there and feel whole again for just a few minutes, a few short minutes. "*Damn!*" I spat, and my mind forced itself to gear. Rolling off her, I was on my feet.

"What *is* it!"

"Something bad," I answered, turning around in a full circle. "Can we see out of here?"

Lynn rolled to her knees, crawled the few feet to the big round coffee table, and began fiddling underneath the thing with her hand.

"Hurry!" I yelled.

"I can't find the switch for the outside cams."

I got down there with her, running my fingers along the edge of the table. I found a series of toggles and began flipping them. Scenes started changing on the walls, all of them dark and nasty-looking: the sack of Rome, the fall of Berlin in a world war, the repatriating of the Panama Canal. Then the walls went white, gradually darkening to the outside cam-view of the grounds.

We watched, still kneeling naked on the floor. As Lynn grabbed my arm, I felt the breath catch in my throat. The domes stretched out all around us, one by one bursting into flame—reddish orange balls of fire, seemingly suspended in the air like stars come down to earth. It was perversely beautiful, like the debris cloud of a nuclear explosion.

I jumped up, pulling Lynn to her feet. "Come on, let's go."

Her eyes were darting, mouth working. "Where?"

"Out of here! You got any cash?"

"I . . . I . . ."

"Look!"

She stumbled for the stairs, pulling herself along by the banister. Grabbing her tunic, I tossed it to her.

"Get dressed."

She slid the fabric over her head there on the stairscase. "What happened?" she asked as her head popped into the open again.

I was charging around, grabbing my own clothes. "Go on!" I said, and she disappeared up the stairs.

Fumbling into my clothes, I found my boots and zipped into them. The bullet keys were on the table. I scooped them up. Outside, the fireballs increased in number, got closer. Lynn was gone too long. I started up the steps after her just as she started down. I met her halfway and pulled her arm to hurry her.

"What happened?" she asked again.

"Someone turned in the neighborhood," I said. "Would you come on!"

"Why?"

"Get into your coat," I said, and moved to the down-tube to press the button.

"The place is fireproof," she said, slipping her arms through the imitation-wool sleeves.

"So's an oven," I returned. "Come on."

The tube hatched, and I grabbed Lynn, shoving her in before me. Spinning the weight dial to the max, the tube plunged us at near gravity level to the ground. We jerked and fell with the impact. I was up before the door slid open again, pulling Lynn to her feet.

We moved into withering heat and petroleum smells. The air was alive with it. The fireballs were everywhere, pouring thick black smoke straight up into the smog, and all I could think of was that the wind had died down. People running, shadows charging in all directions. Smoke shadows. Government goons in their white suits and black goggles for eyes were pumping napalm onto the domes from large wheeled machines, liquid fire dripping in globs from the sides of the homes like ice cream cones melting in the summer heat.

There was confusion all around us, screaming and running. They were going for the parking garage, and I knew down deep inside of me that the parking garage had already been taken care of. Our bullet was still parked in front of the house. I moved for it, keeping an arm around Lynn so as not to lose her in the confusion. People were stumbling from their burning homes, only to be doused and ignited as they came out.

And all of it was moving toward us.

The bullet glowed in flickering patterns that danced along its contours. I got open the door and shoved Lynn inside. It was getting difficult to breathe as the firestorm ate up all the oxygen. I was running around to the driver's side when I caught sight of something moving in the shadows.

It was a woman—*that* woman, and I immediately knew who turned in the alarm.

I started for her, saw the death machines moving up on us from down the block, and thought better of it.

"I'm coming for you!" I screamed at her from across the yard.

Something glinted in the firelight in her hand.

"Get down!" I yelled to Lynn, and watched the pink laser-line slide right past my face. Ducking behind the hummer, I cracked the door open and scooted in. Keying the whine, I hummed off, just as another line slid past my right shoulder to burn a penny-sized hole in the windshield.

I saw her in the rear-view, in the middle of the lawn, stiff-armed for another shot. Then the yard erupted in flame around her and she charged for the shadows again.

We turned. We had been heading in the wrong direction, and went for the wall. Lynn stayed down on the seat, hands covering her eyes. Bodies running across our path, grabbing for the hummer. There was no way I was stopping for anything. A napalm machine was blocking the road. I swerved to avoid it, but glanced the thing anyway. It spun crazily and erupted on the roadway behind us. We were animals escaping a forest fire, and that was the only level my instincts were working on. I knew one thing, though. If that damned woman knew we had escaped her original death attempt with the poisoned water, it was because someone had told her. Someone from Springmaid.

The roads were straight and level. We opened the whine full and screamed through them. Nobody could lay a glove on us. I looked for the exit, but it was gone. A monstrous pile of stone rubble from a massive explosion lay scattered along the roadway. Roger was gone. The noise that we had heard.

We hit the rubble at full speed, and began buffeting horribly. Lynn was back up in the seat, watching behind us. I didn't know whether she was looking for pursuers or saying good-bye to her home. I didn't ask.

Making it through the debris, we hit straight roadway again and opened the magnets up full. I leaned up close, glaring through the windshield at the road, afraid to use the headlights. Straight ahead, in the distance, the sky glowed angry orange—the air force making good on its threat of martial law.

I couldn't get the clown parade out of my head. What was the difference between their illness and what was controlling the people we had just gotten away from?

"Did you find any money?" I asked Lynn.

# 14

Even through the fuzz of the screen, Juke's eyes looked like he had treated them to forty coats of varnish with a plastic sealer. I never asked him what he took; I didn't want to know.

"Where are you?" he asked.

"In a pay vis," I returned.

"You're out on the streets? Don't you know there's a curfew?"

I turned to Lynn, moving sideways to give us a little breathing room. The vis chambers were never designed for more than one person.

"Got no choice," I told him.

A drink came up to his lips. It was orange with red speckles. He took a sip. "So, what do you want?"

"I want to talk to you."

He chuckled. "Not over this fiber," he returned. "Say, you'd better get out of there. It won't take the soldier boys long to trace down a working vis-booth. Go home."

"Tried," I said. "Couldn't get near it for checkpoints and patrols."

"Oh," he said, and just looked at the screen.

He didn't believe me, but I figured that he'd believe even less the story about a blonde with long legs and murder on her mind who knew where my house was.

"We need a place to hole up for a while."

His eyes got wide. "We?"

I pulled Lynn into cam range. She smiled automatically. She was bearing up pretty well considering what she'd been through. "We got burned out, Juke. We need a hand."

"What, do you think I'm nuts!"

"We're desperate," I returned. "I'm asking you as a friend."

He leaned up close. "Friends are for borrowing cigs, or getting a lift somewhere, gumshoe. This kind of shit cuts a lot of ties."

"That's a hell of an attitude," Lynn said.

His face screwed up. "You stay out of this."

"Whatever you say," she answered. "I guess that's the kind of attitude I'm going to have when they catch up to us, Juke Carver."

The putty of his face relaxed to a sag. He knew that I'd never turn him in, but Lynn was another matter. The drink came up again. "How close are you to Belton Street?" he asked.

"What hundred block?"

He held up five fingers, and I nodded in return. He shook his head and mouthed an address without actually saying any words, just in case someone had tapped in. I mouthed them back to him.

"Thirty minutes," he said. "The door will be open."

We blanked and I looked at Lynn. "We're going to have to leave the bullet," I said. "It'll be too easy to spot where we're going."

She backed up a step, banging into the cold steel of the chamber. "Out there?" she said, cocking a thumb. "On foot?"

I cracked the door and snuck a look out. The broken streets seemed empty. I could hear the *swish-thunk* of clankers, but the sound was far off.

Opening the thing full, I stepped out into the night. It wasn't as cold as it had been. The wind wasn't howling and the smog layer tended to seal in whatever heat there had been that day.

I turned back to Lynn. She was reluctant to leave the safety of the booth. "They'll zero it in," I said. "Now's the time."

She took a breath and stepped out into the night. "Let's get it over with," she said sternly, and stalked off down the street.

"We'd better start by going in the right direction," I called after her.

She stopped, turned slowly, then walked back to where I stood. "Don't say anything," she told me, and took off walking again. This time it was in the right direction.

I caught up to her and pulled her in closer to the rotting buildings, more in the shadows. "The trick is to keep moving," I said. "Don't stop for anything."

We moved quickly, mostly in silence. The clankers went by from time to time, chewing up the already chewed-up streets, pushing the city a little farther into oblivion; but they weren't too difficult to avoid. We heard moaning, crying, the entire time we walked. It came from every place and no place, and could have almost been the city itself. We kept moving.

The night was dark, so the only lights were the bonfires that we passed on street corners. We avoided them whenever we saw them. They were government body burnings. The meat machines weren't flying anymore.

It was nearly three in the morning when we arrived at the address on Belton. It was a legal drug parlor, the store front window filled with the multicolored rainbow emblem of such places. It was totally dark within.

I tried the door; it was open.

Lynn started to move through it. Putting a hand up to stop her, I shoved her away from it. "I don't trust Juke that much," I said. "Wait out here. If anything happens, run like hell. Try and get to another pay vis. You may be able to hide out for the night in one if you don't use it."

She wanted to protest, but I stuck a finger on her lips to silence her. "My way," I said. She backed up against the wall and nodded.

I winked quickly and went through the door. There was a night light shining from somewhere toward the back of the place, but all it did was define the edges of the black forms that made up the inside.

Moving slowly, cautiously, I got into the center of the room and tried to adjust to the darkness. "Juke," I whispered harshly.

Nothing.

I moved in farther, toward the light source. It was coming from a back room, the door cracked partway open, squeezing out a quota of harsh white fluorescent lighting.

I crept up on it. If there were going to be any surprises, I wanted to be the surpriser, not the surprisee. I inched my hand toward the knob, and—

The door flung out, knocking me aside. A figure was there, framed as black against stark white. I jumped at it, knocking it back into the lit room.

We went down hard, and a putty face was moaning beneath me. It was Juke, and he was so loaded he was barely human.

"Swain," he slurred. "What are you doing here?" Then his distant eyes narrowed as if that would close the distance

107

somewhat, and he rolled his head around. "What am *I* doing here?"

"You invited me, remember?"

I climbed off him and helped him to his feet. "Oh, yeah," he said, as he grunted up his stooped frame. "That damned jane of yours. Would she have really turned me in?"

"Ask her yourself," I answered, moving toward the door. "Don't move. Let me go get her."

Moving quickly through the shop, I hurried to open the door to give Lynn the good news. The news was good all right; it was just a little too late.

Lynn was gone.

# 15

I ran.

I ran for several blocks in each direction. It was mostly the adrenaline pumping itself out, the frustration charging my legs to work like pistons. But it didn't do any good. I couldn't find her.

And when the exhaustion overtook the frustration, I went back to Juke's place. I found him sleeping on a small bed in the back room, and it made me mad to think that he could sleep while Lynn was missing.

I grabbed him by the front of his sweat-soaked, dirty one-piece and shook his scheming eyes awake. They rolled out slowly, like draftees at boot camp.

"What did you do with her?" I barked, holding the weight of his upper body with just my arms.

He was foggy, lost in the mist. He wasn't faking. "W-Who? What?"

"The woman."

"Woman?"

I let him drop back to the bed. "Stay awake," I told him. "We've got some talking to do."

A small bathroom with a shower stall was set off the back of the small room. Going back to the cot, I put an arm around Juke and helped him to his feet. He was light, filled with air like the people he invented for the computers.

I got him into the stall and turned up the cold water. He started screaming and shaking when the spray hit him, like he had the Rapture or something. But I held him in.

Finally he started yelling. "Okay . . . okay! I'm awake. Get me the fuck out of here."

Shutting off the water, I let him out. We went back into the bedroom, where he sat on the bed again, shivering, his tufted hair plastered to his putty face, running tiny rivers along the creases of his skin. There weren't any towels, so he wrapped up in the blanket to where only his boil-white face was poking through. I paced back and forth in front of him. I couldn't sit still.

"You're an asshole, you know that," he said.

"I'm an asshole," I repeated, "and you're the man with all the answers. Tell me what you remember."

"About tonight?"

"You catch on quick, Juke."

He sat there in thought for a minute, trying to get it all straight. "I was pretty well into my . . . ah . . . milieu when you buzzed me." His face creased deeper and he shook a finger at me. "You had a woman with you and she threatened me. I don't like to be threatened, Swain."

"Sure, sure. Go on."

"Can I have a drink?" he asked.

"Later."

"Just a pill?"

"Later."

He frowned, waving his arm around like a radio antenna in a stiff wind. "This place is a little sideline of mine. I reroute NCO Club booze shipments to this address, and in return, the owner lets me stay here when I get scared that I'm going to get caught. So, I came on down through the back alleys and opened it up for you. When you didn't show right away, I . . . passed the time as best I could. That's about all I remember."

"You came here alone? Didn't tell anybody?"

"I always work alone. You know that. What happened?"

I stared at him, just to check his eyes. "I had her wait outside while I checked the place. When I went back for her, she was gone."

He pulled the blanket up over his head, and began using it to dry his hair. "I quite often have that effect on women myself," he said.

His eyes betrayed nothing. I turned and began pacing again. Lynn was gone; I had to find her. But where? "Who the hell could have nabbed her?" I said absently.

"Maybe nobody," Juke returned, as if it were a real question.

I turned to him. "What?"

He looked at me, puzzled. His thin, spider fingers appeared from under the blanket and moved ryhthmically in the air. "Well . . . people just walk away all the time, you know? Maybe nobody took her. Maybe she just . . ."

"No," I said. And I said it so quickly that I realized I was afraid of that possibility myself. I sat beside him on the bed. "Maybe she heard the commotion we made and ran to hide in a vis booth like I told her to do."

"Sure," he said. "That's it."

But neither of us believed it.

The thought forced me to stay put, though. If she had, in fact, hidden in a pay vis, she would come out with the morning light, and most likely walk by here to check things out. I'd have to wait for her.

"Can I go to sleep now?" Juke asked me.

"Not hardly. We got business, pal."

He was trying to lay back down, curling into the fetal position. I pulled him up. "Springmaid Corporation," I said. "Tell me everything you know."

There must have been something very strange on my face, because Juke took one look at it and sighed with resignation. "Okay," he said. "Let's get it over with. What do you want to hear?"

"What it is, for starters," I answered.

He finished drying his hair, then ran long fingers through it to lay it down on his skull. "I don't know, actually. Well, I know, but I don't know."

"Great," I said, standing up to pace again. "What the hell is that supposed to mean?"

He pulled the blanket a little tighter around himself. "Let me start from the beginning."

I rummaged through my waistcoat until I found a pack with a few crumpled cigs in it. I fidgeted, just touching things with my mind, but never dwelling on them. I needed to be out there looking for Lynn, but there was no way I could do it right then. I lit the smoker and tried to concentrate on what Juke was saying.

His fingers were back out from under the blanket again, wiggling. I offered him a smoker, but he acted like he didn't even see me.

"I had a hell of a time getting to it, see?" He was awake now, getting into his trip, his pleasure in life. His fingers were stroking the air in a staccato rhythm. He had very musical fingers. "I slipped into the net of the Corporation Commission's pipeline: credit bureaus, D and B, stuff like that. Coded myself as an auditor. Well, on the Corporation Commission's data files, there ain't no such animal."

111

I stopped pacing and looked at him. "No Springmaid Corporation?"

His hands were fists now, punching the air, his eyes alive, on fire. "Let me finish, damn it. I'm a pro. I dead-ended every time I tried to crack through to it. It was buried under piles of subsidiaries of subsidiaries of other corporations that nobody ever heard of. It was a classic deep-six job. I'll tell you what, the guy that programmed that poop into the Commission's computers knew his way around a relay board."

He threw the blanket off himself and stood up. Walking up to me, he pulled the cig right out of my mouth and began sucking on it like a baby with a clogged nipple on his bottle. "An ordinary man would have gotten lost forever in *that* quagmire," he said. "But not old Jukie, no sir."

I watched the cig physically disappear before my eyes. He just sucked it right in. I only had a couple left. I held the pack out for him to take another. He ignored it. "See," he continued, "there are three letters that strike fear into the hearts of all corporate bureaucrats. Know what they are?"

I had to admit that I didn't.

"SEC," he said proudly.

"Securities and Exchange Commission?"

He pointed a bony finger. "The feds. Business makes the world go round, my son. No matter what bleeding hearts like you want to say. And when business is in control, for their own protection they need a strong regulating and cohesive force."

I lit another cig, barely got a drag off it before Juke grabbed it away from me and began sucking again. "There's a paper middle management guy I invented years ago who works for the SEC. I used him to get into the tax records of some shaky business ventures so that he could extort a little green stuff from them. His name's Edmond McKibben, and I resurrected him yesterday."

Juke would walk and stop, walk and stop, all the while puffing like a son of a bitch on *my* cig. And every time he'd stop walking, he'd leave a little puddle of water on the floor that was dripping off his still-soaked one-piece. I decided to light my last smoker while he still had one going.

He walked, then stopped and turned to me, smoke jabbing out of his mouth as he talked. "Well, old Edmond's a mean one," he said. "He hit those mothers hard. He tied into their nets with every official document I could steal from the feds.

112

Demanded to cut through the red tape to Springmaid. Told them that the programmer was going to be arrested for conspiracy to defraud, and that the whole Corporation Commission was under investigation."

"And?"

He started walking again, his words coming faster. "They did the leg work themselves and got me through to it. It turned out that the programmer was none other than the Corporation Commissioner himself."

"What's his name?"

"It won't do you much good."

"Why?"

"He died a few weeks ago. Heart attack."

I turned the same time he did. I stared at his eyes which were staring at my cig. He had finished his. "The name," I said quietly.

Juke took a few steps toward me. I back-pedaled to match his pace. "Parkhurst," he said. "Simon Parkhurst."

I recognized the name, but grabbed the paper out of my pocket anyway. I quickly unfolded it, and felt as if I had spent my whole life folding and unfolding that damned paper.

"What's that?" Juke asked, and walked toward me some more. "I knew that something crazy was going on here. What the hell have you dragged me into?"

I kept my distance from him. "Nothing," I said. Running a finger down the column, I found his name, a line red as blood gouging right through it. "Jesus," I whispered.

Juke was coming for me, for my smoker. I just kept walking too, staying just out of reach. "So, what about Springmaid?" I asked.

He stopped, froze, hands up like claws ready to strike. "Oh, yeah. Yeah! Well, it's nothing."

"What do you mean, nothing?"

His hands came up empty palms, then dropped to his sides. He began stalking me again, slowly, like maybe I wouldn't notice. "It's declaration of purpose says that it's in business to manufacture disposable shoes."

"What?" I took a deep drag on the cig; he was closing in.

He came right at me, but I sidestepped and avoided him, getting about half the room between us. "Their quarterly statements show no business at all being generated in any direction."

"Then what's the point?"

"It's a dummy," he said. "It's not real—all paper like me."

I got tired of the game. Walking up, I handed him the cig. He looked disappointed and handed it back to me. I was through. I dropped it on one of his little puddles and it sizzled itself to extinction.

"There's got to be more," I said.

"Okay," he returned. "Here it is: on its original application for corporate status Springmaid showed three million dollars worth of assets, all of it in cash."

"Where did it come from?"

He raised his bushy eyebrows. "There's a question. I don't know. I was able to get into everyone's bank records who had anything to do with the company, and no cash transfers were shown on anybody's. It's like the money mysteriously appeared one day."

"And what happened to the money?"

"A little of it's still left, less than a million. The rest was all drawn out a bit at a time by the corporate treasurer, co-signed by the chairman of the board. One Amanda Pitcher, and Harvin Fuller."

"Cash withdrawals?"

He went over and sat on the bed, wrapping the blanket around himself again. The eyes were beginning to dim. "All listed as salary for one Dr. Max Erickson."

Just what I needed, a new name. I sat down next to Juke. "Did you . . ."

"Yeah," he said, nodding. "I got into the AMA records. There's no such doctor by that name licensed anywhere in the U.S."

"You don't have any . . . ?"

"I got no addresses."

"That's it?"

"Yeah . . . no. They also listed as an asset a warehouse in the DMZ. It had originally belonged to one Robert Hampton, but he invested it in the corporation."

"How about *that* address."

"Sure," he said, and thought for a second. "Corner of Main and . . . Hudson." He watched me commit the address to memory, then shot me a got-you-again smile. "It'll be all right, if you want to look at the ruins. The place burned down last December."

"On the up-and-up?"

"Clean as a whistle. Hell, it was even underinsured."

"Who with?" I asked, and I had a feeling.

114

He made a sound down in his throat and lay down. "I don't know . . . wait. Continental, I think. Yeah, Continental. Struck me as odd because the policy was underwritten by one of Springmaid's board of directors. You'd think they'd look out for themselves better than that."

I stood up. "Yeah," I returned. "You'd think so."

I got off the cot and walked to the door. Peeking out, into the store proper, I could see the first dingy light of day beginning to seep into the place.

"Think I'm going to wait out here," I told Juke, but he was already asleep, snoring lightly.

I moved into the business end of the building. What had been dark before was defined now. There was the booze section, all the bottles filling aluminum shelves and tables in neat military rows; then the smoke section—tobacco and dope, prerolled or loose, dusted or not. That sat next to a holo of a floating cumulus cloud, the gas section: freon, nitrous oxide, ether, party helium—the bubble stuff. The chemicals took up a whole wall, pills displayed sensuously, seductively, fingers of pain and delight to tug on the fibers of needing brains. And all of it glowing sleepy gray in the morning light, colors beginning to come alive as they awoke to the smog-bottled sun.

There was a large glassed-in case, called the Fuller Line. It was all stuff manufactured at Fullerchem, including their special tiny-tot variety. I thought about Harv Fuller. The man was worth incredible amounts of money. Why would he need to tie himself up with something illegal just to make a little more? But, why would any of them?

I walked to the rainbowed window and looked out. The streets were coming to life. At first there were only government vehicles clanking on the broken concrete. Then people joined the flow. Civilians with masks, military in white suits with masks. The world's largest masquerade party. It was like everybody was hiding under a false face so that they could fool Death into thinking they were somebody else.

Lynn didn't show; I wasn't surprised. Someone had snatched her and was doing God only knew what with her. It could have been the blond woman; it could even have been the troops. It could be important or mean nothing. She could be alive and well or have been dead for hours. The only thing I could be sure about was that I had no idea where to start looking.

Business as usual.

# 16

The long counter in front of the big storefront window looked out on Tremaine Avenue like it was some kind of vis show. The place was called the Soy Shack, and they had the worst coffee that I'd ever tasted in my life. I ordered another cup and stared out at the life parade.

An electro-junkie was sitting next to me, wires dangling, unattached, from the alpha band around his forehead. He was all burned out, crashing like Wall Street on Black Tuesday. His eyes were wide and staring, the color of a Russian flag. Head held firm, his eyes moved methodically across the window space, watching some movement that he picked out as important as it went across our life screen to disappear off the other side. Every time he lost another one off the end, he'd say, "I'll be damned." Then the eyes would move back and pick up something else. The usual white mask covered nose and mouth, and to drink his coffee, he had to pull it down over rotted teeth, then pull it back into place. A small brown stain had saturated the mask where the coffee dribbled back out of his mouth. He'd halfway gag every time he took a sip. It was that kind of coffee—good coffee, painful coffee. The kind of coffee that always jerked you back and reminded you where you were.

"I'll be damned," the guy said. "I'll be damned."

The streets were different. They were not the same streets I remembered. The people were not the same people. They were people trapped, without options and knowing it. They were like political prisoners in an Arab country, just marking time until the day they'd be lined up to have their heads chopped off. The military didn't make it any easier. They were always there, anonymous behind their white suits, watching, watching. They'd stare at people or stop them to observe their behavior. And sometimes, they'd drag some poor soul away, kicking and screaming, never to walk past our window again.

"I'll be damned," my brain-fried buddy said.

I watched the crowds, too, but I was looking for someone. I didn't know what else to do. Every once in a while, I'd see a woman who looked like Lynn and I'd feel this little jolt of excitement inside, even though I knew it really couldn't be her. When you can't get anything else, you settle for the small stuff.

The refill came on my coffee, and I didn't know whether to thank the waitress or curse her. I settled for a half-assed smile. She may have returned the smile, but I couldn't tell under her mask. It didn't matter anyway. She was just like the people on the streets, moving mechanically, obliviously, waiting for the grinder to finish sharpening the ax.

Whoever grabbed Lynn had a reason for it. The way that the blond woman had been going for us, it seemed that she would have just blown her away, not bother to kidnap her. And it seemed that the military would have made a lot more noise. That didn't leave me with too much: her friends at Springmaid . . . or Lynn herself.

I had to concentrate on the death list. To understand why those murders were being done, would have to make me understand a whole lot more. Lynn was being held; I had convinced myself of that. If she wasn't, then everything was a lie. I'd be ready for Terra Firma then, ready to throw in the towel for good. I tried to shake off those damned doubts. They'd just get in the way of the work. I had to keep my head, move properly.

That was the supposition anyway.

The insurance thing bothered me a great deal. Human beings don't do things without reasons. For a top executive at Continental to mistakenly underinsure a building that he had a vested interest in, was just too much stupidity for me. Maybe it was time to pay a little visit on Mr. Jasper.

I wondered about Dr. Max Erickson, too. A person didn't have to be a medical doctor to use that title. Hell, a person didn't have to be any kind of doctor to use the title. I needed Juke to do some more checking on that.

And the woman? A total blank. Did she work for the Springmaid people, or some of them, or one of them? What was her interest in the whole affair? She wanted Lynn dead. She sure as hell wanted me dead. Death seemed to be what I had in common with the strange blond woman without blue eyes. One of us would accommodate the other in that regard the next time we met. I was positive about that.

An altercation broke out on the streets. A group of citizens had jumped on several soldiers and were beating the faceless snowmen to the ground. I shook my head. What a waste. There were siren sounds and the far-off clanking of armored vehicles. Then a large, gray-white cloud of nausea gas rolled down the street like a thunderhead down tornado alley.

It rolled past our window, rolled over asphalt and cement and brick and two-legged animals who had been venting their frustrations in a very primal and direct fashion. Then it rolled on down the block, and in its wake everything that had a stomach was down on hands and knees bringing it up.

"I'll be damned," me and my buddy said at the exact same instant.

We turned to each other; his eyes were narrow and suspicious. I smiled at him. A smell like rotten eggs had drifted into the diner—rotten eggs and at the very bottom, something worse.

Getting up, I left a fiver on the counter for the coffee, then walked out the door into the dissipating smoke. I was like a king, people on their knees all around me. Moving in front of the window from the outside, I saw my buddy make a tentative reach for the money I'd left behind. I knocked on the glass and shook my head. His bloodshot eyes went wide, and I didn't need to see beneath his mask to know what he was saying. Sulking, he went back to his vigil and I moved on.

The army was all over the streets, an occupation force. In a way I wasn't unhappy to see them. If they could keep some control over the situation, maybe the city still had a chance. Their armored vehicles were everywhere, all of them sprouting those large napalm cannons, a constant reminder of the alternative.

I walked toward the bullet Lynn and I had abandoned the night before. I should have been tired, but I really didn't have time for that.

The public vis-stations on the corners were jammed with people looking for news of the plague. The screens kept up a dutiful list of grisly images of the massacre at the freeway the night before, and a running body count that grew inordinately higher each time it flashed on the screen. There were never any names, only numbers. Businesses were shutting down all over the city because the workers weren't showing up. The banks had all shut down to avoid runs, leaving everyone broke and in the same boat. A man in a tweed toga came on to report that the air force had already used fifteen thousand gallons of napalm on the city, and that two hundred thousand gallons was the total budget the feds were willing to spend. He looked meaningfully at the screen, as if there was something we could do about it all.

I moved on.

There was one really good thing about the Air Force being there—it reduced the Fancy Dans to the status of ordinary citizens. They no longer controlled the streets. Fact of the matter was, it looked to me as if the soldier boys would just as soon fry a Dan as look at one. The punks became a lot less visible on the byways.

The bullet was right where we left it, a little the worse for wear. Something had scraped all along the driver's side, tearing through the aluminum in big, jagged strips. The driver's door wouldn't open. I went around and climbed in the other side, sliding over.

Keying the whine, I felt the machine rise uneasily off the broken concrete. It listed slightly to my side, but it wasn't anything I couldn't work with.

I hummed toward my flat and a working vis. Without Lynn with me, I wasn't afraid of the blonde. Juke wasn't going to be real happy to hear from me, but that was his problem. He had signed on for the ride, and nobody ever told him it would be a smooth one.

The checkpoints into the decay were gone. The insanity had spilled over and it was useless to try to keep it out. I hummed into my end of town and didn't see any soldiers at all. They had written us off the way the cops had done.

The streets seemed quiet enough, but the fear was so thick on them that it hung in the air, a physical thing, like the mothball smell when you unpack your winter coats. I wished that I had a winter coat to unpack.

I heard loudspeakers again and saw the helis through my windshield. They were announcing an evacuation. Everyone was to leave the city at once and go to the appointed holding areas. It was getting down to it.

I slid up to the curb and let the hummer settle onto the street. Sliding back to the passenger side, I climbed out and got down the landing to my door. There was still some drifting snow down there, but it was the only amount of gray stuff I had really seen in a while. I guess the wind had blown most of it away.

Hand-printing in, I went searching for cigs. I found a beat-up pack underneath the couch, and pulled one out. It was bent in half, partway broken. Going into the kitchen, I got into my tool drawer and took out a small roll of electrical tape. I broke off a strip, taped my cig back together, and lit it.

Moving over to the kitchen table, I sat down and juiced the vis. Tilting my chair back, I put my feet up on the table and buzzed Juke's fiber. He didn't answer.

"Time," I said, and 11:14 flashed on the screen.

Early for Juke. He was probably still at the place where I left him. I tried information for the coordinates. It took a long time to get through, which meant that city systems were beginning to fail.

I got the number and punched it up. Nobody answered for a long time. Finally a runt of a man with a plastic nose sticking out of his mask and a powder blue tunic focused. His hair was rumpled, his clothes torn and wrinkled. All I could see behind him was a solid wall of people, all grabbing and shoving. The sound was deafening.

"What?" he yelled at me.

"I want to talk to Juke Carver," I returned.

He cupped a hand to his ear, squinting his eyes. "Huh?"

"Juke Carver," I said loudly. "I want to talk to him."

"Nobody here by that name," he answered, then turned his face to the crowd. "All right. Keep your pants on!"

It looked like a banner day at the drug store. If people couldn't get any relief physically, they'd at least get their minds to a tolerable place.

"I know he's there!" I yelled. "Put him on."

The man straightened, hand going to his fake nose just to make sure it was there. "Piss off," he said, reaching to blank me.

"You don't put Juke on, I'll come down and frump your store."

"Bullshit," he replied.

"You want to take a chance it's bullshit?" I asked, glaring at my cam.

He only hesitated for a second. "Hold on."

It didn't take long. Juke was back on before I had even smoked down to the tape. He was rubbing his eyes.

"Oh, Jeez," he said when he saw me. "Don't you ever put it back in your pants?"

"Wake up," I told him. "You got work to do."

"Go to hell."

"We're there."

He turned to the crowd behind him, eyes narrowed. Putting a finger in one ear, he leaned the other one closer to his speaker, which put his face right up on the cam. It filled my screen. "What do you want?"

"Insurance," I said. "Find out about everybody in the corporation. See who's had claims lately."

He grimaced, but didn't say anything.

"And Dr. Max Erickson," I continued. "I want you to check and see if he's a doctor in the educational sense."

He screwed up his doughy face. "What?"

"A Ph.D.," I returned.

He let his face widen again, like the yeast was beginning to rise. "Anything else?"

"Yeah. How are you on police records?"

"I don't have one," he said with a straight face.

The cig turned bitter in my mouth. I was smoking black gooey tape. I threw it on the floor and wiped my tongue on the sleeve of my waistcoat.

"That'll taste better with salt," Juke said.

I didn't answer him. "See if this Dr. Erickson has a record, would you?"

"What would make you think . . ."

I sighed. "Illegal activities and criminals tend to go together," I said. "Now will you please get started?"

He frowned, nodding. "You can get me at home," he said.

I gave him the thumbs-up and we blanked.

I sat there, tilted back in the chair and closed my eyes, letting myself drift for just a minute. I heard the sound, but knew it was coming before I heard it. It was almost as if I were expecting it.

"Long time, no see," came a voice.

I opened my eyes and turned my head. Bob Hampton, back from the dead, was standing right beside me.

He had a laser leveled at my left ear.

"I hear you're seriously into dismemberment," I said.

121

# 17

He gave me a great big smile. I guess people who are seriously into dismemberment do that. He looked nearly like I remembered him, but not quite. He was slim and dressed like a gigolo at a Junior League meeting. His hair was clipped short, and he still had his boyish good looks, kind of like a grown-up cherub; but there were hard lines of cruelty around his eyes and the corners of his mouth—deep lines stretched on an evil face through the constant strain of trying to look human. The burner was rock steady in his hand, and I sensed that killing me would be one of the easiest things he'd ever do in his life.

"Couldn't stay away from my wife, could you?" he asked.

"Come on, Bob," I returned. "You can do better than that." I started to straighten my chair, but he stopped me.

"I like you right where you are," he said.

I smiled back at him. "Still afraid of me after all this time, huh?"

The smile faded, and the creases around his lips got deeper. "You've been a source of never-ending pleasure to me over the years," he said. "Every time I got in bed with Lynn, it was you I was fucking."

"I'll bet you pulled the legs off of flies when you were a kid," I said.

"Did she tell you how afraid of me she was?" He chuckled softly. "I'll bet she did. I can picture it now, moist eyes, pleading face. I'll bet she didn't tell you what I used to do to her, though."

"Let it go," I said, and my voice was hoarse.

"I used to tie her up, and pretend you were watching..."

"Let it go!"

His face took on a look of mock anguish. "Is that any way to talk to a dear friend you haven't seen in such a long time, a lifetime nearly."

"You're crazy," I said.

# Introducing the first and only complete hardcover collection of Agatha Christie's mysteries

Now you can enjoy the
greatest mysteries ever written
in a magnificent
Home Library Edition.

# Discover Agatha Christie's world of mystery, adventure and intrigue

Agatha Christie's timeless tales of mystery and suspense offer something for every reader—mystery fan or not—young and old alike. And now, you can build a complete hardcover library of her world-famous mysteries by subscribing to The Agatha Christie Mystery Collection.

This exciting Collection is your passport to a world where mystery reigns supreme. Volume after volume, you and your family will enjoy mystery reading at its very best.

You'll meet Agatha Christie's world-famous detectives like Hercule Poirot, Jane Marple, and the likeable Tommy and Tuppence Beresford.

In your readings, you'll visit Egypt, Paris, England and other exciting destinations where murder is always on the itinerary. And wherever you travel, you'll become deeply involved in some of the most ingenious and diabolical plots ever invented ... "cliff-hangers" that only Dame Agatha could create!

It all adds up to mystery reading that's so good ... it's almost criminal. And it's yours every month with The Agatha Christie Mystery Collection.

**Solve the greatest mysteries of all time.** The Collection contains all of Agatha Christie's classic works including *Murder on the Orient Express, Death on the Nile, And Then There Were None, The ABC Murders* and her ever-popular whodunit, *The Murder of Roger Ackroyd.*

Each handsome hardcover volume is Smythe sewn and printed on high quality acid-free paper so it can withstand even the most murderous treatment. Bound in Sussex-blue simulated leather with gold titling, The Agatha Christie Mystery Collection will make a tasteful addition to your living room, or den.

**Ride the Orient Express for 10 days without obligation.**
To introduce you to the Collection, we're inviting you to examine the classic mystery, *Murder on the Orient Express*, without risk or obligation. If you're not completely satisfied, just return it within 10 days and owe nothing.

However, if you're like the millions of other readers who love Agatha Christie's thrilling tales of mystery and suspense, keep *Murder on the Orient Express* and pay just $9.95 plus postage and handling.

You will then automatically receive future volumes once a month as they are published on a fully returnable, 10-day free-examination basis. No minimum purchase is required, and you may cancel your subscription at any time.

This unique collection is not sold in stores. It's available only through this special offer. So don't miss out, begin your subscription now. Just mail this card today.

# BUSINESS REPLY CARD

FIRST CLASS    PERMIT NO. 2154    HICKSVILLE, N.Y.

Postage will be paid by addressee:

The Agatha Christie
Mystery Collection
Bantam Books
P.O. Box 956
Hicksville, N.Y. 11802

"Not really," he returned. "I just don't give a shit about anything except myself. I'm extraordinarily selfish."

"What are you doing here?"

He rolled those nasty eyes. "Well, I'm going to kill you, naturally. This isn't just a social call. I'm a businessman; I have a lot of important things to do. And you coming in here at the last minute trying to queer my deals is really pretty aggravating."

While he talked, I righted my chair and waited for my shot. He was a decent jump away and was underestimating me. "Where's Lynn?"

He pursed those lips and the creases went nearly to his chin. Ten more years and he'd have jowls. "She's in my . . . protective custody. Away from you. You really surprise me, you know? I never took you for a home wrecker."

I sat up straight in the chair. "Cut the bullshit. Right now. You seem to want to talk. Why don't you just spit it all out."

"Okay." He walked over and sat across the table from me. I was tensed, ready. The hand really is much quicker than the eye. All it ever takes is the guts and the opportunity.

"I want to know what your stake in this is," he said.

"Why don't you tell me?"

"It can't be just Lynn," he replied. "She ain't that great. Is it the money?"

"Maybe."

"You're an asshole, you know that?"

"You're the second person who's told me that today. Who died in Detroit?"

Our eyes dueled across the table. He was daring me to make a move. "Just some poor geek I picked up on the road. I bribed the fingerprints. Money talks."

"Yeah. And bullshit walks."

He rested the hand holding the laser on the table. Just a kick away. "Who else have you told about this?"

"Everybody," I returned. "I stop people on the streets."

I watched his jaw muscles tense, but he didn't betray the tension in his eyes. "You're not going to give me anything, are you?"

"Nope."

"Even to prolong your life for a while?"

"I wouldn't give you the satisfaction."

That he understood. He smiled again, and raised the laser. "Well, I guess . . ."

The vis buzzed. His eyes flicked away for just a second and I was on him. Coming off the chair, I shoved the table at him, knocking him to the floor. I was over the table and on him. He was in my ballpark now and way out of his league. Getting the burner away from him, I showed him what it was like to be looking down its barrel. The vis stopped buzzing. I wondered who to thank.

"Where is she?"

"Never-never land."

Grabbing a handful of hair, I banged his head against the floor a few times. "Where?"

His eyes shut with the pain, but when he opened them, they were clear and bright with hatred. His words came through clenched teeth. "You'll get no better than you gave me."

"I'm going to hurt you bad, Bob."

He forced a smile then. "No you're not, either."

I laid the barrel of the thing right up against the side of his head. "Damn it, Bob. You people are driving me crazy. What the fuck is going on?"

"The end of the world," he said.

I squeezed the trigger, and the pink-hot light burned a pencil thin line along his skull just above the ear. A large charred place appeared on my floor.

He began laughing, not even feeling the pain. The smell of burned flesh drifted up to me and I climbed off him in revulsion.

Still smiling, he elbowed his way to a sitting position. "Listen to me, you flat-footed son of a bitch," he said. "This is a high-stakes game, too rich for your blood. Believe that if you've ever believed anything in your life."

I brought the burner up again. "I do permanent damage this time. Where is she?"

There was noise outside, mass movements of people. Wave after wave of legs was passing by my window. Bob got to his feet, straightening his shiny blue waistcoat. Walking right up to me, he let the laser barrel bump him in the chest. "Let's get down to it," he said. "Go ahead, kill me. Get it over with. Of course, that will be the end of my darling wife."

We just stood there, eye to eye, while the world moved past outside. He finally took an index finger and pushed the burner out of his chest.

124

"I told you," he said. "High stakes, and I always cover my bets. You're not in our class, Mathew. Face it."

He juiced my vis and turned it to monitor. Turning the burned place on his skull toward the cam, he looked at the larger-than-life reflection on the vis screen.

"Boy, you really did it, didn't you?" He lightly ran a fingertip along the smoking black gouge that ran the entire length of his head. "Going to take me some time to even get a good growth of hair to cover this." He sighed theatrically and stood, shutting down the vis. "Alas. But I'll forgive you. If you're a good little detective who doesn't meddle in things that don't concern him."

"Think you've got it all wrapped up, don't you, Bob?"

He put his hands on his hips, his dominant pose. "You bet I do, honky tonk." He leveled a finger at me. "See, you got a weakness. And I'm in control of that weakness. I got you by the ying-yang, partner, and don't be forgetting it. Lynn's my insurance."

I tried something on him. "Has Max Erickson got insurance, too?"

He recovered quickly, but couldn't keep that second's worth of surprise off his face. It was worth a million bucks to me. He suddenly wasn't so confident anymore.

"So you know a name," he said.

It was my turn to smile. "Oh, I know lots of names. I'm a regular vis directory. And you're not the only one who knows about insurance, either."

He jolted again. Two lucky shots in the dark. It was better than I ever did at the track.

His hands went to the lapels of his jacket. "I've still got Lynn," he said. "And in case you haven't figured it out, if you don't get out of my life, I'm going to take it out on her."

He turned and walked toward the door. "I'm leaving now," he announced. "Got things to do."

He stopped walking, turned back to me with a smile. Reaching into his pocket, he pulled out a wad of bills and threw them on the table.

"For your trouble," he said, and his voice was nasal and patronizing. He moved back to the door. Opening it, he stepped through. "And you're right," he told me over his shoulder. "I *am* seriously into dismemberment."

I watched his legs disappear up the steps before following.

I could have tried to stop him, but I was hoping he would lead me to Lynn if I gave him enough rope.

The streets were full of people. A string of government helis were floating low overhead, blaring orders to the citizens over their loudspeakers. It was a roundup. The refugee camps were being set up on the outskirts of town, medicamps where people would be scanned for the plague and divided into categories. What they weren't telling was what would happen to the plague carriers. They were leaving in droves, carrying enough belongings to sustain them for a short time. Their faces were set, grim. They were off into the movement, because it was better than not moving, better than having to think about it. They were all movement, and thankful for it.

I caught sight of Hampton; he was moving against the flow, heading back farther into the decay. Getting into the human river, I tried to fight its current too. I was bucked around angrily, the people on the streets too intent upon their unity of purpose to deal with obstacles.

The smell of fear was on them, fear and deadly determination. They spoke very little, and when they did, it was in murmurs. I kept Hampton about a half block in front of me, keying on him by where he broke the flow. I was able to stay on his tail for several blocks down Tremaine, but then, all at once, he jerked around to look in my direction.

I squatted immediately, nearly getting knocked over by the shuffling feet that wanted nothing more than straight line movement. When I dared to get back up again, he was gone, like he had never been there at all.

Shoving my way through the masked crowds as quickly as I could, I reached the place where I had seen him last. Nothing. It was like Bob had decided to return to the dead. I wished that were true.

I turned around and let myself get pushed along with the flow, let their determination become my own. And the city was a shambles around me, a manic vision of twisted alleyways and crumbling dreams. And the breaking of glass mixed with the bullhorn blare of the helis and the shuffling of mechanical feet to form a new sound, a sound that was very much like total surrender. The city was crying; the tears were people. The tears slid in cold, runny strands down the broken streets and avenues to puddle in salty bogs in another city, a city of canvas, a sterile city of tents and food lines and alphabetical order where even the tears would lose their reality.

I barged down that river of tears until passing my own flat. Then I swam to shore. I wasn't ready for that last ride yet. There was too much to do.

And so little time.

I got back into the apartment, and my insides were jangling like a rich boy's change purse. The people on the streets were trooping past my window, so many feet and legs marking the time left on the city's life clock. I was struck by how little time I really did have. The city was a dead thing, rapidly decomposing before my eyes, and I had to hurry to get my business done before the maggots set in.

Bob had Lynn, but I didn't know where. I had lost him back in the decay, farther into the craziness. I didn't like that at all, but then I didn't like anything about this whole mess.

He had said something strange to me also. He had told me about the money, said that I'd never get it. Money. The bottom end of almost everything, the deep-dish crust on the apple pie. And another question mark was added onto the bottom of the list. It was time to start answering some of those questions.

I had left Hampton's laser on my kitchen table. Picking it up, I checked it over. It was a small charge burner, good for about thirty seconds' worth of use before needing recharge. It was a lady's gun, a small one. They had taken my permit and weapons away when they revoked my license. This wasn't the kind of thing I'd normally carry, but it would do in a pinch. I stuck it in my pocket.

The wad of money Bob had left was still sitting there too. It was a horse choker, folded in the middle and secured with a rubber band. Going over to a kitchen drawer, I came out with a long knife. Slipping the wad onto the blade, I went to my sink and held my bundle over it. Getting out my lighter, I started the money burning. It went up with a flickering blue-and-yellow flame which eventually dropped off the knife and finished burning in the basin. I watched the sheets of ash curl and crumble for a minute, then walked over and juiced the vis.

Siggy Harris was still on my mind. He was the only living board member I had never talked to. Going through vis assistance, and it was another long process, I found that he had no listed numbers. Normally, I would have gotten a supervisor on the fiber and greased my way into the listing, but apparently computer control was all that was operating anymore. The people were all fleeing.

I'd have to get that number from somebody else, and Jasper, the insurance question-mark, seemed like the place to start. I was feeling strange, inhuman. I was a part of the movement all around me, unable to extricate myself from it. The frenzied twitch of the city's death nerve had me caught up. The feelings kicking around inside of me hadn't been there since the worst days at Terra Firma. I was losing my grip, and it scared me.

Going to the cabinet, I found Black Jack where I had carefully hidden him yesterday. Finding the biggest glass I could, I poured it full and drank it down like it was spring water I'd found on the desert. It all meshed with the hopscotch fire that was stoking up in my brain.

Grabbing the table top with both hands, I rode out a wave of nausea and poured another glassful. Something was happening to me. I pushed it aside and jangled Juke's fibers, thoughts of Lynn the only thing keeping me going.

He came on like a spring day in Oklahoma, all bluster and swirling winds. His pupils were the size of beach balls.

"You know what's going on out there?" he said when he caught my focus.

"You had a chance to do anything for me yet?" I asked.

"Do you know what's going on out there?" he asked again.

"Yeah, I know. I can't do anything about it."

He had a drink, raised it to his lips. I think it just gave him something to do with his hands. "Well, maybe *I* want to do something about it. Maybe I want to get to one of the camps with the rest of the citizens."

"Sure," I said. "Sure you do. I can see you in the soup line now, holding your bowl out for just a little more; or bending over so's the good doctor can stick something made of stainless steel up your ass. You're riding this out with me, Juke, and you know it. Now, what have you got?"

"You didn't give me much time."

I brought my own drink up and sucked down nearly half of it. "I need as much as you've got."

He nodded and his face was more amused than anything. By all accounts, Juke Carver was sixty-two years old and had never done anything even remotely like other human beings in his life. He was like a computer changeling, substituted for a real baby at birth. I wondered what the real baby was doing.

"I did the insurance thing first," he said. "Because it was the easiest."

"How does it look?"

"Clean sweep," he said, and the drink was to his lips again. "Every one of the board of directors of Springmaid has had a claim in the last year."

"All of them?"

"When it rains, it pours," he said, and dumped the rest of his drink over his mangy old head to make the point. The liquid was pale green, the consistency of mucus. It slid down his head in sticky globs.

"How much money are we talking about?"

"Haven't figured it," he returned. "But it runs into the millions."

"What's the breakdown on the claims?"

A glob of the green drink ran down the bridge of his nose and hung like mistletoe on its end. It focused all my attention; I couldn't look at anything else.

"Different things," he replied, shaking his head, and the glob wiggled back and forth as he did, but it didn't fall off. It was beginning to really get on my nerves. "Lots of vandalism, though, and a better-than-average loss to fire damage. The woman who runs the art gallery had a bunch of stuff stolen that the insurance paid for."

"Anything else?"

He had another drink. It came up to his lips, his nose disappearing into the glass. When it came out, he still had his glob.

"Yeah. I've just gotten started on your Max Erickson, and it seems that someone by that name did, in fact, receive a doctorate from Cornell University about eleven years ago."

The glob was driving me nuts. "Would you please get that thing off the end of your nose," I finally said.

His eyes narrowed for a second, getting lost in the putty; but then they widened in amusement. "You mean this glob?" he asked, pointing to it.

"Get it off."

He smiled broadly. "No," he said, and a second later, it fell off all by itself.

I sighed and finished off my drink. "What was Max Erickson's field of specialty?" I asked.

His eyes narrowed again, thinking. I could watch it dredging up slowly from somewhere far away.

"Genetic engineering," he said at last.

# 18

I hummed along with the tear flow down Tremaine Avenue, then turned north onto Fourteenth Street. The government people were everywhere, like ants at the picnic, gumming up the works, blocking up the streets. People and machines were cramming in from all directions, beeping horns and shouting—a human logjam on the river of tears. And overhead, helis of all shapes and descriptions clogged the airways, blotting out the smoglight, plunging the streets in cold shadows, a manmade eclipse.

Continental Insurance took up almost the whole west side block between Tremaine and Harvey. It was a massive stone structure, very straight-up and respectable. It had that look of most government buildings, neoclassic and old. They built them to look old, so that people would be fooled into thinking they were stable.

I bumped partway up on the sidewalk just to be out of the crush. Sliding out on the passenger side, I started shoving my way to the building. There was a wide driveway that led into the center of the thing. Steel garage doors had rolled back, revealing a dark, cavernous belly in the stone monster.

A caravan was rolling out of the dark passage. Security punks in their green latex uniforms, walking beside large armored hummers with the Continental insignia—a big red C encircling a stylized map of the U.S.—stenciled on the sides. Every punk on their payroll must have been there, and they all had big shooters strapped to their backs. It made me think that the hummers must have been carrying money—gobs and gobs of money.

All the rats were deserting the sinking ship.

I was sick and mad and more than a little drunk, and I just didn't give a damn anymore. I zeroed in on the open belly of the building and pushed my way right up to the guards.

They started knocking me away when I got up to them and

I used the opportunity to kindly roll down the line until I got right up on the entrance itself. I tried to move through.

There was a punk there who was chewing the sap out of a toothpick. His face was smooth and drawn beneath his mask, like he had had plastic surgery to remove scars. The toothpick stuck right through the material. His eyes never opened wide; they were smoky slits. When he stared at me, he did it by simply tilting his head back a little.

"Where d'ya think *you're* goin'?" he asked, as I tried to slide by him.

"Came to pick up Mr. Jasper," I answered, and knew he wouldn't buy it; I was too far down the road to convince anybody of anything.

He took the toothpick out, looked at the frayed end for a second, then put it back in, other end first. "Well, you're goin' to have to pick him up from out here, on accounta you ain't gettin' past me ta go in."

"Don't you know who I am?" I asked, eyes wide like his could never get.

"Lemme guess," he sneered. "You're Governor Lamb come to pay a visit."

I folded my arms and looked angry. "Aw, come on," I said. "You're not really trying."

He turned his eyes from me. "You're gettin' on my nerves, buddy. Hit the streets."

"But you didn't guess who I am yet."

"I said, move along!" He put his hands on the rifle he was shouldering to make the point.

"Okay," I returned. "I'll tell you."

His smoke-filled eyes returned to mine. I motioned him closer, and leaned toward him. When we were practically nose to nose, I whispered. "I'm the Sandman, and you're going to take a little nap."

His smooth face began to stretch into a look of surprise, but it never got that far as I followed my words up with a right that dropped him like a wrecking ball on a wooden shack.

I started running, and was ten feet into the darkness of the building before I heard the first shouts behind me. There was another punk on the inside, but I hit him on a dead run before he could even clear the visions of sugarplums out of his slow-witted brain. He went with a grunt to the floor, and I kept moving.

I was in a huge, low-ceilinged garage that sprouted cement support pillars as if it were a storehouse for them. The lighting was minimal, the atmosphere depressing haze.

A steady stream of armored bullets was inching its way toward the open door which, at this moment, was pouring in equal amounts of smoglight and punks who were all chasing me.

Running past rows of parked bullets, I began thinking exit. They were behind me, shouting, their sounds jumbling together in the echo to monkey-house clamor.

Exit doors were lit in the distance by neon arrows, but I steered away from them, positive I'd never get through their security. Instead, I followed along the line of moving bullets, tracing them back to their source. And footsteps were thundering behind me.

The line bent around in a slow curve, then dipped through a wide portal that was a long down-ramp. The ramp curved downward in a lazy spiral. The bullets took up almost all of the ramps, and I was moving sideways most of the time just to keep from getting hit. I passed several security points, all of them shut down to allow the passage of the money hummers. And, God, there were a lot of those.

The curve went down and down and down and I thought I'd never stop going down. The ramp finally bottomed-out way underground in a wide, well-lit area. There was a big holding pen to my right where the armored bullets were being drawn from. Next to that, a gleaming vault that sparkled gold in the harsh neon lighting. It was a large, round door, twice the size of a man. The door was open, and a hummer was backed up to the open vault. Little bald men in glen-plaid business togas, wearing lifting exos on their backs and legs and arms, were carrying huge stacks of money and gold bars, and laying them in the back of the bullets. When one would get full, it would pull away up the ramp and another would take its place. None of the bullets really held too much, and I figured that it was only good business. If something would happen to some of them, Continental wouldn't be losing too much at one time.

I thought it interesting, though, that they would always be prepared for such an emergency. That's insurance for you.

I skidded to a stop on the shiny aluminum floor and sauntered up to one of the little men involved with carrying the cash. I was standing near the most money I'd ever see in my life, and somehow, it was all so much junk to me.

"How's it going?" I asked one of the men.

He fidgeted around, his little eyes darting between me and the burden he was carrying. Every time one of his little arms would move up or down, a puff of gray-black smoke would squirt out of the steel joints of the exo.

"We'll be done on schedule," he said, his eyes only meeting mine for an instant.

"Well, keep it moving, huh?" I told him, and wondered if I asked him for a gold bar or two if he'd oblige.

"I've got the situation well in hand," he answered, and I thought I detected something high-handed about his tone, but figured I wouldn't report him this time.

I turned around to make sure my pursuers hadn't caught up to me yet. So far, nothing. "I'm looking for Jasper," I said. "He down here?"

The man was busy setting a crate of fifties into the back of a hummer. The exo ran all the way up his spine and cradled his head so that he couldn't turn it without turning his whole body. "He's in the catacombs," the guy replied, and directed me with his eyes to a hallway to my left.

"Keep up the good work," I told him and trotted off down the hall.

This corridor sloped downward too, although at a much steeper angle than the one I had just come down. I moved quickly, not figuring the punks to have given up on me just yet.

The hallway was all aluminum, and it spiraled also; but the curve was so gentle you barely noticed it. The lighting was by dry-cell bulbs hooked to large batteries. It was pale blue, like an old man's protruding veins. The walls occasionally juiced vis pictures of various forms of recreational gambling: the horses, cards, roulette, life insurance. It kind of kept you in the right frame of mind to appreciate the business.

There was something very strange also. It was a phrase, in holo, that floated in the air in front of me as I moved along. No matter how far I traveled, and I was traveling a great distance, the words were always there, hanging just out of reach: PROBLEMS ARE JUST OPPORTUNITIES DRESSED IN WORK CLOTHES.

Small cams were stationed at various intervals along the hallway, but they didn't seem to be taking much notice of me.

I decided that life at Continental was in such turmoil at this point that their security was getting a trifle sloppy.

I kept jogging the hall, feeling like I was never going to reach the end. I jogged until my legs stiffened and my knees started to hurt, and then I slowed to a walk and kept going.

I shouldn't have started drinking; it was wearing me a little thin about now, and I didn't have anything else to replace it with. One of the unshakable rules of the universe is that once you start drinking, you can't stop until you're ready to crash.

The hallway finally terminated in a large holding area. I hadn't seen anybody on the walk down, but there were plenty of people here. They were workmen and clerical people, some with masks, some without. They were pushing machines around on squeaking wheels—computers. They were all talking at once and getting in each other's way.

There was no building per se down here, just a cavern, a real one, carved out of solid rock. I had the feeling that this place, "the catacombs," they called it, could withstand nearly any manmade or natural disaster.

Fanning out from the holding area were five tunnels. Reaching things, they were like fingers on a grasping hand. The machines were being moved down the various hallways like they were being put in storage.

I stood on the periphery of the activity for a moment, getting my breath and figuring my next move. I looked around for Jasper, but he was nowhere to be seen. I did see another familiar face, though, and pushed my way through the crowd until I got up on him.

He was bent over the readout screen of a computer that was being pushed by two burly workmen in battleship-gray tunics, and kept walking sideways with the thing, the same way I had come down the first ramp. He had his back to me.

"Foley!" I called, and he jumped nearly out of his socks at the mention of his name.

He turned, all lanky and disproportioned, his black hair tumbling all over his forehead like it had been poured on. "Swain!" he said, and his eyes got like full moons.

"In the flesh."

"That's the trouble," he returned.

I had done some work for Foley's computer-claims center at one time, but got fired because I kept finding other things to do that seemed more important to me at the time. Mr. Foley, apparently, was into holding grudges.

"Good to see you," I said. "No hard feelings, I hope."

He pursed his lips, and turned back to the computer. Unfortunately, the computer had already moved on. He clucked his tongue and looked at me sideways. "You want something," he said.

"Foley," I said. "You got a suspicious nature."

He shook a long finger at me. It was lanky and clumsy like the rest of his body. "I want you to know that my time limit ran out on those policies you were supposed to be following up. We were in the process of selling off our life policies to Mid American, so I had to go ahead and approve the lot of them. It put my budget through the shredder."

"What the hell," I shrugged. "If you can get within a few bucks of it . . . you know?"

"Gaaaa," he choked out from somewhere down deep inside of himself. He was wagging those clumsy hands. "How do you survive with that kind of an attitude?"

"The best way I know how," I returned. "Say, what the hell's going on down here anyway?"

He ran a hand through his slick hair, then wiped it off on his tunic. "All our records, everything . . . are in the computers. If we don't protect them, we've got no business left when this is all over."

"Over," I said.

"It has to end sometime."

Just then, a contingent of cucumbers from the vegetable farm came charging into the room. They were panting heavily; their rifles were in their hands. They began filtering into the crowd, looking.

Foley smiled wide. "I knew it," he said. "Swain, you're a lunatic. What do they want with you?"

"Minor disagreement," I told him. "Will you vouch for me?"

"Why should I?"

"'Cause we're pals?"

He started gagging again, and I had to slap him on the back to help clear his throat. It raised a small turmoil, and brought one of the punk guards over to us.

His eyebrows tried to join the space program when he saw me. His burner came up to jam into my stomach.

"We may be tired," he said, "but we're always ready to have a little fun."

Foley was still bent over, coughing, banging himself on the chest.

"Fol—ey," I called very softly.

He straightened, half smiling, waving his hand at the Dan. "He's with me," he said, and shook his head. "Go back to your station."

The man frowned deep, the corners of his mouth dipping down like the GNP during a recession. "He broke into the building," the man said.

"He's with me," Foley said.

"Yeah," I said. "I'm with him."

"He decked two of the guards," the man returned, incredulous. "Made Georgie swallow his toothpick."

"I'm getting tired of saying it," Foley announced loudly.

The guard pouted out his lower lip and stalked away.

Foley sighed deeply. "God, where do people like you come from?"

"I guess they broke the mold when they made me," I replied. I turned a full circle, letting my eyes linger on the people working. The guards were all filing out noisily.

"You know where I might find Jasper?" I asked.

"Marion Jasper?" he returned. "The vice president?"

"How many Jaspers you got?"

"What do you want with him?"

"Business," I said. "We've got business."

He drew back his head theatrically. "You're working for us again?"

"Sure," I said, and slipped my hands into my waistcoat pocket. "Something like that. What's the story on Jasper?"

There was a commotion nearby. A young woman in a lavender one-piece and no mask was screaming and crying, throwing herself at the workmen who were moving one of the machines.

"Sharon!" Foley called, and started moving toward the scene. I followed.

The woman had jumped up on the back of a big Mexican guy and was pounding on his broad back with her fists. "Leave him alone!" she screamed. "Please!"

*Por Dios!*" the man yelled, flailing his arms back behind him. His partner was leaning against the computer on the other end, laughing.

Foley went up and grabbed her around the waist, pulling her away from the man, but her legs were still linked around his waist in a death grip.

"Give me a hand, will you?" Foley said.

"Anything to oblige," I returned, and unhooked her tight clamped legs. She and Foley immediately fell to the floor.

Holding her tightly, he motioned for the workmen to resume pushing the big machine. "Go on. Go on."

Sharon was on top of him, wrapped around him, sobbing. His eyes looked up at me, pleading. Reaching down, I took her under the arms and helped her to her feet.

When Foley stood, she fell into his arms. "Oh, Mr. Foley," she cried. "You can't let them take him away."

He stroked her hair, gently, soothing. "There, there, Sharon. You know that we have to put him down below for a while. It's for his own good."

"But he'll be so frightened," she said. "He's never been alone before. He'll feel like he's dead."

He pushed her away from him, holding her at arm's length. The whole left shoulder of his tunic was soaked with tears. "I'm sure he'll understand," he said, his voice low and comforting. "We're all having to make sacrifices right now."

It looked to me like Foley's eyes were misting over, too.

He let his misting eyes drift up to mine. "They're putting her computer into storage," he said softly.

I cocked a thumb, and I knew my lookers must have been the size of lemon-meringue pies. "You mean that damned machine?"

His eyes flashed at me, and Sharon began crying in earnest again. "Have a little compassion," he snapped. "Can't you see what this poor woman's going through?"

I really couldn't, but I guess it takes all kinds. He took her in his arms again, and she leaned against him, quieting to an occasional sob.

"So what about Jasper?" I asked again.

"I thought you were working for him."

"Just trying to get a feel for the man."

He kept patting the woman's back, and the pats were beginning to look suspiciously like caresses. Maybe I wasn't giving the old transistor brain enough credit.

"He's up from the ranks," he said. "Used to be a Bible salesman, and came right up the ladder very quickly. Some people say too quickly."

"What's that supposed to mean?"

He put his other arm around Sharon and hugged her a little closer. "He's a real businessman," he said. "A real insurance man."

"In what way?"

"It's a business of odds, playing the odds. An insurance company risks its money with the odds, the percentages. Jasper's got Freon in his veins when it comes to playing the odds all the way out. He gambles big. So far, he's never lost. It's not only made him a successful insurance man, but a very rich man also. He's slick, Swain. He'll own this company one day."

"You know where he is right now?"

Foley nodded. Reluctantly taking his hand off the woman's back, he pointed down one of the appendagelike corridors, the third finger.

"Thanks," I said, and walked up closer to look in the woman's face. "It was nice meeting you," I said. "And I hope that you and your machine get back together again *real* soon."

She started crying again, and Foley bared his teeth at me.

"What'd I say?" I shrugged and wandered off before I made any other mistakes.

I walked through the tangle and entered the cave. The floors were still reflection-distorting aluminum, but everything else was rock, cropped off in smooth sections where it had been blasted. It was cold in there, but not damp, and there was no smell. No smell at all. In the distance before me, some computers were being creaked along that shiny floor. The workmen talked in hospital voices that echoed back to me in a pleasing jumble. I tried to focus on their words for a minute, but it was too much of an effort and I gave it up.

The hall eventually emptied into a large chamber that stretched upward for six stories. It was like being on the inside of a tower, the various levels ringing around the inside. Each upward level was a wide balcony defined on the outer edge by a steel railing painted red and yellow. The rock itself formed the inside boundary. Each level consisted of a series of doors set into the rock. The doors were thick metal, probably titanium. Every door was embossed with a large picture of a human brain dangling an electrical cord and plug. Soft organ music drifted down from unseen speakers, and the smell of incense wafted past me from time to time. The lighting was provided by man-sized candles that flickered the whole place in and out of darkness. The entire floor was a vis, juicing a continuous picture of blinking readout boards and chattering typers. A barely audible whisper said over and over: "They're only sleeping... they're only sleeping."

An open elevator linked the various levels together. The

people who had been pushing the machine in front of me were busy loading it onto the platform. I hurried over to join them.

"Howdy," I said, climbing in next to their machine.

One of the men, a tall Africk, put a finger to his lips.

"Howdy," I whispered.

"You a friend of the family's?" he asked in the same voice I had used.

I shook my head. "Curiosity seeker." I winked.

The man rolled his eyes, then turned his head away.

I looked at his partner, a fat little man with dead head eyes and a filthy-looking plague mask.

"Looking for Marion Jasper," I said to the guy.

He pointed a stubby finger into the air. I followed it with my eyes. On the top floor was a glassed-in cubicle which protruded slightly over the edge of the balcony. I could make out a couple of small figures in there.

I thanked the man, and we continued the ride up in silence. There was a crudely done painting on the side of the computer. It was of a pair of dice, rolled up to reveal the lucky seven. I thought about that for a minute, then thought about how seven was a crap-out if you had a point to make.

My buddies got off on the third floor; I had farther to go. As they pushed the machine off the platform, I kissed my fingertips, then touched them to the dice. I needed all the help I could get.

I took the 'vator up to six, the top floor. The glassed-in place was around the curve opposite me. I started in walking around. A number of people were up there, sitting sadly next to those closed doors. Some of them were wailing softly. Several of the doors even had greenhouse flowers lying beside them. Reaching down, I plucked a carnation and stuck it in my lapel.

I got around to the office, trying to stay in the rock-face shadows.

The cubicle was lousy with bright light, reeked of it. Jasper was in there, along with Amanda Pitcher. Double play.

I could barely hear their voices through the thick glass. They were arguing.

# 19

Jasper was bent over in a semi crouch, his stone features strained and rigid. He wore a shiny black one-piece with a gold ascot. He moved very slowly, in jerky mechanical motions. He was trying to get at Amanda Pitcher.

There was a stainless-steel bowl-type desk between them, and the Pitcher woman was very careful to keep it there. Whenever Jasper moved, she mimicked the action and always stayed just that far away from him. She was small, like a bobcat is small. Her floral-painted toga showed off a little too much of chubby legs, but there was a tension evident in her, a physical manifestation of some seething inner turmoil. Her vibes were strong, her karma withering in its darkness.

"Arm's length, Jasper," she kept saying. "Arm's length."

"How do I know it's not you?" Jasper said, and his mouth was moving like a scream that came through the glass to me as a whisper.

"Because I'm telling you it's not!" she screamed back.

I slid up a bit closer to the clear booth. There was a glass door within reach and cold stone gouging my back. The booth was like a hydroponic bulb, glowing hotly from bright overhead lights.

"You and your 'stolen' art treasures have been ripping off my company for years, honey child," Jasper yelled, and tried to get closer. "So, where'd your sudden dose of religion come from?"

"You gotta trust somebody!"

He leaned across the bowl; she backed away the same distance. "That's not the way I see it," he told her. "To me it looks like I'm alive because I *don't* trust anybody."

"You're just so much bullshit," she said, drawing her small frame up as high as it would go.

His head went to the side like somebody had slapped it.

"Clean your own house, Tinkerbell," he returned. "You're just all fucked up because you've never met a real man."

She folded her arms. "Well, if you ever find one, *Marion*, why don't you send him along."

He started to lunge for her, but his eyes drifted up for just a second and caught sight of me. He did a take, then his hard face hardened some more like an ice sculpture on a banquet table.

The jig was up. I stepped out of the shadows and knobbed through the adjacent door to stand in the little room with the glass floors and the two big mouths chewing each other up.

"I was in the neighborhood," I said. "Thought I'd drop in."

Jasper yelled and dove for the floor behind his desk as Pitcher went spinning away from me, her right hand reaching into the folds of her toga.

Without thinking, the little laser was out of my pocket and in my hand, instinctive reaction to what the woman was doing. A second later, we were all looking at each other over the barrels of our burners.

"So, we've all got guns," I said. "Maybe we should open a pawn shop."

"Yours goes on the floor," Jasper said, his head and gun just barely visible over the lip of the desk.

"I was just about to make that same suggestion to you," I returned. My burner was hovering halfway between Pitcher and Jasper, and I hoped that my reflexes were as good as they used to be.

"Swain . . ." the woman began.

"Can it!" I snapped. "And listen to me. I'll put mine down, but not until everybody else's goes down too. Now, we're not going to debate this or take any board votes on it. I'm strung up tighter than a fourteen-year-old hooker right now, and I'm going for anything that moves. Are we all in agreement?"

Nothing.

"ARE WE?!" I yelled.

Jasper stood up slowly, the laser easing to his side. I let my eyes drift to the woman's. They smoldered at me, crackled. She wasn't even a little bit afraid.

"You too, lady," I warned. "Believe it or not, I'm on your side."

Her laser faltered, lowered.

I untensed, straightened, and lowered mine. "Okay," I

said. "Now we're going to put them, very carefully, on the floor at the same time. Ready?"

They nodded. I began to crouch down; they did the same. A few centimeters from the glass floor, I stopped. "Far enough," I said. "I want to hear them hit the ground."

There was a click of a dropped weapon, two clicks. I added mine to fill out the list. I stood. So did they.

"What hole did you crawl out of?" Pitcher said, her pop eyes wide and staring, her tiny lips drawn tight.

"Holes don't come any deeper than this," I replied, and looked around the room for a chair. Beneath my feet, the machine sarcophagus stretched down level after level, all flickering candles and wailing mourners. Far below, I could see other machines being pushed to other resting places. There were no chairs in the room, no other furniture save the shiny bowl desk with its multiple control panels.

Going over to it, I eased one leg up on its edge and balanced there. Getting into my pocket, I fished out that cig pack I got at the house and stuck its last smoker into my mouth. "You seem to be prepared for the worst," I said.

"Our own insurance," Jasper replied, and sliding the swingaway section of the bowl, he stepped in and took a seat in the doughnut hole. "Other industrial cities have fallen in the past. Odds-wise, it was advantageous of us to be ready."

"Don't talk to him," Pitcher said. "Don't tell him anything."

"Somehow, I get the feeling that you don't like me very much," I returned. "How come?"

She stamped right up to me, so I could better read the hatred in her eyes. "You're a leech," she said. "You've got your hooks into this and you're trying to milk it for a few bucks at our expense, at Lynn's expense." She shook her head, and her pixie hair bobbed around her. "God, you make me sick."

"Did you know," I said, "that in the reflection of the floor glass I can see right up your dress?"

She turned away from me. "You're disgusting."

I slapped pockets until I found my lighter. Pulling it out, I thumbed the coils. "Besides that, what else don't you like?"

"No smoking in here," Jasper said.

"Sure," I answered, and fired up the cig, blowing a long stringer of carcinogens in his face.

143

"How come you didn't go to Detroit to hunt with Bob Hampton that last time?" I asked him.

"Because I didn't," he answered.

"He's still alive, you know."

I heard Pitcher gasp beside me. Jasper just stared at me for several seconds before the corners of his mouth turned up in a slight smile.

"Don't believe me?"

The smile got wider. "Oh, I believe you," he answered.

"How do you know that?" Pitcher asked.

I turned to face her. If she would only learn to relax every once in a while, she wouldn't be unattractive. "While you people have been in here trying to rank each other to death, your friendly neighborhood leech has been doing a little detective work."

"What about Bob?" Pitcher asked, her voice rising in pitch.

I took a big drag, stretched it out, smiling at the woman's frustration. "I told you: he's still alive. He's kidnapped his own wife and is holding her to keep me off the case. He says that I'll never get the money. Do you know what money he could be talking about?"

Michaelangelo may as well have carved them out of marble for all the reaction I got. I kept prodding. "Found out quite a bit about your little corporation, too," I said.

Jasper laughed through his stoic face. "Swain," he sighed. "You are no end of amusement to me. You waltz in here off the streets and think you can play with the big boys."—he stopped for a second, then nodded in Pitcher's direction—"and girls. Now you know there's nothing that you could find out. Why do you keep trying to bait us along?"

"Is it my face?" I replied, and touched it with my free hand. "Do I look dumb, or is it the way I talk. Not much I can do about either one of those things." My leg was beginning to go to sleep where the edge of the bowl was cutting off my circulation. I climbed off the thing and began hobbling around, trying to get the feeling back.

"You know, Jasper. For a smart guy, you're the one who's dumb. You keep underestimating me."

He was laughing again. He barked out the words. "I'll have to hand it to you, you sure put on a good show."

The numbness was going away, and the pin prickles took its place. I grimaced and shook my leg. "How about a dummy corporation supposedly making disposable shoes that attained nearly three million dollars' worth of assets through bogus insurance claims. Claims, I might add, underwritten by you." I pointed to him; his forehead creased with rock-hard wrinkles. "And how about most of that money being issued for equipment and salary to a certain Dr. Max Erickson, who just happens to be a genetic engineer. Making shoes that walk by themselves, are you?"

I stared hard at Jasper. He looked like one of those old-fashioned nutcrackers of the wooden soldier, where the mouth drops open real wide to take the nut. It probably wasn't a good idea to spill everything I had, but it sure felt fine to kick that bastard in the ass.

Somebody must have pulled his handle. The mouth closed up tight. "A hundred thousand to walk away from this," he said. "Cash money. Right now. No questions asked."

I shrugged wide, my cig making a little smoke ring when it went up with my hand. "And, see, Bob told me I was wasting my time." I turned to the Pitcher woman. She had backed away from me, hand to mouth, looking like she was holding it closed.

"What do you think, Mandy? Should you go ahead and pay off the leech? Huh?"

She just popped her eyes out a little farther.

"Well, come on, say it. Say: 'Take the money, Swain.'"

"Take the money, Swain," she mumbled around her knuckles.

"That's better," I said. "Now that we all understand each other." I wandered around to the swingaway and pulled it open. The anger surged in me. Reaching down, I grabbed Jasper by the front of his one-piece and jerked him, grunting, out of the bowl. I threw him hard on the floor and got down with him.

"Listen to me, dog hunter," I hissed. "You can take that money and shove it up your corporate ass. I want to know what's going on. I want to know where Lynn is. I want to know the bottom line on this paper corporation of yours. I want to know who that damned woman is who's been trying to kill me."

"W-Woman?" he stammered, and through the masonry of his face a large crack of surprise appeared. "Who're you talking about?"

"You tell me."

"That's about enough," came a voice behind me.

I really was slipping. The Pitcher woman's voice was cool

145

precision. When I turned to her, I wasn't surprised to find that she had recovered her burner.

"Shouldn't turn your back on a lady," she said in a voice so snide she could have checked it into the Hilton.

"You're no lady," I returned.

"Kindly get off Mr. Jasper."

I did like she said. Jasper's laser lay on the floor a couple of meters away. I hoisted myself off him so that I'd be closer to it.

"Don't even think about it," Pitcher said, reading my mind.

I grunted with a little back pain and got slowly to my feet.

"Nice going, Mandy," Jasper said, and scrambled up. He moved past me to get his weapon.

"That's fine right there," she told him, and he froze in mid-reach.

"What're you talking about?" he asked in that friendly business voice that they all seemed to use when they were putting moves on each other.

"I'm sure you're a wonderful guy, kind to dogs and children," she said, "but I don't trust you any more than I do the hired help."

"That means me," I told him. "Looks like we're all in the same boat."

"Go to hell," he said.

I shook my head. "This is great, isn't it? And you people are supposed to be friends, birds of a feather and all that . . ."

"Shut up!" the woman snapped.

"So now what?" Jasper asked, his eyes still drifting lovingly to his gun on the floor. "We sure as hell can't let him walk out of here alive with all he knows."

"He's not the one I'm concerned about," she replied coldly.

Jasper drew his head back. "Now come on, Mandy," he said, and the good-time edge was missing from his voice. "Let's don't do anything foolish."

"I've been thinking," she said, "that it's not paranoia if they really *are* out to get you."

"Think about it," he said. "If Bob really is still alive, it would make sense that maybe he's the one."

"Are you people responsible for the plague?" I asked straight out.

"In case you haven't noticed, Swain," Pitcher returned. "I'm the one running the show here."

"She has got the odds," Jasper said, as if he needed that confirmation.

"What would be the point of creating an epidemic?" I asked.

Her eyes flashed, but she didn't say anything. Then: "Tell us what you know about Max Erickson."

"Yeah," Jasper added, happy to have the conversation away from himself and his improbable future. "What's the deal?"

"Why the big interest in the good doctor all of a sudden?"

"I'm rapidly losing patience," Pitcher said, and as near as I could figure, she hadn't so much as blinked since she got charge of the gun.

"The story is that you fine folks hired a genetic engineer to perform highly illegal and extremely dangerous DNA experiments." I looked hard at both of them. "The question is, why, for God's sake?"

"You haven't answered *my* question," she persisted.

Well, now that I had convinced them I knew everything, it was going to be damned hard to tell them that I really didn't know anything. I was sure of one thing: If I didn't do some fancy footwork PDQ, I'd be laid to rest behind one of those computer doors, the only difference being that there'd be no one to mourn for me.

"You know, Mandy. I'm the only one you *can* trust around here," I said. My smoker had fallen on the floor sometime back and lay smoldering on the glass. I bent down and picked it up, a tiny barrel of ash staying perfectly formed in its place.

"How do you figure that?" she asked.

I was partway in front of Jasper, blocking him from her view. He seemed to be easing himself toward the bowl, inching toward the control panel.

"I've only been in it for two days, and I've already given you more information than you've gotten in a year."

She licked dry lips. Her features seemed to be softening.

"He knows, Mandy," Jasper said, and he was threatening to break our uneasy partnership. "He *knows*."

"You can get us in a lot of trouble," she said, her eyes freezing up again.

I caught Jasper out of the corner of my eye. His hand was resting on the edge of the bowl, fingers stretching toward the controls.

I dropped the rest of my cig on the floor, freeing up both hands. "You're already in a lot of trouble," I returned. "And I can help you out of it. But you've got to tell me everything."

"He's not one of us," Jasper warned. "He won't understand."

Damn him. He was using me as a shield and trying to get me popped at the same time. I guess he was playing the odds. I had to go with him now; he had turned her against me.

She raised the gun, steadied it.

"Don't be a fool," I said, and never got to say any more. The lights went out.

Everyone went down, and I saw a long streamer of pink light rake a blurry line just over my head. It cut through the glass and refracted off into the crypt itself. Coming up low, I caught Pitcher around the waist and took her, grunting, into a wall.

My eyes had adjusted to moving shadows now, light flickering up eerily from the floor. She groaned loudly, the laser clattering to the floor. I was reaching for it when Jasper hit me, and I guess our partnership was over.

We went down, and he was as strong as he looked. I got him beneath me, all animal cries and gouging fingers, reached back to pop him good, and the woman was on me again.

We rolled, all of us, a jumble of pounding arms and flailing legs, and I knew right then that there was too much darkness and too many burners lying around for my own good, and when my legs got free I kicked out hard at anything that had give to it, and the flesh gave and the voices brought up gut sounds and I physically threw someone off me and staggered to my feet.

They both scrambled in different directions, and I knew what they were going for. The door was close to me, closer than our bargain basement of lasers; I opted for the quick exit instead of the bad odds. I guess Jasper was getting to me.

I was through the office and running, pounding past door after door of sleeping odds-makers, the reduction of life to its most simplistic, uncaring form.

I could hear sirens bleating around me as I got to the 'vator. They'd get me for sure this time. My friends from before were unloading another machine off the ramp.

I patted the thing on its shiny top. "He had a rich, full life," I told the Africk. He turned his head away again.

The fat guy winked at me from behind his mask, and they

were off down the aisle. I followed them around until they reached one of the big doors and swung it open.

The inside of the thing was marble, veined black. It had small pillars climbing up the sides that looked like twisted bread dough. A perpetual candle burned steadily in a small alcove set in the rear wall.

The tomb was barely big enough for the machine. They turned it so the fat guy led in first, pulling, while the other pushed from the outside in. They nearly had it all the way in when I added my weight to the pushing.

"Let me give you a hand," I said, and put all my muscle into it. The computer jammed hard against the fat guy, wedging him between the wall and the body. He whistled out a strangled cry and tried to push the thing off him. But caught the way he was, he just couldn't get any leverage.

The other guy yelled and made a grab for me. I swung up hard with a braced elbow and heard his nose crack. He banged back against the door and slid gracelessly to the cold floor.

"Sorry," I said, and began pulling at his clothes. Unconscious bodies tend to be uncooperative in the extreme, but I've always been a perseverent guy. The horns kept bleating, and I hoped that Jasper wasn't watching me from above. Although, I had the feeling that he still had his hands full with Pitcher.

Wrestling the man out of his gray coveralls, I dragged him into the tomb and laid him over the computer. The fat guy's eyes were not quite so dead head anymore. He was choking sounds out of his throat.

"Not a word," I warned him, and pointed a finger.

He gulped loudly and nodded.

Taking off my waistcoat, I threw it down, my last good jacket, and started getting into the overalls. There was a little blood on the collar from the Africk's nose, but it didn't look like it would show too bad.

Finishing up, I stepped out of the mausoleum and closed the door to click behind me. I looked up just in time to get face to face with one of those green-suited security punks.

"They're only sleeping," I told him.

# 20

I just kept walking, like that was all I had to do in the whole world. I walked through the crypt, through the tunnels, through the vault, and out the up-ramp, and nobody even so much as asked me for a potty pass. I guess they were preoccupied.

The street crowds were getting a lot thinner. They were all herding like cattle farther north. Stragglers were on the streets, stragglers and patrol clankers full of white suits with no eyes and napalm for brains. Soon they would be gone, and all that would be left would be the crazy ones, the ones so crazy that they even knew they were crazy. The crazy ones and me.

Lynn's neighbor's bullet was still sitting on the curb where I'd left it. I walked up to it and got out of the Continental overalls and down to my one-piece. It wasn't even that uncomfortable anymore; the weather was beginning to warm up a bit.

Climbing through the passenger door, I slid into the hummer. Keying the whine, I headed it in the direction of Juke's place. I had had one purpose in mind when I went to see Jasper: Get an address on Siggy Harris; and I never even got around to asking him. Maybe Juke could help me.

My head hurt like an infected tattoo, and my stomach kept wanting to climb out my mouth and try life on the outside for a while. The head I chalked up to the booze, the stomach to the fact that I couldn't remember the last time I had eaten.

There was lots of extreme craziness going down here, layers on layers. For instance, why wasn't Jasper surprised to find that Bob Hampton was still alive? And what was the intense interest in Max Erickson? I had become convinced of a connection between Springmaid and the plague, but I couldn't see any motivation for it. It was like humming into a

150

residential area where the streets all turn and twist. After a time you lose your sense of direction and you're just moving—lost. I needed a compass.

Juke lived pretty solidly in the decay, just off a garbage dump that had once been a park. It was a fairly safe area, though, because the dump bred such incredible rats and smells that not even the street animals could handle being around it. I made sure my windows were rolled up and put a handkerchief to my nose when I passed the place. They had used cranes to lift the trash on top when the park filled, so what was ultimately left was a compost heap ten acres big and four stories tall. Somebody told me once that the stench could kill birds flying overhead as high as the smog cover.

I slid up to the middle of the block, the only bullet within sight in either direction. It was a long block of prefab aluminum residences and small businesses, most of which were failed and boarded over. Juke lived in a place called the Veterans of the Cuban Blockade, Post 109. Since the last veterans of the Cuban Blockade probably died thirty years previously, it was a good place for Juke Carver to hang his hat. Fitting that a nonperson should have a nonaddress.

The foundation for the building was stone, as were the steps leading up. I took them two at a time and tried the sheet metal door. It was open.

I walked into a narrow foyer papered with tiny patterns of bluebirds that led into a large, open meeting room. The room had a dull sheen plastic floor and folding chairs that ringed the four walls all around. At the far end of the room was a long table covered with a white tablecloth. There was a punchbowl on the table about half-full of some red liquid, with clear glass cups hanging on its edge like mountain climbers on the Matterhorn. Paper plates full of sandwiches and cookies fanned out around the bowl. A big sign hung on the wall behind the table. It said: WELCOME VETS. Red, white, and blue bunting drooled down from the ceiling and table edges.

I walked up to the table and went for a sandwich. It was plastic; so were the cookies; so was the punch. Story of my life.

Walking around behind the table, I started pushing on the

wall. The section that had the sign on it was hinged. I creaked it open and walked into machine heaven.

It kind of looked like a little house back there, with rooms and a kitchen, but every bit of wall space was filled with machines: chugging, whirring, beeping machines. They went floor to ceiling, and left only a footpath between them. There was a smell of overheated circuitry in there that was real grating, but I got used to it pretty quickly.

Making my way through the machine jungle, I found Juke's bedroom. It was also filled with machines, with one wide low one taking up the middle of the room. It had a pillow and blankets on top. Juke was there. He shoved some of the blankets aside and was filling a suitcase with clothes that were lying around on the floor. He was very intense about his work.

"I'd hate to pay your electric bill," I said.

He didn't even look up. "So would I," he returned. "City Hall gets all my bills."

"What are you doing?"

"Getting my narrow ass out of here. What does it look like?"

"We're not finished yet."

His eyes rolled up to meet mine. "I won't die for you, Swain," he said.

"Who said anything about dying?"

He coughed and shook his head. "In case you haven't noticed, it's epidemic out there."

I went over and sat next to his suitcase. Every time he'd bend down to put another piece in, I'd take one out and drop it back on the floor. He never seemed to notice.

"You got anything for a headache?" I asked him.

"I've never had a headache," he replied.

"How about something to eat?"

"You like baby food? That's all I can keep down."

I thought about that. "What kind?"

"Strained peas."

"Find out anything else about Max Erickson?"

He stopped packing and sat down too. "Yeah," he answered. "Fact is, I did."

"What?"

"You going to let me go if I tell you?"

"No. I still need you."

152

"Hell, Swain. The systems are shutting down all over the place. I can't get arrested right now."

"I still need you."

"You don't give an inch, do you?"

"I'm not that clever."

He sighed and shoved the suitcase onto the floor. "It's not going to be worth a damn out there anyway," he said. He rubbed a hand across that dough face and let me see the surrender in his old gray eyes. "Your buddy Erickson did a stretch for illegal experimentation with DNA. Served his time in the federal prison at Stringtown, Oklahoma."

"Stringtown," I said. "Does that strike you as odd for some reason?"

He shook his head. "Should it?"

A little buzzer was ringing in my head. "Something..." I started, but the pounding up there kept driving it away. "When did he get out?"

"About a year ago. And he didn't get out, he was sprung."

"How?"

Juke folded his legs in the lotus position and locked his hands behind his head. "Good question, and a very strange answer. A full pardon came down for him, signed by the president of the United States and the attorney general and all in proper order. Max Erickson walked out free as the breeze."

"Only the pardon wasn't real."

"Bogus as a transvestite in a beauty pageant. I checked it back, just as a matter of course, and the government has no record of such a pardon."

I stood. This was getting stranger and stranger. I walked up to one of Juke's machines and leaned, stiff-armed against it. I felt faint, disassociated. I stared at the dials. They blinked a pleasing red and green, gentle, soothing. I wanted to get lost in the soft lights for a time, just forget about everything else.

"You okay?" I heard his voice say, and had to forcibly drag myself back to the present. It amazed me how far back I had to come.

"Did you keep records on all the stuff you snooped out for me?" I asked.

"Sure."

I turned around to face him. He was looking at me strangely.

"What?" I asked.

"You sure you're okay?"

153

"I'm okay!" I said, much too loudly. I waved my hands. "I'm sorry. I'm just on edge. It's this damned headache."

He stood and came over to me, feeling my head. "You're feverish," he told me. "Maybe you'd better take it easy for a few hours."

I pushed away from him. "We don't have a few hours. I want to see the stuff you got from the Corporation Commission."

"Sure, Swain. Whatever." His voice was uneasily quiet, almost patronizing. It made me a little angry. I shook it off.

He had one wall bare of machines. It was completely covered with a vis screen. We walked over to stand in front of it. Juke began playing spider on his coordinate keys, moving faster on them than any human being I'd ever seen. His eyes would physically glaze over when he did it, so lost was he in his machine dreams.

Readouts began appearing, marching across the screen like electrons in a vacuum tube.

"What are you looking for?" he asked.

"Addresses," I replied. "I want addresses on Springmaid's board of directors."

He fast-forwarded the readouts until they were just blurs, then slowed them all at once, as if he knew exactly where everything was.

"Who're you looking for?"

"Sig Harris."

"You got it."

Siggy's name came into focus, attached to an uptown address. I memorized it, then asked for Amanda Pitcher's. Hers was listed as her fine arts gallery, and it was *definitely* uptown. I got others after that, home and work on Fuller and Jasper. If I was going to be doing some moving around, I wanted to know where I was going. I wasn't too worried about them leaving for the camps just yet. Every instinct I had told me that a deal was going down, and I intended to dog them until I came across it.

"Well," he said, slapping his hands together. "Anything else?"

"Don't think so."

He clucked once and blanked the screen. He seemed in good spirits when he turned to me. "I guess that's it then, right? Nothing else for me to do."

I shook my head very slowly. It hurt when I did it. "You and me have got to take a little ride together."

"Where?"

"Uptown."

"Why?"

"Breaking and entering," I said. "Things are getting too dull around here."

# 21

The smog cover was angry, churning. It blanketed the city with a patchwork quilt of strung-up tension and frustration. The cover was darkening, getting somber, laying a melody in a minor key on the concrete forest. We hummed along the jungle pathways, watching the shadows lengthen.

"Gonna be dark before we get out of here," Juke said.

"Yeah."

"How's the head?"

"I'll live."

There was almost no movement on the streets. We could travel for blocks without seeing any, and those we did see were mostly government clankers and sentry outposts. They would eye us as we went past, the turrets on their armored guns following us until we'd get out of range. All that would change when the darkness came. The crazies would take to the pavements to loot and feed their insanity. That's when the bull would really be out of the pen.

And we'd be right in the middle of it.

Juke sat fidgeting in the seat beside me. He was there not by choice, but it didn't bother me. I knew him well enough to know that if he *really* didn't want to be here he wouldn't be. When the time came, he'd bail out.

"What's this Sig character gonna do for you?" he asked.

I went through a red light at Melrose and jogged around the small park with the bronze statue of Gordon MacClendon, Texas' great-granddaddy of media hype. "I have no idea," I replied. "But he's the only one I haven't talked to. Lynn liked him a lot. I hope it was for a reason."

He rolled down his window for a second, spit out it, then closed it. "Sounds like the real long odds if you ask me."

"I'm not asking," I snapped, thinking of Jasper.

"Touchy, touchy."

"Sorry."

I still felt awful, like I had just done ten rounds with an industrial andy. The lack of sleep wasn't doing me much good either. I could have laid out for a day or so, but from the looks of the streets, the city may not have had that kind of time to give me. I tromped on the magnet release and sped up a little.

"There it is," Juke said, pointing.

Harris lived in the penthouse of a high rise called Nixon Towers. It was an easily recognizable building, owing to its flattish elliptical shape and sandy brown color. It was designed by an architect who later committed suicide by sticking the end of a vacuum cleaner hose down his throat and turning the machine on reverse. It was very famous locally. Folks around here called it the Big Burrito.

I pulled up to the curb in front of the place and unwound the hum. The building was a good fifty stories tall and had no windows. The lobby door was recessed in an arched alcove. It was heavy steel, polished to reflection, and opened hydraulically. A vis was inset in the alcove wall. Beneath that, a small grilled mike and indented hand-print.

We walked up to the door. Photocells on either side of the arch set off the entry procedures. They were dark, non-op.

"Nobody home," Juke said.

I put a hand up to touch the cells. "They must have evacuated." I backed up into the light and stared straight up the side of the Big Burrito. "All except the penthouse, anyway."

"Too bad," Juke said, but his voice didn't sound like it was too bad. He stuck his hands into his pockets and wandered back toward the hummer.

"Where're you going?" I said.

He turned to me from the bullet, hands coming back out of his pocket to stretch sideways. "Well, it's locked up, in case you haven't noticed. We've got to get off the streets."

"Come on back here," I said.

He closed about half the distance to me. "Are you crazy, or what?" he asked, voice rising. "They're going to tear us to pieces out on these streets. They're going to kill us eight ways from fucking Sunday. What the hell are you using for brains these days?"

"Come here," I said quietly, motioning with my fingers.

He twisted his face into a flabby grimace and walked up to me. "What?"

I leaned up close. "Get us inside," I said.

157

He slapped his forehead and turned a complete circle out there on the empty streets. "Just like that," he said loudly, and puffed out his cheeks. "What am I, Houdini or something?"

I put an arm around his shoulder, and hugged him until he grimaced some more. "I know you can get us in, Juke. So why don't we stop wasting time?"

He sighed loudly and pulled away from me. Walking back to the door, he ran his long fingers over the vis.

"How about through the parking garage?" I asked.

He shook his head. "Naw. It'd be just that many more systems to crack." He stepped back a pace and folded his arms.

"Something?"

He pursed his lips and flicked me with his eyes. "It's the usual stuff," he said. "Common garden variety. The vis is for a security-guard eyeball check, but it's not integral to the system. Hand-and voiceprint can do the trick, and they tie into one of the place's computers, probably... bookkeeping. Bookkeeping would be netted with the credit bureau, which would be netted with practically every other credit source in town. You got good credit anywhere?"

"Nope."

He frowned. "How about filed records at another security apartment?"

I thought about that. "No, I ... wait. There was a woman ... Ginny Teal, but ..."

"What?"

"That was a long time ago. She may have taken me off the list by now."

"My son," he said. "Women never take you off the list. It's not their nature. Where does she live?"

"The Henry James."

He cooed, impressed. "Some friends you've got. Okay. We'll give it a try. First thing we've got to do, though, is get the system operational."

"And how do we do that?"

He raised a finger and wagged his eyebrows. Leaning against the wall, he slipped out of one of his shoes. His socks were worn through at the toes. Moving up to the vis, he bashed the screen with the shoe. The glass popped loudly, and a puff of gray smoke drifted lazily out. He put the shoe back on and reached into his pocket, extracting a small tool that looked like a miniature soldering gun.

"Reflected sig," he said with a wink, as if that would clear everything up for me. Then his hands disappeared into the vis.

His face got real serious while he worked, and just about the time it seemed that nothing was going to happen, there was a loud hum and Juke went flying away from the screen, banging into the other side of the alcove and sliding to the ground.

I bent down to him. "Are you okay?"

He groaned and rolled his eyes. Getting slowly back to his feet, he pointed to the photocells. They were glowing, ready to go.

He stood there for a minute, shaking, getting himself back together. Knotting his shoulders, he rolled his old head around like a ball bearing in a vaseline jar.

"There," he said, and started off down the block.

"Where you going?" I called to him.

"Wait here," he said, and I watched him until he vanished inside of a public vis on the corner.

He was gone for quite a time. I searched through my pockets for a cig, but had finished my last one at Continental. My teeth were on edge, tension in my jaw. I found a fraying string coming off my one-piece. Wrapping a finger through it I pulled it off and stuck it in my mouth for something to chew on.

It got darker as I stood there, Juke's vis booth getting lost in the long shadows. Remnants of drifted snow still clung to the recessed parts of the buildings, where the light never got. It had become smog-dirty by now and began to look like part of the buildings.

A fed clanker came by, a contingent of white ghosts fanned out behind, rifles at the ready. I sank back into the shadows of the archway and sweated it out until they went by.

As the darkness settled in, I began hearing distant sounds: explosions, voices. The battle for possession of the city was beginning. If the government lost this round, they'd simply tear the place down.

Juke showed up a couple of minutes after the clanker left. I was almost surprised to see him. I had become convinced that he wasn't coming back.

He was smiling, proud of himself. "Step right up," he said, and extended a hand to the ID station.

I walked through the electric eyes to the broken vis.

"Name, please," a tinny voice said through the speaker grill.

"Matthew Swain."

The handprint lit up with a bell sound. I placed my hand in the recessed palm and the bell rang again. Juke repeated the same process, and as soon as the bell rang, there was a hydraulic hum and the big front door slid open.

We walked into the lobby. It was dark in there, the only light coming through the door space with us.

"How did you do that?" I asked.

"Just reversed the process," he returned. "Nothing really. Got into the credit bureau's net with one of my paper people, and programmed our info back through to here. Life can be simple if you know the tricks."

The door slid shut behind us, plunging us into darkness. It was an uneasy darkness, a fearful thing. I moved cautiously, eyes continually searching out the darkness, formulating visions of the dark. I shook my head. I hadn't been uncomfortable in the dark since I was ten years old.

We moved to the up-tubes. They sat dark and quiet, on the far wall. They were shut down, without power.

"I'll get it," Juke said, and disappeared again. I began to wish that he wouldn't do that so often. I leaned against the tubes and listened for sounds. I couldn't stare into the darkness in any one place for too long. It would start moving on me, shapes looming out of the blackness. My head was pounding. I kept shifting my eyes, darting my head.

The tubes hummed to life behind me and I nearly left my skin on the floor. Juke came charging around a corner.

"What's wrong?" he yelled.

"What? What?"

His eyes were locked on me, glowing in the pale light of the tube panels. "You screamed," he said. "I thought something happened."

"No. I'm . . . okay. Fine."

"You're sure . . ."

I flared around and grabbed the front of his one-piece. "I said I was fine!"

The dough of his face hardened, and the shadows shifted around on it. It became a nasty face, a demon face. His hands came up to force mine off him. "Just keep away from me," he said, low and menacing.

160

My arms dropped to my sides. I wanted to apologize, but I had done that too many times already today.

Juke turned from me, still angry, and punched the door button on the panel. The tube hatched open and we stepped in, setting our weight on the dial and punching up the fiftieth floor.

There was light in the tube. It made me feel a little better. My insides were still jangling. I took deep, controlled breaths to calm myself.

Juke kept a distance from me. He tried to be subtle about it, but I could see him sneaking looks at me out of the corner of his eyes. It made me mad, but I let it slide by.

The tube stopped on floor forty-nine. It wouldn't take us all the way up. There was a special box attached to the panel that contained the digit code that took it to the penthouse. Juke opened the box door to reveal ten number keys.

"Great," I said. "There must be millions of combinations."

"Billions," he said smiling. "Billions and billions."

"What the hell are we going to . . ."

"Shhh."

He kept his head down to the box, and leaned his ear flat up against it. Then, very delicately and carefully, he let his fingers dance across the keyboard, never pressing, just touching. He did this for several minutes, always shushing me if I made a sound. It began to get close in there to me, hot, confining. I pulled at my collar and unzipped the front of my one-piece just a bit.

Finally he pressed a button. He was beaming, ecstatic. He winked at me and began the process all over again. This time he found the second number quicker than the first.

"How many numbers?" I whispered.

He shrugged with his eyes. "When we hit the right amount, we'll know."

He played around and found a third number, then a fourth, and with a slight jerk, the tube started up again.

The thing stopped almost before it started. It hatched us into a well-lit foyer, narrow and long. The place had been full of furniture, mock-velvet, French provincial. It was just a junk pile now. The furniture had been ripped to pieces, stuffing and coverings everywhere; drifts of white, like the snow outside. The frames were wood. They had been broken up as much as possible. The walls were scarred and, in places, broken through. All I could figure was that someone

161

had picked up furniture and bashed it against the wall. The reason for such action was unclear to me.

A door was set in the middle of the foyer. We walked up to it. It was metal, heavily dented. It was leaning against the frame, but not attached to it, as if it had been battered down.

Juke and I looked at each other, and I could tell by his eyes that he wanted to be anywhere else in the universe right then, including the refugee camps. There were sounds coming from the other side of the door. Strange sounds.

Inhuman.

I took a breath and pushed against the door. It fell inward, crashing loudly to the floor.

We walked through the entry and into the end of the world.

# 22

The smell was the first thing, first and foremost. A stench, a decay whose nature couldn't quite be fingered. It was nearly overpowering. I heard Juke gagging beside me.

I wasn't gagging.

There was light, bright light, everywhere. There was no darkness. The floors were lit, the ceilings; every corner was bathed in the light of heavy kliegs that were positioned all over. The light brought heat. It was like an oven in there, or like the desert at noon. I was drenched in sweat immediately.

There were people, or the remnants of people, or the shells of what had once been people but were now just shells, like what's left when a turtle dies.

They were all young and beautiful, no older than twenty, any of them. They were all naked and huddled in small groups on the floor. They were dirty, filthy. Their hair was wild, their nails bitten down to the bloody nubbins. But they were mostly eyes. They all had the same eyes. Their eyes were encased in fleshy shells of the brightest crimson. Their eyes were open wide, wider than human eyes can or should open. Their eyes stared, fiery blasts of hatred and mistrust, overpowering doses of fear that physically oozed from those open gates to seep in an ever-growing pool on the floor. They weren't so much eyes as they were bleed-off valves to keep the internal turmoil from building too much pressure and causing the people shells to explode in a fury of instantaneous combustion. I had seen those eyes before. In Terra Firma. I shivered.

It was all happening again. I had stepped into the mire of insanity and was being sucked down— the harder I fought, the stronger the pull. The tar-baby syndrome.

I felt Juke's hand scrabbling on my sleeve. "Swain," he whispered. "These people... they've..."

"Get out of here," I told him.

His other hand was on my arm. "What?"

I was forcing the bullet key into his hand. "You got me in here. I don't need you anymore." I couldn't look at him, couldn't extract myself from the attraction of those eyes. There must have been twenty people-shells in there. They were all staring at us.

"But, Swain . . ."

"Run, you stupid son of a bitch!" I yelled. "Get back down that tube and start running and don't ever look back."

"Will you be . . . ?"

"Don't say it. Just get out. Now!"

Without a word, he turned and ran back out over the fallen door. Seconds later, I heard the ding of the tubes, and my last hold on reality was gone.

I stood there in my drenching one-piece, listening to the pounding of my own heart. A deck of playing cards was nailed up on the walls in neat, precise rows. Nails were driven through the heads of every face card. Sweat had plastered my hair and was running down my face. The atmosphere was total, all consuming. Seductive.

Many of the naked people stood up, crouching defensively. Others slid back to the wall, bracing against it. The place had once been a luxurious apartment. Now it, like the people, was merely a shell. All the furniture had been busted to pieces: chairs, sofas, end tables, knick-knack shelves, vis screens, everything. Except for the lamps. The lamps were all still there, standing amid the rubble piles, burning bright. Strange, unearthly music drifted in from another room. Christ, there were more of them.

The people on their feet began circling me, but kept their distance. I stepped another couple of paces into the madness, sank deeper into the mire.

I wanted to speak; no one was speaking. I tried to get the words out. "S-Sig Harris," I managed finally. "Where is he?"

"Who are you?" a young woman with platinum hair said from the floor. The words were venom and she was a viper.

"A friend," I said, and it sounded stupid as soon as it came out.

Her hand came out to encompass the room. Her fingers were dried blood. "The friends are here," she said, and didn't leave a lot of room for anything else.

The singing was still going on, setting me on edge. The heat was unbearable. I unzipped my one-piece to the navel and slipped my arms out of the sleeves, so that it hung from the waist, trailing me like a tail.

"You're from the outside," one of the boys who was circling me said. He had a diagram, like blueprints, scrawled all over his chest in lipstick. "Siggy said you'd come. Outsiders to infect us."

I turned a full circle, making sure everyone kept back. "You've done a pretty fair job of that yourself," I told them. "Where's Siggy?"

"He's here to do us harm," the platinum woman said. "Here to ruin everything." She also stood. So did several of the others. The blonde had a large comb with most of the teeth missing. She kept combing her hair, continually combing her hair.

"I just want to talk," I said, putting my arms out in front of me. "Then I'll leave. I promise."

"Leave to get more infecters," she hissed through perfect white teeth.

They closed in on me.

A forest of milk-white bodies covered with dirt and smeared blood lumbered slowly toward me. They were all hands and those horrible, staring eyes. Fish eyes. And the smell, that stench, was coming from them. From them.

And I got lost in that forest, went off the pathway into the dark and twisted roots that slither down into the deep, black earth, reaching, reaching.

"Wait!"

It was a voice. I heard it.

"Wait!"

Again. I opened my eyes to the sound, and was surprised to find that I was wrapped into a fetal ball on the floor, arms covering my head. The forest had been cut down. I was alone in the center of the room.

A man strode up to me. It was an old man with hair an iridescent white, radiant hair, a beacon. He was naked, too, but not beautiful. His face was lined and slick, the result of one-too-many lift jobs. His neck was wrinkled like an elephant's knee, and the rest of him had gone to seed long ago. His flesh sagged on the brittle bones, his paunch hung down from the sheer weight of the flesh that encased it. He had bird legs and scrawny feet, and I don't suppose that there was ever a time when he was nice to look at naked.

"I'm Siggy Harris," he said, and his eyes were just the same as the others. "You wanted to talk to me?"

I stood and extended a hand. He recoiled from it in horror. "I'm a friend of Lynn Hampton's," I said.

He tried to narrow his eyes, but all it did was crinkle his nose. "Lynn," he said finally, sharp and clear. He had remembered and he was proud. "You're a friend of Lynn's?"

"She's in trouble," I said. "And I need your help to help her."

He ran a withered hand through that bright hair. I almost expected the hand to come away white. "*Ohhh,*" he moaned. "That's a lot of help going down here. Lot of help. I'm not much on help these days."

"You won't have to do anything but talk to me."

"Talk," he said.

"Talk."

"Lynn Hampton, you said."

"Yeah."

"Bob Hampton's wife."

"Will you talk to me?"

His eyes searched mine for a long moment. "You're from the outside," he said. "But you're not like the others."

I wasn't sure if that was a compliment or not. "Is there somewhere we can go?"

"My office," he replied. "We'll go to my office." He turned and started walking into the guts of the house. I made to follow. He turned around to face me. "But we'll have to leave the door open. Closed doors are not allowed here. We're protecting ourselves from the plague, you know."

"I know," I replied, and I was thinking about how Terra Firma had no doors.

The living room led into a large dining area. An oak table stood, still intact, in the center of the room. But it was dug out, stained and sticky. Broken glass was everywhere, and the carpet was covered with blood from all the cut feet.

I looked behind me. The door was being replaced in the entry, closing me in. The whole place seemed almost to be physically throbbing to me, a living organism that had eaten me up. But it was somehow comforting. Safe. The heat was even beginning to feel good, my sweat proof positive that my heart was beating, that I was still alive.

We entered a long, fluorescently lit hallway. A young

couple lay on the floor trying to make love, but the man couldn't get an erection. He was laughing; she was crying.

We came at last to the office, the bathroom. The house had completely swallowed me, and was digesting, making me one with itself. The thought of eventually having to leave was not something I wanted to dwell on.

The bathroom was all tile, antiseptic-white tile everywhere. But there was a great deal of blood splashed around, especially in the tub. It caked on the tiles, then broke off in flakes, leaving only the grouted areas permanently stained. I didn't mind the blood. I didn't mind it at all.

Siggy sat on the stool. I climbed into the tub, liking the feel of the three walls so close around me.

"You're only halfway with us," he said, indicating my hanging clothes. "I can't talk until you belong."

Zipping out of my boots, I slipped out of my one-piece and dropped it on the tub floor.

Siggy smiled a smile that didn't really seem to be connected up with him in any way. "They won't get us," he said. "While that plague terrorizes the rest of the city, runs through those fools out there, we're going to stay up here and party. Have a *goood* time. Old Siggy knows how to live." His voice was hoarse, strained.

"How do you like my women?" he said, and winked at me. "Picked them all out myself. And the young studs to keep them busy when I want to watch." He cocked that old white head. "Yes, sir. While the rest of the world suffers, old Siggy's going to weather the storm in style."

I sank down to sit in the tub. Harris was sick and didn't know it. None of them did. They didn't have anything to compare it to. And there I was, sitting naked in his bloody bathtub.

"I want to talk about the Springmaid Corporation," I said.

"You're the last," he told me, and put a finger to his eye. "The last we're going to let in." He pointed to me. "You're okay," he said. "I could tell right off. Why didn't Lynn come with you? I'd bet that she's okay, too."

"She's missing," I said.

"Oh," he said, wide eyes wandering. He turned to stare at the tiles on the wall right beside him, reached out a gentle hand to touch them.

I wanted to reach out and slide the shower door closed, so

I would be totally boxed-in, safe. As if reading my thoughts, Siggy smiled and slid the thing closed on me.

"How do you like that?" his distorted shadow said from the other side of the glass.

"I like it fine," I answered, and I did.

"Yes, sir," he said, and laughed like shaking a box full of broken glass. "We're safe here. Safe as houses."

I wanted to lie in that tub, stretch out, and close my eyes to rest for a minute in the security. Things had been so hectic lately. I felt myself starting to drift. Shook my head and came back.

"What do you know about the Springmaid Corporation?" I asked.

"Springmaid . . . Springmaid . . ."

"A deal that everybody from the Steering Committee set up."

"Why do you want to know?" he asked, and his voice sounded odd.

"It'll help me find Lynn," I said.

"Bob's wife?"

"Yeah."

"Well, didn't you hear?" he said. "She's missing."

"What was the corporation for?" I asked.

He did that broken laugh again. "To make money, of course."

"How?"

He got off the stool and climbed up on the edge of the tub so that he could peer his wide eyes down at me over the sliding glass. "It was a weird deal," he said. "I didn't want any part of it. But all the others went along, so I did too."

He slipped off his perch and went crashing to the floor. He lay there groaning for a minute, then sat up. I watched his shadow slide the door open just a crack, so that he could look in with one eye.

"It was one of those genetic deals," he said. "Jasper told us that he had this doctor who could invent some kind of bug or something that could eat smog, you know? We could sell the little buggers to people to keep around their house to keep the dust and grime out."

"Where did the assets come from to run such a company?"

His head wagged around for a minute. "Jasper said he was willing to run insurance deals on everybody that wouldn't cost us anything, if we promised to use the money we made to finance the company."

"For instance?"

He stood and began pacing back and forth. "Well, like I have this little electronics firm. They needed some electronic gear for the business. Jasper arranges for a lot of stuff to be stolen so that it can be used in the corporation, then fixes it so that I get a payoff on all the stuff and can replace it without an investigation. I think he did everybody else the same way."

I spread out a little more in the tub. It was beginning to look bigger to me. "Did you know Max Erickson?"

"Who's that?"

"The person they hired to do the experiments."

He slid the door open and peered in at me. "All I did was agree to the original deal," he said. "After that I wanted no part of it. I never knew anybody else connected with the project. Most of the others didn't either. They told us it was a clean deal and that none of us would get burned, and that was good enough for me."

I stood up so that we were eye to eye. I felt removed from my body. Ethereal. The atmosphere was really getting to me. "Why did you do it at all?" I asked him. "You know that unlicensed genetic experiments are illegal."

He stepped into the tub with me, backing me against the wall. "What the hell are you talking about?" he snapped. "We're talking money here, you dumb shit. Legal. Illegal. Those are just terms to use on the little people to keep them in line while we do our business."

His face was angry, the loose skin suddenly stretched tight over the angular skeleton of his aged face. "Money's it. Everything. What this whole life is all about. It's moral no matter how it's stained, legal no matter how you get your hands on it."

He reached out to grab my throat. His grip was savage, unrelenting. "How do you think that people get to where I am?" he whined through clenched teeth, the sweat oozing out of his face in thick globs. I knew he was choking me, but I could barely feel it.

My hands locked onto his shoulders, pushing. "You're wrong!" I screamed. "Wrong!"

His voice was up now, high and screeching. "You stupid bastard! You stupid asshole bastard! It's God!" His eyes were lit up, on fire. "It's God and heaven and sex and sweet gooey chocolate and music that rolls around in your head. Don't you understand? Nothing else is real. Nothing else is . . . pure. What else could it be? What? Oh, God, what?"

His hands were no longer choking me. They were holding on, holding on for dear life. He was crying, the salt of his tears mixing with the salt of his sweat. One and the same. Always the same. "It's so fucking useless," he sobbed. "So fucking useless."

I pushed him away from me and stepped out of the tub. He sank down in my place and cried into his hands like a baby. I was crying, too, and I didn't even know it.

"What right have you got to come up here and try to tell me anything," he sobbed, his words muffled in the blank wall of his palms. "I've worked hard for what I've got, and I always pay my own way." He looked up and shook a fist at me. "*That's* morality," he said sternly. "Hell, I wouldn't even let Harv give us the vaccine for free. I paid for it. Paid good, too. Full price."

I was over there, my face right up to his. "Harv Fuller vaccinated you?"

"Sure," he said. "And all my friends. You don't think we'd stay here unless we were safe?"

I backed away from him, and the room was hard and cold, like a tub of formaldehyde for the dissection students. And I was the cadaver, dead and stiff, two hundred-plus pounds of lifeless meat waiting for the stainless steel scapel of German metal to hack out my internal organs. I was gutted, laid bare. Harv Fuller, vaccinating his friends with a placebo, getting rid of them subtly, untraceably. God, he may even have vaccinated with the disease.

I didn't want to face it, didn't want to realize the unalterable fact that Siggy Harris accepted me because I was just like him. I walked to the mirror and froze in horror at the wide-eyed monster that stared back at me. We were dead, all of us. Walking corpses—animated, lifeless flesh.

I turned to him and he smiled at me. Comrades. Brothers. We were of a kind, united by ties as deep as the subconscious. *He* understood.

Reaching out a hand, I helped him out of the tub. Siggy, at least, was spared the horror of it. He didn't even know. I would have cut my arm off for such a luxury.

There was screaming from the living room. It sounded like a pig's squeal. Siggy's hand reached out to take my arm.

"Come on," he said. "We've got business."

We moved out of the john, into the glowing hallway that seemed to tilt and roll to me as we walked. My head was still pounding, but it was pounding in time with the lifebeat of the apartment. In sync.

The couple was gone from the floor. The hall seemed wider than before, the edges harder. I walked that hall like I was born there, like it was the friendliest place in the whole world.

We got through the dining room and into the activity. Everyone was there, on their feet, squirming and shaking. One of them, a woman with short brown hair and red flaring eyes, was being pinned to the floor by some of the others.

She had deep-ended, I could tell it immediately. Her head was jerking from side to side, and the strength in her limbs was unbelievable. Men, big men, were sitting on her legs, and she was kicking out, nearly knocking them off. She was gone totally, an animal. She was human only by biology. She was a vicious, snarling creature. She was dangerous.

Siggy and I walked up close and looked down at the thing that was pinned to the floor. Sounds were coming out of its throat, gurgling, hissing sounds.

"She's turned," he said to me. "Gone bad. We have to deal with it."

The creature lurched, nearly coming off the floor. Its strength was incredible.

"We'll have to hurry," he said. "This thing is capable of anything."

I agreed.

Siggy nodded to the men on the floor, and they brought the creature to its feet. It strained against them, nearly breaking free. I backed away in revulsion.

More hands moved in to subdue the thing, grabbing hands in the bright white light. Their voices were chattering all at once, a battlefield of voices, clashing against one another; rising in intensity, vying for control. And the women all looked quite beautiful to me, their faces mirroring the intensity of their souls, their breasts heaving rapidly in the flush of their excitement, nipples stiff and jutting.

The sea of hands picked up the creature and carried it above their heads, its animal cries rising to pierce the clamorous din that filled the room to the bursting. I was yelling now too, swept along with the cresting wave of emotion. My mind began to touch on the mob at the Fullerchem plant, but the thought died quickly, withered on the vine. This wasn't the same thing.

I gave myself over to it.

We carried the monster into the dining room and banged it down on the table. There was a second of hesitation, then the hands went for it. Its screams lasted no longer than the hesitation.

They tore into it, bare-handed, tore it apart, destroyed the evil totally.

And then they ate. Warm fresh meat, meat you killed and ate yourself. Survival meat. Meat you could trust. Someone was shoving something warm and slippery into my hands, and the forest of flesh was dancing all around me, throbbing in and out with internal rhythms, and I was one of them, caught in the music, at one with the beat. The beat. The heartbeat. I brought the safe meat up to my lips. The smell was sweet, overpowering.

I ate.

Then I threw up.

Then I passed out.

# 23

The dream went like this:

I was back in Terra Firma, back in my nut-house grays. It was close in there, hot and suffocating. I was lying in my room, on my bed with the thin mattress and broken springs. I was wet with sweat; so was the bed. It was like lying on a sponge.

I got up, wanting a drink of water. When I went to the tap, blood came out. "Oh no," I said. "Not again."

Leaving the room, I walked down those dark, dirty halls, feeling like a concrete termite that had burrowed itself into solid rock. There were noises behind all the other doorways that lined the hall. Sex noises mostly, or pain. I began to look in the door spaces.

The rooms were filled with people in small groups. They were people I'd known for my whole life—good and bad. All of them. A family reunion.

Some of the rooms were occupied by the women I'd known: Lynn, Maria, Ginny Teal, Porchy Rodgers, Les Heenan, and others who went back to my earliest experiences. They were all wearing straitjackets and sitting around card tables. The sex noises were coming from them. They'd take turns doing them, like some sort of contest. When one would finish, they'd all laugh, and the next one would start. It went on and on. I'd call to them, and they'd look up and smile at me, but the contest went on. I moved along.

Behind every door were faces from my past, all confined, all restrained. Mad. Comfortable in their madness. They'd call to me and I'd wave, but I moved on. There was someone I was looking for.

I found his room finally, went in. He was dressed in a tux tunic with a ruffled front and black bow tie. A pink carnation was stuck in his lapel.

"Swain," he said. "Come in. I've been waiting for you."

"I'm thirsty," I told him.

"I know."

He held out a glass to me. It was filled with clear, cold water. I brought it to my lips.

"Not yet," he said, and took it away from me.

He sat in a swivel chair at a big desk. I wasn't dressed in my grays anymore. I was in a tan one-piece, with the dark brown waistcoat I had lost in Freefall City when I crashed on Papa Bear.

"Sit down," he said.

I sat on an overstuffed sofa that sank me down to my armpits. A large coffee table of polished brass was before me. He very carefully got up and placed the glass of water on the table.

"For later," he said.

His name was Charlie Kestleman, and he had spent the first forty years of his life obeying all the rules. He had been a good kid, the kind who always came home when he said he was going to, who never missed dinner or swiped drug money from Dad's wallet. He studied hard in school, and although he never made the best grades, he made the best he could. When he left school, he got a job and designed circuit boards for the same company for twenty years. He married when the time was right, a girl his parents liked a lot. Liked like a daughter. He always brought his paycheck home, raised five exemplary kids, never cheated on his wife to speak of, only drank to excess on special occasions and national holidays. At some point in his life, he had somehow managed to secure a one-acre plot of ground just outside the city. He loved to go there on Sundays and work his vegetable garden. Nothing ever grew properly in the smog-infested, sunless air, but Charlie didn't care. He loved the feel of his hands in the soil. Then one Sunday, he took the family out to the plot, bound and gagged them, laid them out in a neat little row, then ground them to mulch with a solar-powered roto-tiller that he had rented for the afternoon. It was the one violent act in his life. There were never anymore.

Charlie had been my best friend at Terra Firma.

The happiest man I had ever known.

He leaned against the desk and looked me in the eye. "Swain," he said. "You've got to learn to live with it."

"But I don't belong here," I replied.

"The hell you don't!"

"I'm not crazy, Charlie. You know that."

174

He laughed then, in his gentle soft spoken way. "That's what they all say," he told me. "Let me ask you a question: Do *I* belong here?"

"Yes," I said. "No."

He took the carnation out of his lapel and put it to his nose. It turned into a frog as he held it. "I'm a mass murderer," he said. "Only a crazy man would think that a mass murderer shouldn't be locked away."

The frog hopped out of his hand and disappeared under the desk, which was now a laser cannon. Charlie was dressed in an Air Force uniform, a full-bird colonel. He held out his palm to me. It was slick and glistening.

"Damn thing peed on me," he said.

"But you're okay now," I said.

"Don't be an idiot!" he snapped at me. "Nobody's okay. Ever. Some people are just better actors than others."

"I think..."

"That's your problem," he said. "You think too much." He made a throwaway gesture with his now wart ridden hand. "Drink your water."

I picked up the water and drank, and it was sweet and soothing and altogether the best thing I had ever put down my throat. It made me feel better.

I put the empty glass back on the table and stood. "I have to go," I said.

"Yes," he answered simply, and he was dressed like a frowning clown in full makeup. The laser cannon was a trampoline and he began to jump up and down on it. I was in the audience with a bag full of peanuts. The place smelled of popcorn, sweat, and elephant shit. I got up and walked out the doorway.

Going down the steps to the lower level, I went to the front door. The door was gone; just an open space remained. A large number of people were moving in and out freely.

I went to the door. There was a guard, a Fancy Dan with a handlebar moustache. I walked up to him. He saluted me with a big smile. "Good morning, Mr. Swain," he said. "It's a good day out there. See you around."

I returned his smile and went outside. There was a sun shining out there and a blue sky. The asylum had a huge front lawn, and the grass was green, real green, like I'd never seen grass before. The lawn was filled with people, thousands of them, people as far as the eye could see. They all had mallets in their hands. They were playing croquet on the lawn—a mammoth, never-ending croquet game.

I picked up a mallet and joined in.

I opened my eyes to a woman making love to me. She was hunched on top of me, jumping up and down, animal noises vomiting out of her throat.

Growling, I pushed her off me and flashed my eyes at her. She went crawling away from me on all fours, squealing. Most of the others were still asleep all over the floor, rolled up in tight, defensive balls.

I sat up slowly, my mind roller coastering. My hands were stained with dried blood from the night before. I remembered what had happened, and the memory revolted me.

Standing, I looked at the front door. It called to me and pushed me away at the same time. It was the most fearful thing I'd ever seen in my life. It was the ultimate choice.

I had to get the blood off my hands. I walked slowly to the bathroom, focusing my attention in straight lines only. I went into the bathroom. Siggy was perched on the stool. "Do you have an appointment?" he asked me.

"Do I need one?"

He didn't answer.

I went up and looked in the mirror. Blood was smeared on my face. Turning to the shower, I took my boots and one-piece out of the tub from the night before and dropped them on the floor. I got the water going and stepped in, closing the sliding door, not for protection, but to keep the water off Siggy.

"They're going to shut down the systems soon," I called to him over the sound of the shower. "Water and electricity."

"No they won't," he responded.

"You'd better make arrangements."

"We're fine. Everything's fine."

I let the water play on me, let it get the stains from the night before off me—at least the visible stains. The blood dyed the water dark as it swirled down the drain. When the water turned clear again, I stepped out, dripping on the tiles.

"You're going out there," he said.

"I've got to."

"You can't leave," he said. "You belong here."

"Don't make it any harder for me." I slipped into my one-piece, still wet, then zipped back into my boots.

"This is your home."

"I don't have a home."

"Where are you going?"

I ran clean hands through my wet hair, getting it out of my face. "I'm going to find Harv Fuller first," I answered. "Then I'm going to find Lynn."

"But they're all crazy out there."

"Yeah."

I turned from him, and walked back down the hall. My brain was on fire, and the fire was fear, and it was threatening to consume me again.

I took very deliberate steps toward the front door. I ran through the alphabet in my head, recited the primary colors, anything to keep from thinking.

Getting through the living room, my steps slowed as I got closer to the door. My hand was shaking as I reached for it. I wasn't going to make it.

Then Charlie's words came back to me: "Some people are just better actors than others."

I grabbed the door and shoved it aside, strode out of the place and moved to the tubes. It wasn't over yet.

Not by a long shot.

# 24

The bullet I'd been humming wasn't out on the streets. Juke had taken it away. I hoped that he made it.

My mind wasn't working clearly at all; it was all I could do to keep myself from going to pieces. There were things that needed to be done. It was the thought that kept me alive. The work was everything, everything and then some. I keyed on that. My mind became a long underground tunnel that I moved through in a straight line toward the light at the other end. The light in this case was Harv Fuller—the man who was killing off his friends.

I started walking the streets in the direction of the Fullerchem plant. The plant was closer to my location than his home, so I figured I'd start there. I hoped he hadn't evacuated yet.

The streets were a battleground. It must have been house-to-house the night before, the exterminators flushing out the rats and killing them. Lower levels of buildings were burned-out shells, or mere rubble piles. Small fires still burned here and there, swirling drifts of light gray smoke through the deserted streets. Bullets lay dead on the road, burned and crumpled, some squashed like the clankers had run right over them. Bodies from time to time, bodies that had missed the cremation piles. And those were evident enough, stacks of charred carbon, still smoldering on street corners. Very methodical. It was obvious enough physically what they were, but for anyone stupid enough not to realize, there was always the smell that drifted out of the ashes. The smell was the worst. You couldn't shut your eyes to it. I began to skirt blocks out of my way to avoid that stench.

The wind was chilly enough to be early morning, the smog cover still dark, the everlasting overcast. Everything jutted upward around me, stiff and imposing, threatening. I set my eyes straight and continued down that tunnel.

Farther down Melrose, I found an abandoned bullet in the

middle of the street. It was filled with canned food and the card was still slotted in the starter. No sign of what could have happened to the driver.

Getting in, I keyed the whine. It seemed okay. I looked over at the food filling the rest of the seat. I wasn't hungry; I was beyond hunger, but I had to eat. I needed to reassure myself that I still could.

Untabbing some canned-meat substitute, I had to fight down fears of food poisoning to even get it in my mouth. When I ate it, every bite tasted rotted and gamy; but I forced it down anyway. I had to keep control of my mind.

I finished it off and it stayed down. I threw the empty can out the window and wound out the hum, moving for Fullerchem.

I hadn't pegged Fuller for the killer, couldn't really figure out the reason. They took a chance and hired somebody to experiment with organisms, figuring that if it turned out the way they expected, they'd be able to go public with it and forestall any illegality by the overwhelming public good that they were doing. They'd also get a lot richer in the bargain, of course. And money, as Siggy said, was everything. But it backfired. Erickson came up with a deadly virus that couldn't be controlled. They worked frantically and came up with the antidote, but couldn't make enough of it to do any good. Fine. A screw-up on a universal scale. But why would Harv do away with all his friends? Surely they'd all want to keep quiet about it since they were all in it together. It didn't slot together right.

I hummed the remaining blocks to the plant, not looking at the desolation that surrounded me. I think it was awful. I think it was worse than my altered brain was telling me it was, and that was awful. The one thought that kept creeping into my brain, that kept seeping through the cracks that I was desperately trying to keep closed, was that I wasn't seeing anybody on the streets, not anybody. Not even the troops anymore. The city was a ghost town. I think it was getting ready to become a non-town.

The plant loomed before me, as deserted as the rest of the city. Its big iron gates were open wide, inviting anyone to come in and have their way with it. How much different from the last time I was here. I hummed through the place, skirting the fires that still burned in its parking lot, and got up to the door that I had come in before.

I got out and went inside. The doors were gone, missing in action. The lights were gone in there, the only brightness was the red glowing emergency dry-cells that kicked in when the lights went.

So I wandered through a ruby haze. It was the warehouse, shipping and receiving. It was decimated. Vandals mostly, going for the free stuff. Too bad they'd never live long enough to get through even a part of what they took. Junkie heaven. With a catch. Everything had a catch.

Things, monsters, kept moving through the red glowing darkness to get me, but I moved forward, eyes set. There were tubes, but they were shut down. I found some stairs and started up.

I passed a couple of dead ones on the first landing, street types, sprawled on the cold concrete, multiple laser burns tattooing their backs. It looked like the fighting never really got any farther than the ground floor.

By the time I got to the third-floor landing, there was no more evidence of skirmishes. I moved up one more flight and into the general offices.

There was light up here, small pockets of illumination. The kind of lights that the janitors leave on when everybody goes away for a long weekend. It was calm here, peaceful. Everything was neat and orderly—the bowls that filled the programmer pools, the cubby-hole partition offices of the lower- and middle-management people, the real offices with windows for the upper echelon. It was strange to be there, like if I could stay in this world, none of that other stuff would even exist.

I moved on. Grudgingly.

Finding the door that led into Harv's suite, I hesitated only slightly before going in. The music was still seductive, the pills still floating sensuously past. There was a difference this time, though. Harv Fuller was waiting there for me. Not waiting for me specifically, I suppose, just waiting. Always waiting. He was dead.

He lay, face up, in the midst of his erotic drug fantasy. His eyes stared blankly at the substance of his life—one last, eternally longing gaze. His face was serene enough, but then he had worked very hard to maintain the chemical balance that would keep him that way. There wasn't a mark on him, nothing to show how or why he had died. There was one thing, though.

His right arm had been hacked off at the elbow. It was gone, nowhere to be seen. Somebody had cut his arm off and taken it. The blood that pooled around the stump was still wet, fresh.

I sat on the floor next to old Harv and stared at him. "What's the story?" I asked. "What the hell is this all about?"

Harv didn't answer me. Even dead he wasn't willing to tell me the truth.

I checked his body, but it didn't tell me anything. I briefly considered going through his office, but it would take me a year to sift through the mountains of garbage to get to anything real.

I stood slowly, like a man who has nothing to do and all day to do it. Taking one last look at the man who went out of his way to make sure I got my dose of the plague, I turned and headed back out the way I had come.

There was a switch next to the door. I flipped it and the pills and music disappeared to be replaced by deadly darkness. Sorry, Harv.

I retraced my steps to the bullet. I didn't figure it to be coincidence that Harv had been dismembered, since I was hanging out with people who were seriously into it. It came back down to Bob. And Lynn. Doubts about Lynn, nagging doubts. No. I pushed them aside. Mandy Pitcher had said it: You've got to trust somebody. Lynn was my rock, my solid anchor to dry land. I had to trust her.

Uncorking the hum, I nosed the bullet toward the decay, the last place I had seen Hampton. A thought had occurred to me, one that I should have thought about before. Siggy triggered it when he told me about the electronic gear that was "stolen" by Jasper's people to use in the lab, then paid for by insurance money without investigation. Springmaid had a warehouse that burned down, an underinsured warehouse at that. Underinsured translates as nonarson, no investigation. Easy payoff. If everything was so easy, why bother to burn the damned thing down at all, especially with the vice president of the company in your corner.

I remembered the address; it was near my old office. I made the drive obsessed with Harv's arm. It had to be Bob. Who else would do something like that? He didn't just hack it off, but took it with him for a souvenir. Great.

I turned off Tremaine; the desolation wasn't nearly so bad in my section of town. Nothing worth tearing up. Getting onto Hudson I followed it one block to the address that Juke had given me.

It was there all right. Big as life.

Twice as ugly.

# 25

It was burned all right, but it was just outside surface stuff. Just enough to register a fire alarm on the books. It wasn't much of a place. Two stories high, it took up about a quarter of the block without seeming to be there at all. It was aluminum pre-fab, with poured cement on the outside for extra stability. The cement was rough, unfinished, and there weren't any windows.

Passing the front door, I slipped through the alley that ran beside, then behind to the back. Unwinding the hum, I slipped out of the bullet and went to the door.

There was another bullet back there, a new model. It had to belong to someone inside. The door of the warehouse was metal, heavier than the rest of the building. Next to it was a large, garage type door that slid upward. The door had a faded sign painted on it. It read: HAMPTON ENTERPRISES— DELIVERIES ONLY. I tried the handle. It was locked. So was the garage door.

I went through my pockets, and the only thing I could come up with was my lighter. Taking off the shield, I exposed the solar coils. There was a heat-sensitive strip on most buildings that were designed to help in case of fire. Since so many doors were security locked, it was impossible for the fire department to get into many a burning building. The heat strips automatically unlocked doors if the temperature got to a certain degree. It was a pretty good procedure, since it also worked as an alarm to both the coppers and the fire people. Vandals didn't take advantage of it for that reason. I didn't need to worry about it.

Running my fingers along the inner edge of the door frame, I found the seam where the strip joined the frame. Flipping on the lighter, I stuck its exposed coils up on the frame. It took a couple of minutes for the metal to heat sufficiently to set off the trigger, but when it did, the lock clicked open with authority.

I pushed. The door creaked like a pump handle, and I was inside, staring at a wall. It wasn't a real wall; it was a wall made of crates. The crates were like skeletal shells that cradled aluminum containers within them. The shells and the containers both had Japanese writing stenciled on them.

I turned and looked around. Fluorescent bulbs ran in rows along the high ceiling, blinking and buzzing. I was standing in a narrow passage formed on one side by the outer wall of the building, and on the other by floor-to-ceiling crates. I started moving down the aisle until I came to another passage. It was a narrow one with crates forming both walls. The whole place was full of the damned things, bursting full.

I recognized the writing on the crates. It was the same that I had seen on the tape of the call that Lynn had gotten. That call had been placed from here.

There was a single crate sitting on a spot formed by a crate wall corner. It had been partially broken in shipment, the shell splintered and caved in. Going over to it, I pulled apart the broken slats and got down to the container within. The container itself wasn't damaged. It was round, but had a tooled lid that screwed down.

I tried to get the cap off, but it wouldn't budge. Hoping that I hadn't used all the charge from my lighter on the door, I got it back out again and used it to heat up the lid. There was some packing laying on the floor. Getting a handful, I used it to protect my hand from the hot lid, and twisted the thing open when it expanded enough.

There was a clear liquid inside, thick and slick. I dipped my fingers in, and brought them back out to watch the stuff ooze down my hand to drip onto the sleeve of my one-piece. It had a definite odor of fish. I had never seen whale oil before, but I was willing to bet that every drop of it in the entire world was sitting in that warehouse. The proof had been in Bob's tape library all the time, his negotiations—in Japanese. The Japanese had killed off the whale years before. This must have been all that was left of them. While the city was dying off, like the whales, Bob Hampton was quietly hoarding the only thing that could save it.

I heard a scream from somewhere closer to the front of the building. Wiping my fingers on the packing, I moved toward the sound as quickly as I could without giving myself away.

184

I was afraid, really afraid. It was fear like I'd never known it before. I wanted to turn and get the hell out of there. Just get back out and hop in the bullet and hum away where nobody would ever bother me. But I couldn't.

Lynn was connected to that sound. I had promised her I'd never run out on her again. I wasn't anything if I wasn't worth my promise. It was the only thing that kept me going. The only thing that kept my tunnel vision intact.

I hadn't taken ten steps when the lights went out with a loud hum, and I was plunged into total darkness that wrapped me up in cold, clammy fingers. The city had shut down totally, had taken its last, electric gasp.

I stopped moving, the pounding of my heart so loud I was afraid it could be heard. Why did it have to be so dark? Damn it. Damn it. I should have stayed with Siggy; he would have . . . no, Siggy was crazy. Siggy couldn't even look out for himself. Siggy was probably sitting in the dark, screaming.

I could hear Lynn's screams again. Louder this time. I recognized it; it was the call of absolute fear, the kind of scream that would be tearing out of me if I could get away with it.

Then there was some light, jumping, flickering in the distance. A pocket of light in a world of darkness. Whale oil had been used to burn in lamps at one time. I guess someone had lit some. Nothing ever changes.

The erratic light at least gave me something to grab hold of. It made my narrow passage a shadow-filled nightmare, but at least I could see enough to move. And moving at this point was everything.

I zeroed in on the light, homed in on it, and started walking.

Hampton had connections worldwide. He must have bought up the oil as soon as he found out about the antidote, and was selling it in small, precious dollops so that he could get rich off it. That explained the cash deposits in his bank account. He was selling it to Harv, holding back the major supply until he saw how high the market was willing to go. He held it too long.

The light source got closer. It reached for me in long, glowing tentacles. I could hear voices pushing into my darkness, the sounds trying to tame the silence.

I moved up to it, came onto the vortex of the light. It was a cleared area in the middle of the crate city, and it had apparently been home to somebody for a long time. First and foremost, it was a lab, with banks of machines and experiment tables and Bunsen burners. This is where Max Erickson created the monster. It also had a vis, and a bed, and a table with chairs. A small refrigerator sat off to the side, with a mike on top of it. Food trash was strewn everywhere, empty tins and containers thrown just out of the circle of light. Bob was there; he was cursing the blank vis screen that had died with the electricity. Lynn was there; she was tied up on the floor, hands behind her back, feet bound at the ankles. She was moaning softly, the whining song of a mind creating new songs, crazy songs. I didn't need to see her eyes to know I had seen those eyes before.

Hugging the crates with my back, I crept as close to the scene as I could without giving myself away. The light was coming from an open aluminum drum. He had simply put a flame to it.

My eyes traveled the confines of the area. Bob was preoccupied, pacing nervously. He was still dressed to the teeth, like he was waiting at any moment to give a command performance. A large bandage covered his head where I had singed him. Something caught my eye on the table. It was a laser. He apparently had more of those than banana republics had dictators.

"So where is he?" Hampton said, and Lynn just moaned in reply. "He should have been here by now. He's screwing me; I know he is."

"They're waiting out there," Lynn said loudly. "Don't you see them? They're hiding so they can get us when we're asleep."

I watched his face twist in anger. He walked to where she lay on the cold concrete and kicked her viciously in the side.

"You stupid cow!" he yelled. "Crazier than a fucking loon, you know it? You and your water-headed boyfriend both. The nerve of you people thinking you could put one over on me."

He bent down to her. They were partially hidden from view behind the table, but I could see her legs kicking. His back was to me as he reached for her. I needed to move, to do something, but my legs wouldn't respond.

"How was he in bed?" he whined sweetly. "Was he better than me?"

"They're out there," she said. "Don't you see them?"

"Did he touch you all over?"

She was breathing heavy, her voice like a gas motor. "Stay away from me!" she yelled, as his hands moved along her body. "Don't hurt me! Don't!"

His hands moved to her throat. He was chuckling softly, enjoying her agony, her madness. I took a faltering step, fell back.

"Don't like it?" he asked. "But, I'm your husband. If he could do it to you, why not me?"

"Get away from me! Please... please." She was crying loudly, wailing, all of it pouring out.

"Stop that," he said. "Stop it or I'll have to punish you."

She screamed, and his hands went to her throat, and the screams turned to gags as he cut her air off with the pressure of his thumbs.

I was out there, I'll never know how. I was moving toward them, and once I had given myself away, there was no reason to go back.

Bob heard me, flared around. My eyes were on him, but his were on the table, and I realized that I was closer to the burner than he was. I was reaching for it just as he sprang at me.

It was a blur, but I came away with the gun and he hit the table, knocking it over. I kept my distance and steadied it on him as he looked up at me from the floor.

"God, you're timing is really awful," he told me.

"I'll bet you've got some vaccine already made up here, don't you?" I returned.

He was up on his knees, fingers bending back to touch his chest. "Me? Wouldn't I have taken care of my own wife if I had?"

I thumbed up the power and squeezed the trigger. A section of the floor bubbled black next to his knee.

He stood quickly, righting the table when he did. "Okay," he said. "Let's deal." Bending his head a touch, he looked at me through narrowed eyes. "What's wrong with... oh, you've got it too. All messed up, aren't you?"

"Yeah," I answered. "And still man enough to take you."

His frown deepened, settled in permanently. "I've got what you need," he said. "I'm a businessman. I'm willing to negotiate."

"What do you want?"

"A simple trade." He was walking slowly, carefully, getting

187

between me and Lynn. "I give you the cure, and in return, you let me walk out of here."

"Let's see what you've got."

He pointed toward the fridge. "I'm going to walk over there, chief. Okay?" He was bringing me along like a whore with a teen-aged virgin. I must have looked real nervous.

I nodded. As he walked, I snuck a look at Lynn. I didn't recognize her, what she had become. It jolted me. She didn't recognize me either, didn't recognize anything about me.

"I'm going to put my hand up here," he said from the cooler. "I have a rig up here."

"When you come away with it, I want your hands above your head."

"Sure. Sure." He did it. His hand held a small black satchel, like a doctor might carry, if a doctor had any reason to carry instruments.

"Put it on the table."

He did that, too. "See," he said. "I wouldn't shit you. It's the real thing."

"Stand away from it."

He backed off, and I opened it, not ever taking my eyes off Hampton. I got the latch off, then dumped the contents on the table. Sure enough, it was a junkie rig, with a small bottle of clear liquid.

I stepped back. "Do Lynn first," I told him.

"Do we have a deal?"

"Sure," I said. "Why not."

He moved up to the table and started fooling around with the syringe.

"Why did you kill the others?" I asked.

"What others?" he returned.

"You know what I'm talking about."

"Sorry," he said. "I really don't."

"The other stockholders. Did you do it, or was it all Fuller?"

He stuck the needle into the bottle and began drawing back the plunger. "Harv? Are you kidding? He didn't know doodly about any of it."

He pulled out the shiny point and squirted a little out to see how it worked. "And all I'm trying to do is make a dollar. The American way, Swain. Nothing wrong with that."

He moved to Lynn and bent down. Taking a small rubber hose from the rig, he tied it around her forearm to bring up the vein. Then he put the needle in. "I would have taken care of her eventually," he said. "I was just having a little fun first. After all, she is my wife, for God's sake."

"Not anymore," I returned coldly.

"She's all yours, pal," he said. "More trouble than she's worth anyway."

"Shut up!" I snapped. "Can you untie her?"

"Not without a knife."

"Then just back off."

He stood, smiling, and moved back to the table. Dropping the syringe on it, he got out another one.

"What about Fuller?" I asked, as I rolled up my sleeve.

"What about him?"

I tied the hose around my gun hand, reaching down and pulling it tight with my teeth. "We've played this game before," I said. "Why did you kill him?"

His face went immediately white, his mouth fell open. "Harv's dead?" he replied.

"Are you trying to tell me you didn't hack his arm off?"

"How do you know?" he demanded. "Where did you hear it?"

"I saw him," I said. "Right before I came over here."

He slammed a vicious fist down on the table, nearly knocking it over again. Breathing deeply, he tried to calm himself. He swallowed his anger and filled the second syringe, his shaking hands the only outward sign of his inner rage.

"Then who killed him?" I asked.

His eyes sparked fire at me. "We got a deal," he said. "And it doesn't include playing twenty questions." He smiled a tight lipped smile. "Come on and let me innoculate you."

"I can do it," I returned. "And our deal is what I say it is."

"You're the boss," he said, and laying the needle down, walked away from the table.

I kept my eye on him as long as I could, but I had to look down to give myself the shot. When I looked back up, he had jumped at the burning container, pushing it over, screaming with the pain as the super-heated aluminum seared his hands.

It was a flash. Just a second. It was a single motion that turned the whole world upside down. A small flood of flame hurried across the floor, cutting a fiery path between Lynn and me. She was screaming, shrieking, as Bob bolted off into the shadows.

He was gone; I could deal with that. It was me. Me. I turned, ready to run, giving in to the overpowering instinct to preserve my life. I took a step, two, then turned around. The fear was all over me, covering me like fogmist. Through the jumping flames I could see Lynn squirming along the ground, desperate to escape the fire. I couldn't leave her.

I couldn't.

"Goddamn it!" I yelled, and charged back into the midst of it. I dove through the solid wall of flame that was eating the entire area. I hit concrete on my stomach, feeling the air rush out of me, and I was caught in the circle of flame, its heat making me sweat like at Siggy's place.

Back on my feet, I made my way over to Lynn. Grabbing her under the arms, I started to drag her. All the while she kicked and yelled obscenities at me.

I dragged her down one of the aisles and left her there. If the city had a chance for survival, it was by preserving what was left of the oil.

Running back to the place, I dove through again and grabbed the bedclothes off his still-untouched mattress. The oil burned clean, no smoke. It gave me an edge.

Throwing myself on the worst of it, I rolled around, smothering it, my hands and arms burning. It came in flashes, my brain completely out of control. I was out of my mind with fire, given over to the grip of out-and-out fear; and still I kept on, throwing myself at it, not thinking, just moving. Method acting.

I got it out somehow, and lay on the floor a minute just to make sure I was still alive. My clothes were singed, my hair. I put a hand to my face and my eyebrows powdered to the touch. But I had done it. I had faced the worst of fear in my worst possible state, and I had come away in one piece, if just a little the worse for wear. Thank you, Charlie. Thank you, Terra Firma.

It was absolutely dark, no light at all. Oil was still puddled on the floor. I ripped up some of the bedclothes and saturated the material in the oil. Feeling my way to one of the chairs, I smashed the thing up on the floor and used one of its legs to wrap the oil-soaked material around for a torch. My lighter got it going.

Lynn hadn't been making any sounds. I rummaged around

until I found a knife, then went looking for her. She had moved from where I'd left her, had slithered farther along the passageway.

I found her quite a ways down the line. She had really been working at it. Wedging the torch in a crate, I knelt down beside her and got the knife to working on the bonds on her hands. "The way you're moving across the floor," I said. "I'll bet you're a hell of a swimmer."

"Get back," she hissed.

"Whoa, mama. I'm the knight in shining armor."

"Please don't hurt me. I'll die if you hurt me."

I got her arms free. She brought her hands around to massage the red marks on her wrists. I took her by the shoulders. "Hey, come on. It's me. It's all right now."

She made a grab for the knife, murder in her eyes. I wrestled it away from her. She began crying again, face in her hands. I went to work on her feet.

"Listen," I said. "Listen to me. You got a dose of the plague, but it's all right now. Hang on. I know how you feel, what's going on inside of you. You're not alone; I'm here. You can beat this thing. You've gotten the cure. Just hold on for a while."

The ropes on her feet came loose, and she immediately scrambled up, trying to run away. I lunged at her, bringing her back to the floor.

Grabbing, I held her close. She beat on my back with clenched fists. "Let me go," she gasped. "Take your . . . hands off . . . me."

My mouth went to her ear, my voice soft and gentle. "I love you, Lynn," I whispered. "You're not alone. That road is dark, but you don't have to walk it by yourself. I'll help you. Trust me, please trust me."

Her cries were sobs, her beating hands now tugging weakly at my back.

"There's a part of you that's still real, a part that has to hear me. You need a friend, an anchor. Trust me and it will be all right. Lean on me. You can conquer this. I won't hurt you. I'll never hurt you. I will give you the help you need to be right again."

"Matt?" she said from far away.

I held her tighter, tears coming from my own eyes. "That's it, Lynn. Fight it. You can do it. I did. Believe me, you can

191

beat it back. It's weaker than you. Depend on me. Let me be your strength. Let it flow from me to you."

"Oh, Matt, help me," she said, and the fighting hands were holding on for dear life.

# 26

We headed out of the city, toward the refugee camps. I didn't know what else to do. We had managed to drag one of the aluminum urns out to the bullet and get it up in the trunk, and now the thing to do seemed to be to get the news to the powers that be.

There were so many loose ends that looked like they'd never be tied up now. I supposed that Harv Fuller was giving bad innoculations to his friends out of fear for his own life. Figuring that one of them was the killer, he screwed all of them in order to protect himself, to strike first in the only way he knew how. Accepting that, Bob was just using Harv as his bank account as he sold the whale oil. But why did Bob get so upset when he found out that Harv was dead?

"The snow's all gone," Lynn said from the seat beside me.

"Yeah," I returned. "I think we're about through with it." She was talking about inconsequentials, controlling her mind away from the sickness, the way I had taught her.

"Have you noticed that the weather's been warmer, too?"

"A lot of Gulf breezes coming up from the south."

She turned and looked at me, a touch of fear still in those wide eyes. That, too, would pass. "How am I doing?" she asked.

I reached across and took her hand. "You're doing great, lover. Doing great."

"You didn't run out on me."

"Never," I said. "Never."

She smiled, almost relaxed, and settled down a little bit in the seat. "It's going to be a fine spring this year," she said with conviction.

"Spring as in the season," I said.

She gave me a sidelong glance. "Sure."

"Or spring as in water," I said.

"What are you getting at?"

"Or spring as in coiled metal."

"Swain . . ."

I pulled the hummer off the road, let it settle onto the shoulder. I turned my body to face her. "DNA," I said. "The double helix. What does the artistic representation of the double helix always look like?"

She shook her hands around. "Well . . . like a . . ."

"Spring," I finished. I pounded on the steering grips, tried to concentrate. "Springmaid," I whispered, more to myself than to Lynn. "Maid, as in woman. If they'd have wanted it the other way, they would have spelled it the other way." I thought about that.

"Are you all right?" Lynn asked.

I took her face in my hands, kissed her deeply on the lips. "Never been better," I said.

Maid. Maid.

It hit me all at once, the thing that had been bothering me ever since I'd heard that Max Erickson had done a stretch in the Stringtown Reformatory. Stringtown was a women's prison.

"Bingo!" I said, and keyed the hum.

"What?"

"It's falling into place," I said, and we whined a decent hum down the road. "I'm going to have to drop you off for a little while," I said.

"I'll be damned," she returned. "You still work for me, remember?"

I turned and smiled at her. She was starting to return to her old self. "Lynn," I said. "I'm going to have to be able to move around without worrying about you."

"I understand that," she said. "I'll stay out of the way, but I'm going with you."

"Lynn . . ."

"That's it," she said, and folded her arms.

I sighed. I guess that was it.

We had just gotten off the ramp that led onto the freeway when we saw an army clanker, a checkpoint. A lone, white-suited soldier manned the thing.

"Whatever happens," I told Lynn, "just keep yourself together. Tell them about the oil if something happens to me."

She narrowed her eyes, but didn't say anything.

I pulled up behind the steel-plated monster, and the

soldier boy jumped down off its side to accost me. He came to my window, hand on his rifle. But it wasn't in a firing position.

He bent down to the window. "What d'ya need?"

"Where are the camps?" I asked. "I've been moving around for hours . . . hell, the charge is almost gone off my coils."

He turned and pointed down the road, and I got out to see where he was pointing. When he turned back to me, I treated his mouth to a close-up guided tour of my knuckles. He went down like a pillow stuffed with goose feathers.

I ran to the clanker and jumped up on its side. Scrambling up the battleship-gray turret, I hatched the thing and climbed inside. The interior was cramped and cool with circulating air. It glowed pleasantly blue with instrument lights. I had no trouble with their two-way vis; the design hadn't changed a bit from when I was in the service.

I juiced it and a boyish face in a captain's uniform came on the tiny screen. "Who are you?" the face asked.

"It doesn't matter," I said. "Just listen to me. I'm in your clanker at the first highway checkpoint. I had to rough your boy up a little, but he's okay."

"Now, wait a . . ."

"Just listen! Send somebody down here, one of your scientists preferably. I'm leaving a large canister full of whale oil out here on the ground. I've found a whole warehouse full of it."

"That's insane."

"Yeah," I returned. I gave him the address of Bob's place. "You come check this one, and then go downtown. There's enough cure down there to fix up the city and have enough left over to put electric lights out of business. And if you're thinking about not doing it, think about the possibilities of your being a big hero if it's true, then think again."

"Will you be there?"

"I got business," I said. "Bye."

I blanked him. He would have kept me there for two weeks with questions. I hoisted myself back out of the thing and jumped to the ground. I hoped that they would do what I told them. Military people tend to be real hard headed.

Running back to the bullet, I nearly gave myself a hernia getting the canister out, and left it lying there on the ground. My buddy was beginning to stir. I bent down near his face. "It's been real," I said.

Climbing back in the machine, we were off again. Back. Back toward town.

I knew where I was going this time. Knew where Bob was going, too. And I knew why we were all going there. It was great to finally know something.

We slid off the highway and into the good section of town. That's where they keep art galleries, in the good section. Poor folks don't have the time or the capital to appreciate, really appreciate, fine art. They're too busy staying alive.

The Art Attack was located in a nice little security shopping mall where all the rich folks went to make sure their neighbors weren't putting one over on them. Rich people, I've noticed, are very big on that. Humming the parking lot, I noticed that the roof of the sprawling structure was covered with solar panels—self-sufficient, no less. That meant they still had power. I drove around, looking for Bob's bullet, the one I'd seen at the warehouse. Sure enough, it was pulled up by a storefront with a color changing window.

Humming up right next to it, we unwound and climbed out. The front door had a sign on it that read: WELCOME, PEOPLE OF CULTURE. The door was broken, twisted off its hinges. It had been frumped. Damned Bob had a large enough arsenal to start his own war.

"Stick close," I told Lynn.

"I'm glue," she returned.

We went inside, cultured or no, and found ourselves in a dark waiting room. Stairs led down from the end of the room to the gallery below. Light filtered casually up the staircase.

"Matt, I'm scared," Lynn whispered.

"It's all a game," I said. "Between the two of us, we can lick anything."

"Together?"

"You got it."

We started down the stairs. There were sounds, moans, drifting up with the light. They were whispers, but loud, which made me think they were mechanical.

We got to the basement. It was huge; it must have taken up the lower floor of the entire mall. There was a lot of darkness down there, but a lot of light, too. Real soft lighting that highlighted the works of "art."

There seemed to be several different kinds of exhibits. The one that had the sound connected to it, was a series of holos,

196

about twice life-sized, of human beings making love to various animals and inanimate objects: dogs, cats, sheep, chickens, bottles, knotholes, you name it. These giant people were all over the place, grunting and sweating, never seeming to get any real release. I suppose that was the "message." It all went right by me; I guess I'm not cultured after all.

Some of the other things were even weirder. There were things, like bread dough the size of bullets and larger, that just kind of globbed along the floor, just squishing along, bending this way and that. These things would whisper to you as you walked by.

"Take me home," they'd say. "I'm only fifteen hundred dollars, and I'll be your friend for life."

We could hear voices, real voices, coming from the back of the gallery. Angry voices. I felt Lynn's hand tighten on my arm. I stuck my hand in my pocket to reassure myself that the laser I had taken from Bob was still there.

Keeping in the shadows, we crept closer. The exhibits took on a nastier twist. There was a whole line of things that looked like ancient torture devices. Tables where a row of gleaming axes rose and fell, thunking into the wood of the thing. Barber type poles that connected up to long-bladed knives that twirled around, swishing the air. A large steel machine opened up like a flower, only to snap shut on the holo of a naked woman continually lowered on a rope into its waiting maw. It was art all right. No doubt about that.

The voices got louder as we got closer.

"It's Bob," Lynn said in my ear.

I nodded.

A series of stone pillars ran through the gallery for support. We tried to keep those between us and the figures at room's end. There was more light down there, and desks. This must have been the place where all the folks signed over their homes to own some of the lovely work the gallery had for sale.

"Where is it?" Bob yelled to someone. "You give it to me right now, or you go out of here in pieces."

"I don't know what you're talking about," a voice answered. A woman's voice. We got up on the pillar, peeked around it. It was a beautiful blonde, my mysterious woman. And Bob had the drop on her.

It looked like he was getting around to doing her in. I wasn't ready for that yet. "You with me?" I asked Lynn.

"Like a shadow," she replied, but her voice was a little shaky.

Taking out the laser, I walked out of the shadows. Bob's back was to me, and I nearly got up on him before he realized I was there. He started to turn.

"Don't do it," I warned, and he recognized the voice. His hands went up immediately, frump clattering to the floor. "So many guns," I said.

"Don't you stay dead?" he sighed.

"Only if I'm killed properly."

I moved to him, kicking the frump away and shoving him a bit closer to the blonde.

"I don't think we've been introduced properly," I said to her. "My name's Swain. And you must be Maxine Erickson."

"It's Max," she returned, and her eyes flashed at me. "I had it legally changed."

"Well, how original of you," I returned. "I'm going to kill you, you know."

"I know."

"Fine. Just wanted to make sure we understood each other."

Our eyes were vapor locked. It was like there was an invisible conduit connecting us that flowed a never-ending current of hatred back and forth.

"Let me see if I can figure this out," I said. "You got sprung from jail, probably through Bob's multitude of contacts, so that you could make the smog-eating bug. When it turned into a virus that ate brains instead, you cooked up your little whale-oil scheme with Bob here to milk it for as much as you could. Kind of turned the debits into credits, or some such nonsense." I motioned with my burner. "Sit down, why don't you? Anybody got a cig?"

"I do," Lynn said from behind me.

"Well, fire that thing up," I returned. "It helps me think."

Hampton and Erickson sat on desk chairs, behind sheet-metal flat desks. I couldn't see their hands.

"Hands behind your heads," I told them and walked closer. They did it.

Lynn stuck the smoker between my lips, and it felt better already. The smoke helped; it was an ordinary experience in the midst of extreme craziness.

"Now," I continued. "I'll bet Bob wants something from

198

you. I'll bet it's like a briefcase or something. And I'll bet it has a lot of cash money in it. Am I right?"

No response.

I took a long drag. Let it out.

"You guys held onto the whale oil too long, let things get out of hand. When you saw what it had come to, you made a deal with Harv for the whole warehouse—one big cash transference."

I pointed to the woman. "I'll bet you needed the money because you had invested everything Springmaid had given you back in Bob's whale-oil venture."

I looked at Bob. "Harv was supposed to deliver the money to you at the warehouse so he could see what he was buying, but the good doctor got to him first." I clucked my tongue. "Very greedy of you, Maxine."

"Max."

"I got screwed up when I saw the missing arm. Thought it was Bob." I rubbed my chin and took another drag. "The damned thing must have been chained to his arm. You had to take the arm to get it away from him. But why did you want to kill everyone off? I still haven't figured that one out yet."

Max smiled with bright red lips. "I didn't," she said.

"Sorry," I returned. "I saw you at the bar the night that Felix was killed."

"I was following him," she said. "I saw the death pattern and followed him on a hunch. He was the only outsider in the corporation. The only one who wasn't a member of the Steering Committee. That's when I saw you. That's when I started protecting myself. Once the news got to outside sources, nobody was safe. You had to be dealt with. Bob's wife was the same danger— contact to the outside."

"Then . . ."

"That's all, Swain," came a voice behind me, and I knew I'd been had. Again.

I turned around slowly. Mandy Pitcher stood behind a pillar, poking the muzzle of a napalm rifle out at me and Lynn.

"The burner goes on the floor," she said. "You know the routine."

I didn't have a prayer with her. I put the gun on the cold ground.

"Kick it away from you," she said, voice tough as catfish skin.

I did it.

She came out from behind the pillar and moved toward Erickson, who was rummaging around in the bottom drawer of a desk.

"You know, Mandy," I said. "You're the saddest one of all."

"Can it," she said.

"You really are," I continued. "I knew something was odd when you got so worked up about your chum Maxine at Jasper's office. You've got it bad, don't you? A hopeless romantic."

"Shut up!"

"Don't pay attention to him," Erickson said, and she came out of the desk with a briefcase that had a pair of bloody handcuffs attached to the handle.

"True love," I sighed. "All you ever were to her was a shack-up and a place to hide out when things got rough. And you accused me of being a leech. The monkey on your back's a gorilla."

"You don't know what you're talking about."

"Don't I? Let me see if I can set the scenario. Now that you've got the cold cash, you two are going far away to live a life of idyllic splendor in some tropical paradise."

"Why not?"

"I'll handle this," Erickson said, and gently lifted the rifle out of Pitcher's hands.

"She's a killer, Mandy," I said, finishing my cig. I dropped it on the floor. "She's let a whole city die just to make a couple of bucks, and she doesn't need you anymore. In fact, you're getting to be a real millstone around her neck because you know what she's done. That's a hell of a lever."

Amanda Pitcher drew herself up to her full height. "We love each other," she said.

"Sure," I answered. "Then why is the rifle pointed at you right now."

She turned to face her lover. From the distance of no more than a meter, Max leveled the gun at her.

"It's really nothing personal, you understand," she told the woman. "I like you just fine. I really do. It's just . . . business."

With that she fingered the trigger and a stream of liquid fire jumped out and set the woman ablaze. Lynn screamed and grabbed me, as Amanda Pitcher ran crazily around her gallery for a minute, moaning loudly like her sculptures. She finally collapsed on top of one of her dough clumps, like she was trying to bake bread out of it.

Erickson, smiling, turned the rifle on us. "I guess we might as well take care of it all now," she said.

I was just into pushing Lynn away from me when a horrible screeching wail rained down from above, and the whole ceiling was caving in on us. The government. They were destroying the city.

I dove, taking Lynn with me, while everything came apart around us in chunks of cement and steel and fine powdery dust that tasted stale and choked everything up and made it impossible to see.

I heard coughing, and it was me, and Lynn was crying softly beneath me. There was wood on us and small, white, angular rocks, but we seemed to be in one piece.

I moved to see if I could do it and I could. I looked up and didn't recognize any of the surroundings through the fine white mist that shrouded the environment like a thick fog.

There was a figure, dark and shadowy, running through the mist. A man. Bob Hampton. He clutched something to his chest. He ran close by us, moving as quickly as he could through the alien twisted landscape that the basement had become.

I was up, going for him, coughing back the choking dust and plaster. I tripped and lunged, grabbing him by the ankle.

"Damn you!" he screamed, and began using the briefcase to beat at me: one, two, three times.

Releasing my hold on his leg, I grabbed the swinging arm, my hands slipping to the case itself. He was making animal noises down in his throat and his face was white like death with dust as we pulled the case back and forth, me from the ground, him trying to lever against my weight.

"Let go!" he screamed at me. "Damn you!"

He tried to drag me, pulling and straining, and he lost his footing on the rock pile ground. His hands went from the case and he backpedaled.

The pole with the long knives was tilted against the wall, blades still spinning. Bob saw it coming, but couldn't get his balance back. He fell on it without a sound. His body made a pop, like an air-filled paper bag exploding, and a healthy drizzle of bloody rain sprinkled the area, fast soaking into the growing layer of dust.

As for Bob, he was gone. Dismemberment, apparently, was also seriously into him.

Getting slowly to my feet, I went back for Lynn. She still

201

lay on the floor, hands covering her head. "Come on," I said, bending to pull on one of her arms. "Let's go."

She turned her head to me, eyes moist. "Bob?" she asked.

"Gone," I said, and we didn't talk about him anymore.

I got her to her feet, and we made our way back through the mess to the last place I had seen Erickson. I saw her, buried under tons of cement and steel beams, her head the only part protruding from the rubble. She looked like chalk from settling dust.

I bent to her, and her eyes rolled open, piercing like daggers in their white white shell. "I'm dead," she said.

"Guess I don't get to kill you after all," I returned.

"I want to tell you something," she gurgled around a mouthful of frothing blood.

"Yeah."

"You were wrong."

"About what?"

She tried to laugh, but it didn't work. A stringer of red trailed slowly out of the corner of her already red lips and ran down the white of her face, soaking in as it did.

"There was no mistake," she rasped. "I was hired to make the plague."

"But..."

"That's all. You figure it out, smart guy."

That was it. She didn't say anything else.

# 27

The area outside the mall was a wasteland of steel beams and concrete. We had to dig ourselves back up the stairs to stand once again outside. The destruction around us was complete, rolling concrete hills dotted with occasional geysers of exposed water mains. It only went in an area of several square blocks, though. The rest of the city was still intact. They were working slowly, methodically, chewing up the town a block at a time. I was familiar with the routine; it was the standard search-and-destroy procedure. They were calculating the most good out of the least expenditure of energy from the laser cannons. Those babies ate a lot of juice.

The next step would be to come in with the flame-throwers and clear the area once and for all. They'd claim the city, a little at a time, from the outside in. We needed to get out before the soldiers showed up.

"Come on." I took Lynn's hand and began pulling her with me through the rubble piles.

"Where's the bullet?" she asked.

"Where we're going to be if we don't get out of here."

She was looking around like a kid at the carnival as I dragged her through the debris that had once been the rich kids' hangout. "What's that noise?" she asked.

"The hum of the laser cannons," I said. "They're taking out another section of town."

It was just getting dark, twilight in more ways than one. I stopped walking and turned Lynn to the east, let her watch a new sunset, as the cannons would brightly arc the sky in rosy pink. "They come in low," I said, "and angle slightly down into the ground. The heat takes out the bottom of the buildings and the falling debris does the rest."

"How precise," she said, and it was an interesting thing for her to say.

"Let's go."

I turned around to see a squad of white-suits lined out around us, their napalm rifles shouldered and pointed right at us.

"Oops" was all I could think of to say.

"Hands above your heads," a man with sergeant's stripes on his bulky white sleeves barked.

"Do what he says," I whispered to Lynn, and she had already done it.

They closed in, pulling a circle tighter and tighter around us. I wished I could see their eyes, their faces. They were our executioners and they owed us at least that.

"Doin' a little lootin', are you?" the sergeant said, pointing to the briefcase that lay beside my feet. "Lousy plaguers have done your last. You're gonna burn, assholes."

"Loot what?" I returned. "I don't see anything to loot. This bag is my personal property."

"Shut up."

He turned to the others. "Who's turn is it?" he asked loudly. "Jarman fried the last bunch. We gotta do this democratically."

A hand tentatively rose. It had a young, faltering voice connected to it, a female voice. "I think it's me, Sarge," she said.

"All right," the man returned. "Back off and let Birney have her barbecue."

"Just a second," came a voice from outside the circle. It was a thin man in lieutenant's uniform. He wasn't wearing the rad suit like the others, just a portable gas mask. "What have you got here?"

"Couple of plaguers," the sergeant returned, and there was a touch of rancor in his voice. "We're gettin' set to fry 'em."

"How do you know they're plaguers?" the lieutenant asked.

"Well . . . just look at em, all grimy and shit."

"Have you tested them?"

"Aw, hell no. I don't need no . . ."

"It's procedure, Sergeant Mullins," the lieutenant said, and I could feel that we were in the middle of a battle of wills that went way past this scene and had absolutely nothing to do with us. "In my outfit, we go strictly by the book. Now, test them, you lumber-headed moron. Is that clear enough for you?"

The sergeant snapped to a postured attention. "Yes, sir! Lieutenant Harding, sir!"

Mullins turned to the two closest people to him. "Private Franks, you will assist Private Anderson in testing the prisoners for the plague!"

"Yes, sir!" they screamed in unison. It was apparently a game they played all the time.

The soldiers got into their survival packs and came out with the same testing equipment that had been used on me at the Fancy Dan barricades. They came and took blood. We were done for.

Putting my arm around Lynn, I hugged her close. She laid her head on my shoulder, contented that I hadn't run out on her. We got so close, so damned close.

"They're okay," one of the soldiers said.

I looked up, trying to keep my jaw clamped tight. Sure enough, the test tubes showed blue fluid. The antidote must have worked a lot quicker than I figured.

"Ha!" the Lieutenant exclaimed. "Just as I thought. You were about to murder innocent people, Sergeant Mullins. This is going to look bad on your service record."

Lynn and I, arm in arm, walked out of the circle of death and up to the lieutenant. I wanted to catch him in an up mood.

"Want to thank you," I told him. "They nearly had us roasted."

"Only doing my job," the man answered, swelling proudly.

"Do you think it would be possible to . . . I don't want to impose myself, you understand."

"Say it, my poor man," he answered. "We're here to serve."

"Well . . . could we get a . . . lift on to the camps?"

The man's mouth was wrapped around his gas gear, but his eyes were twinkling like marquise cut diamonds. "Certainly," he said. "Sergeant Mullins!" he called. "You will personally escort these people back to the camps, and then place yourself on report. Corporal Wasingski will lead the squad in your absence."

Mullins growled something in return, but he did what he was told. He was, after all, a soldier.

We rode in the back of a half-track, bumping up and over a never-ending series of rocky foothills. I sat cross-legged, the briefcase on my lap. Lynn rested her head on the case, like a pillow. We didn't talk. We were in much deeper communication than that.

I couldn't get Erickson out of my mind. Her dying words still kicked around in the overgrown head-cheese of my brain. Hired to make the plague. Contracted for it. But who? Why? It drove me nuts. It was all so methodical, so mechanical, so . . . bureaucratic.

It didn't take long to get to the camps. They were breathtaking in their vastness, a monstrous, sprawling city of canvas that stretched way into the distance.

We drove through the barbed wire and electronic fences and into the crush of people who wandered through the even rows, the avenues of an overnight metropolis. And something strange was happening here. All the people, the rich ones and the poor ones, and all the shmucks like me who get stuck in between, were all living there together, forcibly rubbing shoulders, interacting, working together because the circumstances forced them to.

It was a specialized moment in time, a focus of history. It couldn't last, these things never did. But, by God, for once I got to see it. The lines had disappeared, the barriers had come down. The common good was the only good and Jesus, sweet Jesus, it was something.

There were tears of loss and displacement, great sadness being shared by all. But there was laughter, too, because that's what people are all about. It was humanity going down here. Serious humanity.

The truck screeched to a stop, and we jumped down from it in its dust cloud. Mullins came back and gave us green tags to wear and told us where the showers were so we could clean up. Then he was gone.

"I'm hungry," Lynn said, her arm linked through mine. "Can we get something to eat?"

"See what we can do," I returned, and led her into the milling crowds.

There seemed to be some excitement rifling through the ranks. I grabbed a guy who was hurrying by and asked him about it.

"Haven't you heard?" he asked. "Word is, they've found a whole warehouse full of the antidote. They're checking it out now. This may be over soon."

"Great," I said, and I could feel my face smiling a real

smile for the first time in months. "That's really great. Say, where could I find the mess tent?"

He pointed toward all the tents. "There's one at the end of each long row," he said, and then flowed off into the crowd.

"Thanks," I called after him, but he was already gone.

"Do you think we need reservations?" Lynn asked me.

"Probably," I answered. "But I'm a personal friend of the maître d'."

"Then what are we waiting for?"

We started walking, and in the midst of all the insanity, I don't ever remember feeling happier. We found the mess tent without any trouble, and as we started in, I bumped into someone on the way out.

"Swain?"

"Juke?" I returned, and took his sorry old frame in my arms. "God, I'm glad you made it."

"Yeah," he returned. "And it ain't so bad either. Ain't a soul who's gotten around to asking me my name yet!"

We all laughed, and it was good to laugh.

"A little scary at first, though," he said.

"What do you mean?"

"The line," he said. "You know, the line."

"We didn't come through any line," Lynn told him.

He rolled his eyes. "Consider yourselves lucky," he said. "They line you up single file, then take you down and test you for the plague. The good ones get the green tag." He pointed to his chest. "The others have to get put in this little room." His face turned dark. "I don't think they ever come out of there at all."

"Where is it?" I asked.

"Matt!" Lynn said.

"Now, you don't want to . . ."

"Where?" I asked again. I was too wrapped up in this. I couldn't let the killing go on if I could stop it.

He pointed to a long green awning off in the distance, toward the end of the perimeter. A long stretch of yard was open around it. No one would even go near.

"Would you sit with Lynn until I get back?" I asked him.

"Sure," he said. "But if you don't watch out, I'll steal her away from you."

I hugged her quickly and gave her the briefcase. "This one I have to do myself," I told her.

She nodded. "I know that," she said.

I smiled. "Get me some coffee, would you? I'll be back in a few minutes."

She returned my smile and touched my face. "Take care," she said.

Turning, I moved toward the awning. It drew me like a magnet. The final indignity of this perverted passion play. Out of the blue, as I walked, something that my old pal Foley at Continental told me that day I was there kept running through my mind. He said that Continental was getting out of the life insurance business and concentrating on property stuff.

That didn't make any sense to me. If a company played the odds alone, it would seem that life insurance would be consistent and predictable. What better odds than that?

I got up to the awning. It was like a cattle pen, long and narrow. Titanium bars slatted longways defined its inside, and that inside was just wide enough to barely accommodate one person at a time. The awning was plastic and admitted the dying rays of the smog-day inside as green atmosphere. It made the people look surreal, unearthly.

On the outside, the people bunched up to get in. The pen itself held about forty. The line kept moving. Its end was a small medical station and a bunch of armed guards in white. I was, of course, contained in my area, separated from the pen by bars. But I ran down near the station anyway.

"What are you doing?" I called inside. "Don't you know they've found the antidote?"

Several of the guards walked up close to the bars. "Move along," one of them said. "You're interfering with the operation."

"But you don't have to do this anymore," I returned. "They've got the antidote. I've seen it!"

Several regular-issue lasers leveled at me, all connected to stern faces. Stone faces. "We've got our orders," the man said. "Until they change, this is it. Move along. *Now.*"

I moved away, walking up and down the pen, looking inside. I was looking. Looking . . . for something.

I watched the faces moving past, noncommittal faces until they got far enough down the line to realize what was going on. And then they turned, dark, deathlike. From time to time I heard a scream from the medical station and I knew without looking that another one had come up on the short end of it. I needed somebody to blame for this, somebody to hate. And when I needed it bad enough, I saw him.

Jasper, dolled up and smiling, entered the pen. He was doing his salesman routine on everybody within shouting distance. I walked to where he was, slow and deliberate. I got the bars right between us.

"Hi," I said.

His face lit up when he saw me. "Swain!" he shouted. "Good to see you, boy. I'd shake your hand, but they won't fit through the bars. I'll be around presently to join you, though."

"They're dead," I said.

"Who?"

"All of them. All of Springmaid. All except for Lynn . . . and me."

He cocked his head. "Well, you know, that's too bad," he said with mock seriousness. "But, these are perilous times, and we have to think about the living."

"You did it," I said. "You killed them."

"Whoa," he warned. "Watch how you throw those accusations around. I wasn't anywhere near those folks."

"You did it for the business, didn't you?"

He stopped the act and stared tombstones at me. "You can't prove a thing."

"I don't need to; I just need to know."

"The city was dying anyway," he said.

"Go on."

He folded his arms, shook his frowning head. The line moved. We moved with it. "It was all going to pieces. Businesses failing, folks going broke, burning down their places to collect on us, or just defaulting payments right and left. We were still in the black . . ."

"Yeah," I said. "I saw the armored cars."

"The profit margin was down." We kept walking. "Computers predicted we'd hit the skids in a few years, a straight plunge after that. We asked them for a solution." He shrugged. "They said to get out of the life-policy business and destroy the city through disaster."

"Why?"

He smiled. "Act of God," he said. "No payoff. Clear the boards, take the profits and find a new game. Simple. Since the plague was manmade, there would be some question about payoffs on life policies, so it was better to just dump out completely."

"And the company approved such a project?"

"Naw," he replied. "It took a go-getter like me to take the

209

bull by the horns. I cooked it all up, financed it without dirtying the company at all."

"And all your friends?"

"Loose ends. Too many people who could tie me in. I used our security people to do them in 'accidentally.' There's always people to do that. And to show you what a good heart I've got, I even paid off good life policies to take care of their families."

I shook my head, and I don't think I'd ever hated so much in my whole life. "What about the security people?"

"You saw one of them the night you had dinner with us at the club."

"It wasn't an android they were cutting up."

"Clever, huh?"

"And what about the antidote deal between Bob and Max?"

His eyes narrowed. "I don't know anything about any antidote. That wasn't in the contract."

"When you lay down with pigs," I said, and grabbed the bars, pushed my face up against them. "When you come through this gate, I am going for you."

"Are you now?" He was back in his salesman's posture, shucking and jiving. "Well, I'm pleased to hear it, because it looks to me like those soldiers here would just love a good excuse to fry your ass."

We were down near the medical station. I looked beside me. The white-suits were watching me intently, hands resting on their lasers.

I flared around. Tried to get my hands through the bars to his throat, but they wouldn't fit.

"See?" he said. "Now why don't you just go off someplace and sit for a while. Get real again. Forget about this; it's got nothing to do with you."

I spit on him.

"Now was that nice?" he said. "This is a new suit." He brushed it off. "See you, Swain." He stepped up for his turn at the table.

I didn't want to die to get to Jasper, so I walked off. I didn't get ten feet before I heard the screaming. Turning around, I saw three soldiers dragging him into the room that nobody came out of.

I laughed so hard that I fell on the ground. Good old Harv. He must have inoculated Jasper himself. Hell, he might even have gotten the plague from me.

A few minutes later, a soldier came up with a message for them to stop the testing, the cure was on its way. But Jasper couldn't stop. He was gone.

The odds had finally caught up with him.

# 28

I sat at my kitchen table and stared at a small mountain of banded up money. It piled way up. I had never thought to look in the briefcase that I had carried away from the art gallery. I had other things on my mind, better things.

It had taken me three weeks to remember I had it. And now that I did, I didn't know what to do with it. It just kind of sat there, yelling silently at me.

Lynn came whistling out of my bathroom, drying her hair on a white towel, wearing my robe open down the front to expose a lot of prime real estate.

"I'm sorry, Matt," she said. "But we are going to have to get a bigger place than this."

"Well, I think it's real homey," I returned.

"You'd think a rat hole was homey."

"Let's not be crass."

She came up to me and bent down for a long kiss. I got my hands up inside the robe and went to town. Laughing, she pulled away from me. "Don't you ever slow down?"

"I'm a kid in a candy store," I returned.

She sat across from me and stared at the money. "How much is it?" she asked.

"A little over three-quarters of a million."

"Hmmm."

She wrapped the towel around her head and put her elbows on the table, her head in her hands. She stared at it.

Old Harv had put one over on everybody. When he made his cash deal with Bob Hampton, he got the money by forging Pitcher's signature on a bank draft and drawing it out of the Springmaid account, cleaned it out. It left a hell of a problem. Who did the money belong to?

"Did you find anyplace to dump it yet?" she asked.

I frowned and shook my head. "Harv had no living relatives." I picked up a bundle and smelled it. Green ink. It smelled like green ink. It also smelled like everything in the world anybody could want, but that was a conditioned response.

"I just got off the vis with Foley over at Continental," I said. "They gave him Jasper's old job."

"Well, good for him."

"I tried to give the money to them," I said. "After all, it was the money from insurance claims."

She shot me a knowing glance. "Didn't go for it, did he?"

"Go for it! He nearly went to pieces over the mention of it. It's not exactly the kind of publicity that a rock-solid insurance company wants to be connected with."

"I'm not surprised."

I tossed the bundle on the table and leaned back in my chair. "You sure I can't talk you into it?" I asked. "It's really yours."

She sighed, reaching up to take the towel off her head. She shook her head, her hair spilling loosely around her shoulders. "I've told you, it's not my money, it's the corporation's, it's Springmaid's."

"But you *are* Springmaid. The only one left."

"Sure. And as an individual, I can't be sued. But if I accept this money in the name of the corporation, everybody and their uncle Frankie is going to be taking Springmaid to court over damages because of the plague. God, I'd be tied up in litigation for years."

She pulled a comb out of the robe pocket and started running it through her hair. "You could always give it to the state."

"Shit."

Reaching over, she laid a hand on my arm. "Then face it, lover. You're stuck with it." She went back to her combing. "Besides, you could do me a favor. Look at it as payment plus bonus for services rendered. Then I won't have to pay you."

"We'll keep it in the family."

"Whatever you say."

I stood up, straightening my one-piece. "Son of a bitch."

"What?"

"What, nothing! I just inherited three-quarters of a million bucks." I started moving toward the bathroom. "Makes me feel like going in and having a shave."

She was behind me, pulling my arm. "Shave later," she said. "Right now, you're coming to bed to finish what you started."

"So this is what it's like to be rich," I said. And I was. I really was.

## ABOUT THE AUTHOR

MIKE McQUAY teaches a science fiction writing course at Oklahoma Central State University. A graduate of the University of Dallas, he has served with the military in Vietnam, Thailand, Japan, and the Philippines. McQuay is addicted to watching B movies on television late at night.

**The eagerly-awaited
return to the fabulous world of
LORD VALENTINE'S CASTLE**

# MAJIPOOR CHRONICLES
## by Robert Silverberg

Journey to Majipoor, the magnificent, exotic planet of LORD VALENTINE'S CASTLE. Come with Hissune, favorite of Lord Valentine, as he probes the deepest secrets of Majipoor's long past. Join him as he becomes one with its many peoples, discovers wonder, terror, longing and love, and learns the wisdom that will shape his destiny.

Buy MAJIPOOR CHRONICLES, on sale January 15, 1983, wherever Bantam paperbacks are sold, or use this handy coupon for ordering:

# OUT OF THIS WORLD!

That's the only way to describe Bantam's great series of science fiction classics. These space-age thrillers are filled with terror, fancy and adventure and written by America's most renowned writers of science fiction. Welcome to outer space and have a good trip!

# FANTASY AND SCIENCE FICTION FAVORITES

Bantam brings you the recognized classics as well as the current favorites in fantasy and science fiction. Here you will find the beloved Conan books along with recent titles by the most respected authors in the genre.

| | | | |
|---|---|---|---|
| ☐ | 22532 | THE WORLDS OF GEORGE O. <br> George Smith | $2.50 |
| ☐ | 22666 | THE GREY MANE OF MORNING <br> Joy Chant | $3.50 |
| ☐ | 20931 | NEBULA WINNERS FOURTEEN <br> Frederik Pohl | $2.95 |
| ☐ | 20527 | SYZYGY   Frederik Pohl | $3.50 |
| ☐ | 20672 | DARKWORLD DETECTIVE <br> J. Michael Reeves | $2.50 |
| ☐ | 20281 | WAR OF OMISSION   Kevin O'Donnell | $2.50 |
| ☐ | 20488 | THE HEROES OF ZARA KEEP <br> Guy Gregory | $2.50 |
| ☐ | 23057 | THE BOOK OF SKULLS <br> Robert Silverberg | $2.95 |
| ☐ | 23063 | LORD VALENTINE'S CASTLE <br> Robert Silverberg | $3.50 |
| ☐ | 20156 | BABEL-17   Samuel R. Delany | $2.50 |
| ☐ | 20870 | JEM   Frederik Pohl | $2.95 |
| ☐ | 22667 | THE MAN WHO HAD NO IDEA <br> Thomas Disch | $2.95 |
| ☐ | 22731 | CONAN THE REBEL #6 <br> Paul Anderson | $2.50 |
| ☐ | 14532 | HIGH COUCH OF SILISTRA <br> Janet Morris | $2.50 |
| ☐ | 22557 | DRAGONSONG   Anne McCaffrey | $2.75 |
| ☐ | 20914 | MAN PLUS   Frederik Pohl | $2.75 |
| ☐ | 22531 | THE KALEVIDE   Lou Gable | $3.95 |
| ☐ | 20592 | TIME STORM   Gordon R. Dickson | $2.95 |

Buy them at your local bookstore or use this handy coupon for ordering: